THE TRUTH SAYER

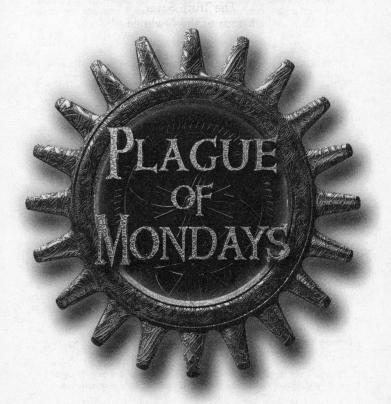

PLAGUE
OF
MONDAYS

SALLY PRUE

OXFORD
UNIVERSITY PRESS

OXFORD
UNIVERSITY PRESS

Great Clarendon Street, Oxford OX2 6DP

Oxford University Press is a department of the University of Oxford.
It furthers the University's objective of excellence in research, scholarship,
and education by publishing worldwide in

Oxford New York

Auckland Cape Town Dar es Salaam Hong Kong Karachi
Kuala Lumpur Madrid Melbourne Mexico City Nairobi
New Delhi Shanghai Taipei Toronto

With offices in

Argentina Austria Brazil Chile Czech Republic France Greece
Guatemala Hungary Italy Japan Poland Portugal Singapore
South Korea Switzerland Thailand Turkey Ukraine Vietnam

Oxford is a registered trade mark of Oxford University Press
in the UK and in certain other countries

British Library Cataloguing in Publication Data

Data available

ISBN: 978-0-19-275537-7

1 3 5 7 9 10 8 6 4 2

Printed in Great Britain by CPI Cox and Wyman, Reading, Berkshire

Paper used in the production of this book is a natural,
recyclable product made from wood grown in sustainable forests.
The manufacturing process conforms to the environmental
regulations of the country of origin.

To Adèle Geras

1

'Truth Sayer!'

A fat man in red leather was lumbering sweatily across the garden of the House of Truth, but Nian, the Truth Sayer, ignored him. Nian was concentrating on the pockle game.

Nian saw a chance, lunged forward, and whacked the pockle cone with his flipper. The pock spun away through the air and Nian saw with a thrill that everything was set up. Alin was running into space and had plenty of time to judge his shot at the drey.

Alin swiped out hard and the pock went up, up, spinning past the trees, the wall, the grey and cloudy autumn sky . . .

'*Truth Sayer!*'

. . . and then slowed to a momentary stop and tumbled down again.

Alin had muffed the shot a bit, though it couldn't have been easy from that angle. The pock was going to miss the drey completely and end up in the brambles.

The pock sailed out of play, hit the smooth trunk of a stoneberry tree and . . .

. . . dived into a hollow tree, trundled out of a wood-knocker hole, got whipped up along the U-shaped shoulder of a wine bush, sailed through the air avoiding seventy-three branches, a startled hayfinch, and one of Hani's old boots that had been stuck up the tree for weeks—and then plunged neatly into the drey at the end of the pockle ground to bring the score to one–nil.

There was a complete and utter silence for about five seconds while everybody's eyes bulged with amazement—and then Hani let out a howl of outrage.

'*Fluuuuuuke!*' he howled.

Alin tried to look bored and lordly, but he just couldn't do it. A great grin of delight spread itself right across his face. He punched his fist into the air.

'*Skill!*' he crowed. 'That was pure skill, that was! And just *immaculate* timing. CITY! CITY! CITY!'

Nian opened his mouth to laugh for ever . . .

. . . and then someone at his elbow spoke.

'*Truth Sayer!*'

Nian made the mistake of glancing at the great mountain of a man who'd loomed up beside him. It was Snorer. Snorer was probably the kindest of the members of the Tarhun who worked in the House of Truth (though that was rather like talking about the *kindest* stink-weasel). And over the fat blob of Snorer's face was a shadow of worry.

Nian's laughter died inside him. Snorer was secretary of the Tarhun Pockle Association. He should have been jumping up and down and hooting like a swing-gibbon after a blatant fluke like that.

2

'What is it?' asked Nian, with a horrible qualm.

Snorer could hardly bring himself to meet Nian's eyes.

'You've got a visitor,' he mumbled.

Hani stooped to snatch up the pockle cone. Even he was grinning, now—and the others were on their knees, sobbing with mirth.

'A visitor?' echoed Nian. 'What sort of a visitor?'

'He says he's your brother, Truth Sayer.'

Tan. But Tan was the most stay-at-home sort of person you could find.

'A fair-haired boy,' said Nian, to make sure. 'Sort of chunky. Valley accent. Not that quick.'

Snorer nodded his great fat head.

'He says he's brought news,' he went on, quietly.

News from home? News worth travelling for a whole week to tell?

Nian chucked his flipper to Alin and started running across the garden towards the great white wall of the House of Truth.

The Strangers' Room was new. It used to be a storeroom for the Tarhun's snowboots, but strenuous and determined airing meant that now, fortunately, it only smelled of whitewash.

There was a stocky sandy-haired boy sitting on the bench against the far wall. He looked up nervously when Nian entered.

'What's happened?' demanded Nian. Home seven days' journey away, and his younger brother Tan

3

could not have been lightly spared from the farm, especially while this fine weather lasted.

Tan squinted doubtfully over Nian's shoulder at the great bulk of the Tarhun Snorer.

'It's Grandy,' he said.

Their grandmother was old, of course, but she was never ill. She always said she was too old and tough and busy to be ill. In fact, she'd said that so often that Nian had come to believe it.

'What's the matter with her?' Nian demanded, fiercely, to hide his sudden fear.

Tan's square face flushed. He gave Snorer another quick look and then mumbled to the stone flags of the floor.

'She's started . . . talking,' he said.

'Talking?'

'About the rocks.'

Nian spent a moment wondering if he could have heard right.

'About the *what*?'

'You know,' went on Tan, miserably. 'Grandy's *always* going on about how she can hear the rocks moving under the earth. About being able to hear the mountains grinding and growing.'

Nian frowned.

'Well, she can, can't she,' he pointed out. 'I mean, she knew when the earthquakes were coming last spring, didn't she. She heard the rocks graunching against each other and made everyone go outside. That was what you told me when I was home in the summer. You said that if it hadn't been for her, then Miri

4

might have been killed when the roof beam fell in the ox house.'

Tan shrugged. He was sturdy, and useful round the farm, but he wasn't one for believing anything that wasn't there in front of him.

'Is Grandy all right except for being worried about the mountains moving?' asked Nian. 'She's not ill?'

Tan wrinkled up his face.

'Well,' he said, dubiously. 'She's not *ill* ill, anyway. I mean, she's up with the first sun, and baking and cleaning and everything, just as usual. But she keeps on and on about the mountains. Getting really agitated. She kept nagging Father about getting someone to come and tell you. Well, Father, he said everyone was too busy, but she kept saying . . . ' he frowned, as if trying to call her exact words to mind. 'She kept saying that someone had cobbled the path of the world. Something like that.'

'*Cobbled the path of the world?*' echoed Nian, completely puzzled. 'Are you sure? What's that supposed to mean?'

Tan shrugged.

'Well, I don't know,' he admitted. 'Mother says Grandy's going age-mazy.'

Nian made a face. That didn't sound like Grandy: she was old, but she'd always been as sharp as a thistle.

Tan sighed glumly and stretched out his legs.

'I don't think all this travelling agrees with me,' he said dolefully. 'My legs feel as if I've been climbing this mountain for days on end.'

Nian sighed, as well. He felt as if *he'd* spent a whole week being interrupted every time he tried to play pockle. One of the things about being the Truth Sayer was that everybody expected you to know what to do whenever there was a problem—and sometimes he really wished he could have a day off. He was feeling like that now. And it was only Monday, so he had just *had* a day off.

Nian wondered rather irritably what on earth he was supposed to do about all this. Go back home with Tan? Try to work out what on earth Grandy was going on about?

A waft of beer breath told Nian that Snorer was preparing himself to speak.

'Probably off her rocker, Lord,' he murmured helpfully. 'My old mother, Lords bless her, she went through a stage of saying that there were mouselets gnawing at the timbers of her shack.' He chuckled, indulgently. 'I mean, *mouselets*! Can you imagine it? And then, when the shack *did* collapse on top of her, she wouldn't accept it was the storm that'd done it. No no, she kept hobbling round waving planks from the wall in people's faces and pointing out the teeth marks.'

'Teeth marks?'

Snorer rasped the stubble along the side of his jaw.

'We never *could* quite explain the teeth-marks,' he admitted.

Tan flexed his legs gingerly.

'Father didn't want to send anyone, but a party of Tourists came through the village and Grandy nagged

6

them into letting me travel with them. But they're still down at the inn, of course, as the House isn't open to Tourists on a Monday. Nian, is there anything to eat?'

Nian's own supper would be waiting for him, but he couldn't take Tan into the Inner House because it was reserved for the Lords of Truth and their pupils. The Lord Rago would go berserk if he found out Nian had brought a stranger in there.

On the other hand, Tan was his brother, and Nian could hardly expect him to spend the night back down in the inn.

Nian turned to Snorer.

'Do you think Snerk would do us a bit of supper?' he asked hopefully. 'And could someone find us a couple of sleeping mats so I can stay here tonight with my brother? And some covers? Oh, and let the Lords know where I am?'

Snorer hunched his brawny shoulders.

'Is that all?' he asked. 'You wouldn't like a rezkler orchestra and a troupe of dancing girls while I'm at it, would you?'

Tan sat up.

'You have *dancing girls* in here?' he asked.

Nian rolled his eyes.

'No, the Tarhun's being funny,' he told Tan. 'The nearest we've ever got to dancing girls was the time Reeklet and Bulls-Eye stepped in a tiger-bees' nest.'

'What?' Nian remembered that Tan had never been the sharpest stake in the fence.

'It's all right,' said Snorer, heavily, as he shuffled out. 'You just take it easy, Lord, and I'll arrange everything.

7

It's not as if I've got anything better to do than run errands for you, is it?'

'I doubt you have,' snapped Nian, tartly, after him. 'Because that means I'll have time to work out what's gone wrong with the fabric of the worlds!'

Nian turned back from the almost-slammed door. His brother was looking around him rather blankly at the bare room, and Nian suddenly remembered all the preparations and fuss that the family made when he himself returned home. The welcome, the feast, the stories. Nian looked at Tan's square, determined-not-to-be-overawed face, and remembered how terrifying Nian had found the House of Truth when he'd first set eyes on it.

Nian swallowed down his annoyance about the pockle game (for this was the first time, after all, that anyone in his family had ever come to the House), and then made a further effort to swallow down his annoyance about the way people kept dumping all their worries and problems on him.

He sat himself down beside his large younger brother and asked him all about the farm, and the family, and Tan's week-long journey to the mountain of the House of Truth.

Snerk came up trumps with a couple of huge portions of fantastically delicious stew. ('What sort of meat is this?' asked Tan, dribbling with rapture. 'Don't ask,' advised Nian, from experience, because Snerk the Tarhun cook was always experimenting with ingredients like mildew and snails' eggs that were best not thought about.) And then Nian and Tan lay down on their mats and listened to the Tarhun having a drunken sing-song and colossal fight next door.

'Do they do this every night?' asked Tan, hugely impressed, as what sounded like another bench thumped and clattered against the wall.

Nian didn't know, because he'd always slept in the peace of the Inner House until then. He'd have thought the Tarhun would have been ready for a quiet Monday evening after the big influx of Tourists that the week-end had brought. But then, knowing the Tarhun . . .

'I wouldn't be surprised,' he told Tan.

There was something very comfortable about sleep-ing beside Tan. He and Tan had slept side by side every night of their lives until Nian had come to the House of Truth.

Nian drifted off peacefully.

Nian woke up on his mat in the pupils' sleeping room in the Inner House.

Nian pushed back his coarse fair hair and wondered what he'd been dreaming about. It might have been something about his brother Tan . . . but no. No, he couldn't remember.

Hani was yawning and complaining and groaning. The Lord Rago was due to take them for a weather-lore lesson that morning, and being taught by Rago was about as safe and relaxing as being trapped in a bottle with a crack scorpion.

9

Nian pushed off his cover. His dream, whatever it had been, had left him with an unpleasant upside-down and inside-out feeling.

Over by the window Alin was doing the horribly bracing exercises with which he felt the need to start the day, and beside Nian Derig was folding up his mat.

Yes. Nian yawned and settled himself into wakefulness.

House of Truth.

Sleeping room.

Monday.

2

The Plain of Hasiris

'Professor! We've found a body!'

Rik gratefully threw aside the duster with which he was supposed to be cleaning a heap of files, and ducked out under the tent flap into the baking sun. He hurried along after Professor Hallam's thin back. Rolan, one of the native bearers, was leading the way across the maze of ditches and mounds of spoil that made up the dig.

By the time Rolan came to a halt there was sweat glistening along the worry-lines of Professor Hallam's face.

'Here, Professor, sir,' said Rolan.

Only a hand was visible above the ashy sand. It looked as if its owner was reaching up supplicatingly out of the ground.

Professor Hallam pushed his hawk-nose over it.

'Excellent,' he murmured. 'And very well preserved, too. Quite a week, this, eh, bearer? First a body, and then tomorrow the opening of the Monument!'

'Yes, sir,' agreed Rolan, expressionlessly.

Rik was only the work-experience boy, and his place was to keep his trap shut. In fact, his place seemed to

11

be to keep as invisible as possible—so quite frankly he'd come to the conclusion that he might as well have stayed at home.

But the sight of that hand . . . it had been desiccated by the centuries it had lain in the ashy sand, so that every joint and tendon formed mountains under the shrunken skin.

'It's really *steel*,' he breathed.

The Plain of Hasiris had been famous for its steel corpses ever since Professor Hallam had dug up the first one thirty years before, but Rik had always assumed *steel* was just an attempt to make *grey* sound more exciting.

Rik, thrilled, peered at the hand more closely. Tiny mica-like flecks in the skin shone back at the red sun.

Rik thought about jumping up and down and saying *Wooh!* but then remembered about being silent and invisible. He pressed his lips together and contented himself with kicking his feet into the sand.

Professor Hallam sniffed at the dead hand as someone might sniff at a fine steak.

'Yes, a typical Hasien body. Very nice. Very nice indeed. You! Bearer-man! Get stretcher! Quick! Chop-chop!'

Rolan turned and jogged away, leaping easily over the ditches, towards the biggest of the square tents. People said the natives looked like ghosts, but Rik had been looked after by a native child-minder when he was small (his parents considered themselves dashingly liberal, and it was very cheap) and, besides, he'd

12

known Rolan for so long that Rik hardly noticed the pale colour of his skin.

Professor Hallam's sand-vulture nose was only a few inches from the steel hand, now.

'Very fine,' he murmured, appreciatively. 'Here, you, boy, what's-your-name, you'll bring a refreshing ignorance to this. What do you make of this body?'

Typical. Rik was finally being asked to say something, and all he could think of was a nursery rhyme Rolan's little sister Aranna used to sing to him when they'd played together in the streets of the Native Quarter.

> *Feet on stones,*
> *Steely bones.*
> *Feet on soil,*
> *Constant toil.*

'The skin looks . . . like metal, sir,' he blurted out.

Professor Hallam's head snapped up, his eyes gleaming alarmingly.

'Yes. Yes, boy. *And?*'

'*And* . . . ' went on Rik. But he hadn't a clue. He'd only chosen to come here for his work-experience because he'd spotted Rolan on the site as he'd driven past in the motor car with Pater. Rik hadn't seen Rolan for years, but Rik had never forgotten him. Rolan had been fantastic: he'd been able to turn cartwheels right from one end of the market-place to the other, and he'd been able to leap from roof to roof across the alleys of the Native Quarter. Finding Rolan's sister Aranna working on the site too had been just a tremendously wonderful surprise.

'Well?' prompted Professor Hallam, waspishly. 'What sort of person might be made of metal?'

Rik almost wished he'd taken the easy option and done his work-experience at one of his mother's youth clubs. He'd come here because of Rolan and Aranna, but it had turned out that neither of them wanted to be friends any more. Which was ridiculous. *Rik* didn't mind that they were pale-skinned natives, and therefore, of course, servants, but Rolan and Aranna seemed to be too embarrassed about it to speak to Rik properly any more.

'Come now, boy! Where might one find a steel man? Eh? Eh?'

Rik did his best to haul his brain into a more efficient gear. What should he say? The trouble was, it was so long since Professor Hallam had spoken to a normal person that he had no idea how totally and utterly bonkers he'd become. The red desert sun had fried his brains.

But Rik had to say something, because Professor Hallam's black eyes were fixed on him, shining with insane enthusiasm.

Rik looked again at the long steel fingers of the body and blurted out the only the thing he could think of.

'Er . . . in space?' he said, foolishly.

Professor Hallam made a triumphant goat-sneezing noise.

'There!' he exclaimed. 'An unbiased mind, you see? Obvious, isn't it—or so one would have thought.'

Rik, having surprised himself by coming up with the right answer, was quite grateful to be able to keep silent as Professor Hallam swept on.

'How else are the carvings on the Monument to be explained?' he demanded, excitedly. 'We are shown men flying in the air. What explanation can there be, other than that this place was visited by creatures from Outer Space? Eh, boy?'

Rolan was returning, now, followed by a squad of other natives bearing shovels and a stretcher. The last of them was Aranna. Aranna had been Rik's best friend for years and years until he'd started Senior School and he hadn't been able to visit the Native Quarter any more.

Professor Hallam's nostrils were flared with insane amounts of triumph.

'What explanation, boy?' he went on. 'Who could deny the presence of a great alien power who had walked in the shadow of *that*!'

And Rik's eyes reluctantly followed the professor's pointing finger . . .

. . . to the Monument.

It rose from the earth, charcoal-dark and as massive as a cliff. Some ancient cataclysm had tipped it out of true, so that it leant threateningly over the little cluster of tents on the plain.

Rik shuddered a little. He couldn't help it. The Monument was only a building, but quite frankly it scared the life out of him. He'd been avoiding looking at it ever since he arrived, and, yes, avoiding walking in the thing's shadow, too, even though it lay blue and cool across the channelled earth.

Professor Hallam let out a slightly manic chuckle. 'The *idea* that the Monument could have been built by

15

the Hasiens, who were then at the most primitive stage of town-dwelling! Or by the Yolek hunters of the forests! The idea that the builders were infected with some plague which gave them psychic powers! Ridiculous! Ridiculous!'

The Monument's walls must be a hundred feet high. They leant forward, balanced, but perhaps only just. The black stone was carved with the pictures that people had been arguing about for centuries. They showed massive people with ugly faces. Some of the people seemed to be flying, and some of then seemed to be dead, and some of them bore mysterious objects which might have been medical instruments, or space-probes, or even, for all Rik knew, sandwiches.

The stone of the Monument reflected the red sunlight a little, so that now the Monument's shadow was criss-crossed with fiery streaks like a leviathan's skin.

Professor Hallam was regarding the Monument wistfully, his back as straight as a lifetime of poking in the ashy sand could make it.

'It has kept its mystery for who knows how many centuries,' he said, quietly. 'But by tomorrow . . . who knows what we shall find, tomorrow.'

And Rik, despite himself, found that his heart was suddenly thumping with the excitement of tomorrow. Tomorrow (one of the very few *tomorrows* that Rik would be on the site) the whole mystery of the Monument would be laid open.

Last week they'd found a large slab of stone in the ashy sand. When they'd dug round it they'd found that, tall as the Monument was, it should be taller still.

16

The winds had buried the Monument deep in the sand, and the slab they'd found was actually the lintel of a great doorway.

At once Professor Hallam, totally bonkers Professor Hallam, had had explosives and experts brought in. All week they'd been blowing away the rocks and earth that hid the base of the Monument, even though the building was leaning at a frightening angle to start with and each blast was vibrating the whole structure and rumpling the sand round it into ripples. The building had always leant too much for it to be safe to blow a hole through the walls, but the door proved to be surrounded by great supporting columns. Tomorrow afternoon it would be blasted open.

And then the Monument, with all its secrets, would be revealed at last.

3

'Truth Sayer!'

Nian was too intent on the pockle game to take any notice of Snorer's shout. He lunged out and whacked the pockle cone with his flipper.

Alin ran forward and swiped the pock hard.

The pock shot up out of play, smacked into the trunk of a tree, bounded neatly down a hollow tree, sailed through the air avoiding seventy-three branches, a startled hayfinch, and one of Hani's old boots—and then plunged neatly into the drey at the end of the pockle ground to bring the score to one–nil.

There was a complete and utter silence for about four seconds while everybody's eyes bulged with amazement—and then Hani let out a howl of outrage.

'*Fluuuuuuke!*' he howled.

Nian stood in what should have been total, complete, and utter gob-smacked amazement—but which, for some reason he didn't quite grasp, wasn't.

The Tarhun Snorer stood by Nian's elbow. His face was strangely solemn.

'Truth Sayer,' he said, awkwardly, 'you've got a visitor. I think . . . I think he's brought news from home.'

Nian felt a qualm of disquiet. It'd have to be very important news to make it worth travelling the seven days' journey to the House of Truth.

He chucked his flipper to Alin and started running across the garden towards the great white wall of the Outer House.

'*Cobbled the paths of the worlds?*' echoed Nian, completely puzzled. 'Are you *sure* that's what Grandy said?'

'Well, that sort of thing,' said Tan. 'Mother says Grandy's going age-mazy.'

Nian made a face. That didn't sound likely: Grandy was old, but she'd always been as sharp as a thistle.

Tan was looking at Nian as if he was expecting him to do something amazing, like lay an egg. People did that a lot.

But what on earth did Grandy expect him to do? Nian opened his mouth to snap a question, but then he pushed away his irritation. He hadn't seen his brother Tan for a couple of months: they should be celebrating.

Nian turned to Snorer.

'Do you think Snerk could do us some supper to eat in here?' he asked. 'I'm afraid I'm not allowed to take you into the Inner House, Tan.'

Snorer sniffed and glowered.

'Oh, of course,' he muttered. 'Of course, that's what I'm grotting here for, isn't it? Running backwards and forwards doing your bogging catering, Truth Sayer.'

19

Nian shot Snorer a sharp look, but Tan was already gratefully sitting down again.

'I don't think I *could* walk to your Inner House,' he admitted. 'I feel as if I've spent a whole week climbing this mountain, Nian.'

Tan did look exhausted, and that wasn't like Tan. Tan was the sturdy sort of person who could work all day around the farm and then be raring to go hunting in the evening.

Hm. First Grandy acting oddly, and now Tan . . . it was strange, and somehow it felt important to Nian. Vitally important, though he couldn't have said why.

Perhaps it was just that last night's dream was still following him about. He'd ask Derig. Derig was perhaps Nian's closest friend in the House, and Derig knew lots about dreams. Mind you, Nian couldn't actually remember what his dream had been about.

Snorer grunted a bit, and shifted from foot to foot, like a bear with belly-ache.

'Well,' he said, hugely put-upon, 'I *suppose* Snerk won't mind the extra work of you having your supper in here, even though he's been really down, lately, what with worrying about his taste buds failing because he says that every day's food tastes the same to him. So I'll be off and see what I can do, then. My head's fit to burst, but never mind.'

Nian, distracted from whatever he'd been trying to remember, glared at him.

'Well, you shouldn't have got so drunk last night,' he told him.

But Snorer's fat face creased into a deeply wounded look.

'*You'd* drink if you were one of the Tarhun,' he said. 'We're always especially in need of a drink on a Sunday night. Exhausted with trudging backwards and forwards with the teas, we are. It's not the drinking, Truth Sayer, we're used to that. No, it's the stress. That's what we all put it down to.'

Nian felt another stab of disquiet. The Tarhun were always moaning and groaning, but it was usually about not getting the chance to cheat people as much since Nian had been the Truth Sayer. Nian had never heard of one of the Tarhun having a headache that wasn't the result of either drink or a fight. Or, most probably, both. And Snerk the cook was generally violent and terrifying, but he wasn't usually depressed.

Again, this was a bit odd; and again Nian sort of felt as if he'd already dreamed something like it the night before.

Hm, Nian really needed to talk to Derig about all this.

He turned to Tan.

'Look, come out into the garden,' he said. 'It's only just through the House, and you can meet my friends.'

The others, having been abandoned by Nian, had given up on the game of pockle and were playing grothead. This was a mind-duel where two people sat and tried to get a flower-pot full of mud to empty itself over the other person's head. It was a good game, but no one would ever play with Nian because his powers were so strong and peculiar that he had a habit, when

21

under pressure, of exploding the whole pot: and none of the boys wanted a blast of terracotta shards erupting in his face.

Hani looked up sideways from where he was pouring water into a pot of soil until it looked like something Nian didn't want to think about.

'Hey,' Hani said, pleased. 'You're just in time to see me beat Emmec at grot-head.'

'Huh,' snorted Emmec, good-naturedly. 'If he does, it'll be for the first time ever.'

'Aha,' said Hani. 'But I have new and cunning strategies. I'm going to use my magnificent ears as focusing dishes for my powers.'

'This is Hani, and that's Emmec,' explained Nian. 'Hey, you lot, this is my brother Tan.'

'You'd better come over here with us and take cover, Tan,' advised Alin. 'Once those two idiots get started that pot might end up anywhere.'

'Yes,' said Gow, seriously. 'Be ready to duck, Tan, all right?'

Tan, looking confused, went obediently with the other boys to where they'd piled up a low wall of stones.

'Derig,' said Nian, quietly, as they laid themselves down on their stomachs. 'Have you been dreaming, lately?'

Derig shook his head.

'I don't think so,' he said. 'I haven't been waking you up, have I?'

Derig was a noisy dreamer. This was a nuisance in some ways because all the boys slept in the same room. On the other hand, if there was anything dangerous going on then Derig could be relied upon to pick up on it and start screaming in the night.

This had proved very useful on occasion.

'No,' said Nian, 'I haven't heard a peep out of you. But my grandmother sent me a message to say that something weird's going on, and I wondered if you knew anything about it.'

Derig frowned uneasily.

'I have been wondering about what she said about the paths of the worlds,' he said, 'but—'

'What?' said Nian, completely taken aback. 'Have you? But you couldn't have been. I mean, I've only just told you about her!'

There was a glurch and a *splonk* from the other side of the wall, followed by a high-pitched howl from Hani, and a lot of laughter from the other boys, but Derig and Nian were staring at each other, confused.

Nian clutched the hair at the back of his neck.

'Something's definitely wrong,' he said. 'I don't know what it is, but something's got . . . I don't know . . . '

' . . . out of joint,' suggested Derig, tentatively. 'I hadn't realized before, but things are sort of . . . bendy at the edges. Perhaps.'

Nian thought about the ceiling in the swimming pool, which was decorated with a picture of the turning worlds. It showed the worlds rayed with spikes, a little like the cogs of a clock, each turning the others as they moved. And although, from Nian's experience of travelling from one world to another, the worlds seemed to be linked in a much more complicated way than that, he found he knew what Derig meant.

It was . . . it was almost as if things had happened before. Except at the same time Nian was sure that some of this was quite new. And how could *some* of it be new? You couldn't take bits of Time and patch them in somewhere else. Could you? Well, he couldn't imagine how. But he did feel as if things were getting progressively more . . . peculiar. Darker. Sort of folded up. Or scooped out.

Nian had absolutely no idea what any of that really meant, but he still had a horrible feeling that whatever was happening was important.

'Hey, will you look after Tan for me?' he asked. 'Make sure he doesn't get grot-headed, will you, because it's not easy to be sure which way the stuff's flying, sometimes. And if you could take him back to the Strangers' Room when it's time to go in, that'd be great. Only I need to make arrangements.'

'Arrangements for what?' asked Derig.

Nian was already making for the door to the Inner House. He glanced back.

'For visiting other worlds,' he said.

Nian would have liked to consult the Lord Tarq, but Tarq was spending the day in fasting and Thought in his room, so Nian hurried along the curving white corridor to the library.

The Lord Firn was there, fussing. Firn spent his every breathing moment fussing—about hartskin moth, or woodmite, or damp, or borrowing slips—the list went on and on. Nian had never actually seen him *not* in a state of quivering anxiety, except that time at a full Council Meeting when the Lord Rago had gone on for so long about the indiscipline and general uselessness of Young People Nowadays that Firn had actually fallen into a deep slumber as he sat.

Nian started talking even before he'd made his bow, because if he gave Firn the chance to get started, he was likely to be there till nightfall.

'I'm leaving the world first thing tomorrow,' he announced. 'My grandmother's sent me a message to say she thinks something might be going wrong with the turning of the worlds, so I need to check everything's all right.'

The Lord Firn stared at him, appalled, like a feeble-minded mole suddenly faced with a drain rat.

'But, Truth Sayer—'

'I'll take great care, obviously,' Nian went on, hurriedly. 'But I'm just letting you know, Lord, so . . . so you know. All right?'

He bowed again, turned away and headed out fast; but of course he hadn't got far before he heard Firn's weak high voice calling after him.

Nian sighed, and stopped. Opening passageways to other worlds was something which only he, the Truth Sayer, could do. And, while everyone agreed it was the Truth Sayer's fate to walk the worlds, none of the Lords were *at all* keen on him doing it. Apart from the understandable objection that Travelling To Other Worlds Had Never Been Thought Necessary When They Were Young, there were a lot of worlds out there, some of which very probably contained dragons and/or worzels, volcanoes, unicorns, murderers, and strangle vines: and, apart from the risk of Something Nasty nipping back through an open passageway, there was also the problem that if people got stuck in the wrong world for more than a couple of days then that set off earthquakes. And eventually, if anyone got *completely* stuck in the wrong world (i.e., eaten or killed by a dragon and/or worzels, volcanoes, etc.) then a couple of the worlds (including, unfortunately, this one) would tear themselves into unliveably small pieces.

Firn waddled up to Nian, panting with haste and worry.

'There might be some hideous danger that only I can avert,' pointed out Nian, reasonably, before Firn could speak.

'Oh yes, yes, of course,' agreed Firn, his white eyelashes flickering. 'Of course. There might be some threat to the House, and that would never do. Especially not when I'm in the middle of reorganizing the library. After all, you're used to danger and all that sort of thing. I'm sure you'll manage very well with all the pain and peril and injury and all that sort of unpleasantness. You'd better take a scarf.'

Well, thanks a lot, thought Nian.

'Yes,' went on Firn, 'yes, indeed. We certainly don't want any danger set loose in the House. I'll see you're woken early, shall I, because if there *is* any danger, then the sooner it's combated the better. A stitch in time, a stitch in time!'

Nian tried to feel pleased Firn wasn't trying to stop him. He bowed again, and turned away.

'Oh, and Truth Sayer! Truth Sayer!'

Nian stopped. Firn wasn't such a bad old stick. He was probably going to say *May the Tides of the Worlds Carry You Safely*, or *Take Care*, or *Come Home Soon*, or something.

'I shall of course require a full written report of your travels,' said Firn. 'In triplicate.'

And then he bumbled back to the library.

Nian cursed quietly but thoroughly; but then he grinned, shrugged, and went to pack.

The Lord Caul caught Nian hurrying along the corridor with his pockets full of food. Leaving even quite small things in the wrong world weakened the whole system of the worlds, so it had been decided that Nian should take his own food with him to other worlds whenever possible; and Nian had decided to avoid visiting other worlds' privies, too, if he could help it.

Caul was by far the youngest of the Lords. He did most of the boys' teaching. He was a quiet sort of young man, but no fool and no push-over. He looked Nian up and down.

'So what's going on, Truth Sayer?' he asked.

Nian tried to scoop together something which sounded sensible.

'I'm going into the abyss between the worlds, tomorrow,' he said. 'And I'm going to . . . look at things.'

Caul didn't look very impressed, but at least he didn't mutter things about missed lessons.

'Is there something wrong?' he asked.

'I'm not certain,' Nian admitted. 'My grandmother sent me a warning, but I don't really understand it.

I think there might be, and so does Derig, but I can't track down exactly what it is.'

Caul grunted.

'Quite honestly, I feel tempted to come with you,' he said. 'I feel as if I've been teaching you lot for weeks on end without a break, and it's only Monday. Come and find me before you set out, Nian, and we'll arrange for someone to go after you if you're away too long.'

The Lord Tarq's door was ajar, and Nian stopped for a moment to look in at the old man who had welcomed Nian when he had first arrived at the House of Truth. Tarq had always been frail, but Nian was suddenly struck by just how thin he was. Tarq seemed hardly more than a skeleton as he sat motionless, Thinking. Nian, rather alarmed, used his powers to search Tarq's old body and found the old man actually shining with weakness. But Tarq should not have been so weak. The Lords were all used to fasting, and missing a day's food was usually a bit of a tonic to them.

Nian made a mental note, as he hurried on his way back to the Strangers' Room, to check on Tarq the next morning before he left.

Nian and Tan had supper, spent a busy couple of hours catching up on all the news from home, and then settled down peacefully side by side to sleep.

'Do the Tarhun do this *every* night?' asked Tan, grudgingly impressed, as what sounded like a bench clattered against the wall of their room.

Nian didn't know, because he'd always slept in the Inner House until then.

'Probably,' he said, grinning.

Tan pulled his cover up round his ears.

'Wake me up before you leave the world, won't you,' he said. 'Because I've got to see that.'

'Don't worry,' said Nian, wriggling himself into a comfortable position. 'I won't go anywhere without letting you know.'

4

Rik didn't know whether he or Aranna had been more amazed at the sight of each other on that first evening when he'd arrived on the site. He'd been heading past a group of saucepan-scrubbing native girls on his way to the wash tent when one of them had looked up—and it had been Aranna.

Aranna, cleaning a saucepan. Aranna.

They'd stared at each other for ages, until one of the other girls had nudged her neighbour and burst into giggles—and then Rik, idiotically, had fled.

Rik had gone back to find Aranna as soon as he'd stopped blushing. He waited by the kitchen tent. She'd been alone, then.

Rik had got their meeting all planned. Once they'd finished jumping up and down with joy at the sight of each other, they'd go to the mess tent and he'd buy Aranna a drink and some supper.

'I can't,' said Aranna, awkwardly. 'The mess tent . . . I'm not allowed.'

Aranna was a servant, a girl, a pale-skinned native: any of those things might mean she was banned from the mess tent—but Rik was so happy to see her that he didn't care. He found himself telling her all about school, and Professor Hallam, and absolutely everything.

She'd stood, eyes lowered, but she'd listened; he was sure she'd listened, because once or twice her face had broken into her wide smile. But then a gong had sounded, and she'd had to run off to her tent before her curfew. She'd said hardly anything, but Rik was sure—was *sure*—she'd been happy to see him. Very, very happy.

Rik had gone to his own tent very happy, too, with the yeasty joy he'd hardly known since he'd stopped visiting the Native Quarter.

Rik had loved going to the Native Quarter to 'Auntie' Marle's house. He'd arrive in his smart school blazer, and 'Auntie' Marle would sling him a bag of root chips and tell him to be off from under her feet.

This had been thrilling to Rik, who spent his time at home being escorted carefully from one improving activity to the next. He'd dump his blazer and dash off into the narrow streets of the Native Quarter to kick stones and annoy the stall keepers in the street markets.

That was how he'd got to know Rolan and Aranna.

Rolan was tall, green-eyed, and could turn cartwheels right from one end of an alley to the other. Rolan was much older than Rik, of course, but sometimes he'd let Rik tag along; until one day Aranna had told him that Rolan had left the city to find work. And after that Rik hadn't seen Rolan for five years, until he'd spotted him from Pater's motor car.

Rik had actually met Aranna under a stall which sold spiced pastries. He'd been hoping for a chance to snaffle one, and all he could see of Aranna at first were the sparkles in her eyes. And then she'd put a bit of warm pastry, all covered in honey and dirt, into his hand, and they'd been friends ever since. Yes, ever since, even though he hadn't seen Aranna for years, and now somehow the fact that she was pale, and one of the servants, seemed to have opened up an awkward distance between them.

That was stupid, because Aranna was clever. Rik would have got into all sorts of trouble in the Native Quarter without her. Aranna was small-boned and delicate, with black hair that swung and bounced behind her like a horse's tail, and she knew lots.

'Not that way,' she would whisper. 'That's Jof's alley.'

'Who's Jof?'

Aranna would pull a face as if she'd just bitten into something sour.

'A friend of Uncle Moram.'

'Uncle' Moram was 'Auntie' Marle's husband. He was cheerful and interesting and tested shops' burglar alarms. Just sometimes, he would ask Rik to help. Rik would have to climb very quietly through a window that was too small for anyone else, gather up whatever he could find, and that way prove to the shopkeeper that his burglar alarms weren't as good as they should be.

'You're a natural, a natural!' 'Uncle' Moram would say, beaming, as he helped Rik down from the window. 'What a help you've been to the shopkeeper, young Rik!'

Back at 'Auntie' Marle's, 'Uncle' Moram even showed Rik how to open locks with the help of some long spindly hook-things. That was interesting, too, and it meant that Rik could do an even better job of checking the shopkeepers' burglar alarms.

'Yes!' said 'Uncle' Moram, delighted. 'We natives are the craftiest locksmiths in the world, young Rik!'

If 'Uncle' Moram had a fault, it was that he had some peculiar friends. Rik tried his best to like them, but they tended to have scowly mouths and curved knives stuck into their belts, and some of them said things that weren't very polite.

'Come come,' 'Uncle' Moram would say, smiling hard. 'The boy can't help the colour of his skin, can he? He's a skilled operator, I tell you.' And once, Rik was almost sure 'Uncle' Moram had gone on to say something about the courts being easy on duns—which Rik hadn't understood at all.

But even picking locks with 'Uncle' Moram wasn't as much fun as being with Aranna. Aranna knew the Native Quarter so well she could vanish like a lizard whenever she wanted.

She laughed, flashing white teeth at him, when Rik asked her how she did it.

'If I could really vanish, do you think I'd live here?' she asked.

Rik felt uncertain. The Native Quarter was grubby

33

and crowded and noisy and chaotic and dangerous, but he just loved it. He loved it so much that he would have been sure he was adopted if he'd been pale like the natives. Going home always seemed like stepping into a newsreel—everything got all hurried and boring and grey.

'Don't you think this is the most wonderful place in the world?' he asked, greatly disappointed.

Aranna looked at him for a moment, as if wondering if she could trust him.

'It was wonderful once,' she said. 'Long long ago.'

Rik's heart bumped. He was at the age when more and more things were turning out to be quite ordinary, but he was still hoping like mad that there were still magical places somewhere.

'What was it like?' he asked, eagerly.

She regarded him coolly, shaking back her long black horse-tail of hair.

'People got a plague that gave them special powers,' she said. 'They used to be able to see right into things. They could see the bones inside people as they walked along.'

Rik took a huge breath of wonder.

'Really?'

She nodded, and then leaned forward to whisper. Her breath smelled of spices and honey.

'They could see past the sky, too.'

Past the sky . . . Rik didn't know what that meant, but it made him shiver.

'What could they see?' he whispered, awed. 'What could they see, past the sky?'

Aranna grinned at him, and suddenly he didn't know if she was teasing him or not.

'Somewhere very beautiful, where everyone was made of steel,' she said.

Rik gasped.

'What happened? What was it like? Tell me, Aranna! What happened?'

Aranna narrowed her eyes until they looked mysterious, and as black as Rik's own.

'The people swelled up until they got as big and strong as oxen,' she said.

'Really? Fantastic!' said Rik, very excited. 'And *then* what happened?'

Aranna frowned, a little.

'And then, they went mad and died,' she said.

5

Nian woke up on his mat in the pupils' room of the Inner House. Hani was lamenting at the prospect of the Lord Rago's weather-lore lesson. Rago was about as easy to be with as a scorched weasel, and Hani was spectacularly bad at weather-lore.

Nian pushed back his coarse fair hair and wondered blearily what he'd been dreaming about. It might have been something to do with . . . but no, it had gone. Whatever it had been, it'd left him with an unpleasant sort of upside-down and inside-out feeling.

Alin was doing the horribly bracing exercises with which he felt the need to start the day, and Derig was shaking out his cover.

Nian yawned, and put his mind tentatively into *forward* mode.

House of Truth. Sleeping Room.

Monday.

The Tarhun Reeklet was whistling as he brought the boys' tray along the path from the Outer House.

Nian, whose turn it was, with Gow and Derig, to

36

set out breakfast, still wasn't really that awake: but his brain gave an astonished and jarring twitch, all the same.

Reeklet. Whistling.

Reeklet? . . . *Whistling?*

'What are you so cheerful about?' asked Gow, disconcerted.

Reeklet beamed at them.

(*Beamed?* But Reeklet was generally the sourest of all the members of the Tarhun. Which was saying a *lot.*)

'Won twenty-five pieces at cards, last night,' he announced, presenting the tray to them with a flourish.

'Oh, that's brilliant,' said Derig, kindly, taking the tray. 'You must have played ever so well.'

Reeklet looked smug. Even his suicidal-caterpillar of a moustache looked smug.

'It's all down to my needlework, isn't it,' he said, tapping the side of his nose. 'Those other boggers in the Tarhun, they may sneer at my embroidery, but look at this!'

Reeklet rolled back a grimy sleeve. There was a playing-card sized pocket sewn inside his cuff.

'Oh yes,' he said. 'I'm going to make a killing at cards with this little secret pocket of mine, I am. Oh yes, indeed!'

Nian and Gow exchanged glances.

'But . . . isn't that cheating, technically speaking?' asked Gow, who liked things to be completely clear and accurate.

Reeklet nodded happily, and nearly burst with pride.

'And none of them could work it out!' he crowed. 'It was fantastic. They were suspicious, of course. Old Bulls-Eye, in the end he got so frustrated he started a fight. Knocked me out with a bench, he did, and I didn't wake until morning. Ha! So here I am, all fresh as a daisy after a nice long sleep, while the others are all crawling about hungover and shattered. But then they should know better than to stay up late on a Sunday, and I've told them so before.'

The Tarhun weren't the only ones who were crawling about shattered.

'Boggit,' yawned Emmec, as they took their places in the schoolroom to wait for the Lord Rago. 'How come I feel as if I need a holiday when it's only Monday morning?'

'Everybody keeps saying that,' Hani yawned back at him. 'Perhaps it's the weather or something.'

Nian was visited by a vague feeling of unease. He was pretty sure that Hani was right: everyone *had* been moaning for ages. But on the other hand, as it was Monday morning they couldn't possibly have been doing anything of the sort.

But here were the Lord Rago's footsteps approaching down the corridor, and even Nian had to keep his wits about him when Rago was teaching. He sat himself down behind Hani, in the hope that Hani's enormous ears would shield him from notice, and dismissed the puzzle from his mind.

* * *

Rik, very bored, had walked round the evening camp six times when he saw a pair of long pale legs disappearing through a tent flap. He hurried after them. Rolan must be off-duty, so perhaps he'd be able to talk, now.

'Rolan?' Rik said, hopefully, to the tent flap. There was no answer, so Rik leaned forward so he could see through the gap in the unlaced canvas.

The sun had paled Rolan's eyes to a startling, unfriendly blue.

'What are you doing here?' Rolan demanded.

'Oh, nothing, really,' said Rik, ingratiatingly. 'Um. Isn't it exciting about the Monument being opened tomorrow?'

Rolan sniffed.

'It depends on what's in there, doesn't it?'

Rik felt a rush of excitement.

'I saw you bringing up some boxes,' Rik said. 'You, and Aranna, and some of the others. Was that the explosives to blow the door open?'

Rolan nodded curtly. 'Sticks of dynamite. Yes, and a great archaeologist Professor Hallam has turned out to be, hasn't he? He can't wait to find out how the door opens, so he's going to blow it into a million pieces.'

'I bet you could open the door,' said Rik. 'You natives know all about locks.'

Rolan grunted.

Rik knew it would be pathetic beyond belief to ask

39

Rolan what he was doing tonight—but then found he'd done it anyway.

'I'm going out,' said Rolan, bleakly.

'Can I come?' asked Rik, breathless with hope.

'No,' said Rolan. 'You're too . . . young.'

Rik thought about walking another six times round the camp in a probably fruitless search for Aranna, who seemed to be always guarded by her silly giggling friends; or else going back to his small tent and having nothing to do for hours except write up his work experience diary.

'I wouldn't be any trouble,' he said.

Rolan waved that away.

'Look, accept it, Rik,' he said, brutally. 'I'm pale, and so are my friends. You can't tag along with us. Now clear off, all right? And don't you go pestering Aranna, either. She's got her own friends. She doesn't need you.'

Rik went away glumly. He hadn't had any luck *finding* Aranna, let alone pestering her, and he was beginning to be afraid that she was hiding from him. But that would be stupid, because they'd been the best friends ever. It wasn't that they were alike, exactly, because she was quiet and clever and neat, and he was a bit loud, really. But they had just had so much *fun*. Fun chasing through the alleys, and fun listening to her stories. So many stories. Stories told under the breath, and probably under the table, too. Stories about the great city of Hasir which was now only ruins under the ash, and of a great black tower, and steel hands reaching mutely towards the end of the sky . . .

Hasir was the greatest city in the world, and it was built, the stories said, on oxen. Well, obviously, it wasn't *really* built on oxen, that was just the sort of silly thing grown-ups said; it was *really* built, of course, on the stone of the plain.

'They were holy stones,' said Aranna. 'Sometimes, if you sat in exactly the right place, you could hear ghosts singing.'

'*Ooooooh!*' howled Rik, happily. 'What happened next?'

Hasir was also built (but also in that silly grown-up way of speaking) on wheat: but all that meant was that the wheat and oxen were as necessary to the city as the foundations were. The wheat flour could be baked, and the milk could be squeezed and salted, until it could all be piled up with the odd bit of ox meat to make a goodly feast which was called in those days a *chee zberga*.

And those *chee zbergas* were so tasty and good that people of Hasir became the mightiest people in the land. They looked out over their fields to the dark forests of the Yolek savages, and they were lords of all they surveyed.

(Rik liked that part of the story.)

The people were so mighty that they began to build a great black tower over the ghost-stones so they could conquer the ghosts, too.

The Yoleks of the forests, who were naked in their ignorance, and also because they hadn't invented clothes, yet (snigger snigger, went Rik, nudging Aranna, who sniggered, too), stared with wonder at the tall black tower, and the mighty people of Hasir listened carefully to the ghosts who spoke through the stones, but lived beyond the sky, so they might learn their secrets.

But one day a woman in the city looked at her child and saw that the infant seemed to be shining; and when she looked more closely, she saw that its skin was flecked with fragments of steel.

'The plague!' exclaimed Rik, excitedly. 'It had caught the plague!'

The woman wrapped it close and took it to the Wise Ones in the great black tower.

They had the child killed.

6

'All right,' sighed the Lord Caul, at last, at the end of the afternoon's lessons. 'That will have to do. Hani, do you think you could go and find a large basket? I expect the excellent Tarhun Snerk will be able to concoct something delicious with all these eggs.'

Derig picked one up carefully.

'I wonder what sort of eggs they are?' he asked, as Hani galloped off. 'Perhaps we ought to send them back.'

Emmec laughed.

'Do you know where they came from, Nian?'

Nian shrugged light-heartedly.

'Not me,' he said. He could easily have found out, but he was probably going to be eating these eggs for days to come, and he wasn't sure he wanted to know. Snerk the cook would be pleased, whatever sort of eggs they were: Snerk's life was dedicated to finding the Ultimate Eating Experience, and he was generally violently enthusiastic about new ingredients.

The eggs had appeared, with a clattering of small clocking explosions, all round the schoolroom ceiling while Hani had been trying to forge the last intricate link in the chain of minds that the rest of them (except

Nian, who made things explode too easily) had been putting together. If the boys hadn't had a lot of practice catching cones at pockle, and if Caul hadn't managed to call up an instant span-deep layer of feathers for the floor, things might have been exceptionally messy.

Derig looked sad.

'Their mothers will be missing them,' he said. 'But I don't suppose they'd hatch, now, even if we could send them back.'

Caul shook his head regretfully.

'I don't think the parents would accept the eggs back, now, Derig,' he said. 'Not once they'd been taken.'

Derig turned his face away and busied himself with rolling up his mat, and Nian wondered if there was anything he could do, after all. He scanned the eggs— and then he laughed.

'They're not real!' he exclaimed. 'They're made of nutpaste!'

All the boys looked at him as if he were mad.

'You're joking,' said Alin.

But Emmec picked one up and sniffed at it.

'Watch out,' warned Gow. 'That thing's probably just come down a bird's backside.'

Emmec scratched the thing with his finger, sniffed again, and finally put a tiny piece in his mouth.

All the boys watched in fascinated suspense.

Emmec's face broke into a triumphant grin.

'Nutpaste!' he shouted, and threw the egg up in the air and caught it.

Even the Lord Caul joined the rush to pick up eggs and take cautious bites.

'Hm,' he said, slurping. 'I can't imagine where Hani managed to conjure up nutpaste eggs from, but they're extremely good. Hm. Yes. And I thought I was so clever to call up that layer of feathers when the things appeared.'

'You were incredibly quick, Lord,' said Gow (which was not sucking up, but simple justice) and the other boys nodded. Even Nian had only been thinking of catching as many eggs as he could, but Caul had acted instantly to solve the whole problem.

Caul looked mildly pleased.

'Yes, I don't think there's anything wrong with my reactions,' he agreed. 'Mind you, being stuck in a room with you lot during mind-joining lessons is excellent training in keeping my wits about me. Still, if we keep practising we'll get there in the end. That's what I keep telling myself.'

Everyone was cramming nutpaste eggs down the front of their tunics when Hani rushed back in. His eyes were bulging with incredible news.

'Hey, you lot!' he called, in high excitement. 'Lord! Oh, Lord! Guess what? The kitchen garden's full of naked hens!'

'Oh *Lord*,' muttered Caul, in his turn; and raced out.

Making warm clothes for the irritable and outraged hens was comparatively easy, Nian found, especially as he'd once met someone in another world who'd made quite a speciality of using weaving Thoughts. Dressing the hens in the clothes once they were made,

45

though, was a nightmare. All the boys were badly scratched by the time the hens were strutting about inside their vests, warm, but stiff with offence.

Alin regarded his lacerated hands ruefully.

'This is really what I came to the House of Truth to learn, isn't it,' he said. 'I can just imagine my father asking what I've mastered since I've been home. And I'll say, *well, I've saved three hens from getting head colds.*'

'You've made real progress with your thought-joining, too, Alin,' pointed out the Lord Caul, putting down the last hen. 'Most of you have. And that's an essential part of being able to see things from more than one perspective.'

Hani shook the sting of his scratches away from his hands as the Lord Caul set off back to the House.

'Come on,' he said. 'Blow all this grandmothering stuff. Let's have a game of pockle. There's still time.'

Nian ran across the garden with the others. Pockle was his favourite time of the day, when he could forget all about the responsibilities of being the Truth Sayer and just . . . *enjoy* himself.

Alin was making the first pass as Nian was running up the ground into position. Yes. This was what he wanted to do. Forget all his doubts and worries and . . .

'Truth Sayer!'

Nian ignored the urgent shout. Not *now*. Not when he was playing pockle. For heaven's sake, he couldn't be on call every moment of every single day. He lunged out irritably and whacked the pockle cone with his flipper, sending it towards Alin . . .

'Grandy said *what*?' asked Nian, staring at Tan's stolid face and wishing he was still playing pockle.

'Something about someone cobbling the paths of the worlds,' Tan repeated. He rubbed at his legs ruefully. 'Boggit, Nian, this mountain's steep. My legs feel as if I've been climbing non-stop for a month.'

Nian sat down beside his brother. He was pleased to see Tan, of course he was—though quite honestly it only seemed like yesterday that he'd last seen him.

'If you think *walking up* this mountain's hard, you should try living on it,' said Nian, feelingly.

Tan made a face.

'You're telling me,' he said. 'When I smelt all those great fat Tarhun blokes I nearly turned round and ran all the way home again.'

'Oh, the Tarhun are all right,' said Nian, in fairness. 'On the whole. They like to look tough, but they're just mouselets, really. Most of the time. As long as they're sober. And not too stressed. Or hungry. No, if you want scary, you should see the Lords. They're enough to turn your hair white overnight.'

Tan's stolid expression wavered a bit. He might even have gulped.

'What do they do?' he asked, not quite carelessly. Nian tried to think up something to say to freeze Tan's insides with terror . . . but then he couldn't quite be bothered. It was odd, but he was really really tired. He couldn't understand it. After all, it was only Monday.

47

'Oh, they just make us work all the time,' he said. 'What else did Grandy say?'

'It was just as I said: a load of cobble stuff. She kept nagging on and on. I think . . . I think she was frightened, Nian.'

Nian felt a first shiver of alarm. That didn't sound like Grandy.

'Mother said she's maybe going age-mazy,' went on Tan, with a blush of shame.

And that didn't sound like Grandy, either. Grandy was old, but she'd always been as sharp as a thistle. *Cobbled the paths of the worlds.* Whatever could that mean?

Nian looked back on the last few days. Everything had been more or less normal. So had today, except that . . . well, it was nothing he could exactly put his finger on, but . . . it was sort of as if he'd seen it all before. He'd been . . . not bored, exactly, because he was never bored; but as if he'd got into a rut.

Nian shook himself. A rut was most definitely where he did not wish to be.

'I'd better check on things,' he decided. 'It sounds as if Grandy thinks there might be something going wrong with the way the worlds are turning. Perhaps I'd better have a look at a couple of other worlds and see if they're all right.'

Tan looked at his brother, awe struggling with suspicion.

'Look at other worlds?'

'Yes,' said Nian. 'But don't worry, we'll have some supper first—Snerk, he's the cook, he's brilliant. I can go and have a look at some other worlds tomorrow.'

7

Rik, having gone to bed early out of pure boredom, woke up before dawn the next day, which was the day the Monument was to be opened. As the work experience boy he'd naturally been put in the tent nobody wanted. It was pitched on an eruption of rib-jabbing rocks, in a place that caught the full blast of the icy evening winds and the even more unpleasant full blast of the rising sun.

He opened the tent flaps as wide as possible and wondered dismally if there was any chance of breakfast.

He peered around through the morning gloom.

No.

No one was moving, not even in the row of women's tents where Aranna lived. He'd decided that the early mornings would be his best chance to talk to her, before anyone else was around—but it was too early even for that. Rik sighed. He was pretty sure that Aranna would have liked to be proper friends again, but Rolan or one of the other girls always seemed to turn up and then she'd have to hurry away.

The sun was not long up. It was glinting on the grey

ashy sand and marking out every ditch of the excavations in sharp lines and hummocks, like the remains of a long-dead war.

Rik crawled out of his tent, stretched, went glumly to the wash-tent, and drew himself a small bucket of water to wash in. The water had kept some of the sun's heat from yesterday, but there was only enough of it (every drop of water had to be carried in, and it was strictly rationed) to make his skin feel slimy. He used his shirt to mop out the bucket in the hope of the wet cloth keeping him cool for another hour or so.

He came out dripping gratefully and discovered he was so incredibly bored that his head was about to explode. He'd left his watch at home because he'd been warned the fine ash would clog the mechanism, but Rik could tell from the feel of the air that it was going to be at least another hour until the clonging of breakfast saucepans began to sound around the camp.

There was still no sign of Aranna, or anyone else.

Being bored during work time was bearable: it was no worse than school, after all, and anyway by the time the working day started it was so hot, and there were so many armour-plated sand-flies everywhere, that Rik could hardly bear to breathe, let alone move or think. But being bored in his free time was ridiculous—especially when he was here, on the site of ancient Hasiris, the scene of so many terrifying stories about people swelling up with plagues, and bitter fighting, and worlds past the sky.

Rik pulled his broad-brimmed hat down over his eyes and went off in search of . . . of *something*.

Anything, almost—as long as it didn't involve Professor Hallam or dusting files.

Rik made his way through the faded tents to the edge of the dig. And there, dark against the rising sun, was the leaning form of the Monument.

Rik winced a little as he laid eyes on it. It spooked everyone: no one said anything, but you could see people being careful to avoid turning their backs on it.

But in just a few hours the doors would be blown open and . . . and what? Rik didn't know, of course. No one did. Rik had listened to all the native stories, but they *were* just stories, obviously. No one even knew what the Monument had really been *for*: Professor Hallam's theories about invaders from Outer Space, were, as far as Rik could tell, exactly as mad as the natives' yarns about plague-struck steelmen.

Of course Rik had swallowed all those native stories, hook, line, and sinker, when he'd been small (yes: Rik could remember the fish-mouthed awe with which he'd gulped down every morsel of story, whether it had been from 'Auntie' Marle's perpetual native radio station, or from Aranna, or even from Rolan).

They were tremendous, terrifying, wonderful stories. Rik had woken up screaming in the night, once. Mater had been quite annoyed.

'We'll have to tell "Auntie" Marle not to tell you such frightening stories,' she'd said briskly, and rather grimly.

That threat was enough to make sure that in future Rik kept his nightmares to himself.

The steel plague-baby was buried (Aranna told him, whispering thrillingly in his ear: of course 'Auntie' Marle never told stories) and all was well until the next baby showed signs of turning to steel, and then so did the next, and then the next after that. And then one day at a Council Meeting one of the Councillor's sleeves got billowed out by the draught from the door and everyone saw that the flesh of his arm was glinting and grey.

'So?' the Councillor demanded, fiercely, glaring round. 'If this is a disease I have, then I believe it is a gift from the ghosts beyond the sky, for it has made me stronger than ever.'

And it was true that he was strong, for when they tried to kill him he fought off six men with ease. The seventh man waited until the fight was at its height and then struck out, fast and deadly as a snake, and clubbed the steel-armed man to death with a telescope.

This seventh man, though, proved to be even more steely-skinned than the first one.

It wasn't long before everyone in the Monument began to show signs of turning to steel. In lots of ways it was rather wonderful, because as someone became affected his eyes grew stronger and stronger until he could see the fabric of the worlds.

Unfortunately, his mind was affected, too: he became suspicious, and then quite certain that the men around him were treacherous. Mind you, in this he was generally right.

The doors to the Monument were soon shut for fear the common people would catch the wonderful steel plague and become strong, too.

Once the doors were shut, of course, no one knew for sure what was going on inside the Monument. Sometimes a body, bloated and grey, would be thrown from the high roof. But soon afterwards there was the great earthquake which lifted the plain and tilted the Monument almost to tipping point.

And after that there was silence from the Monument of Hasiris.

Nian woke up on his mat in the pupils' room of the Inner House. Hani was rubbing his big ears where they'd got creased with sleeping, while having a good moan at the prospect of having to endure one of the Lord Rago's weather-lore lessons that morning.

Nian pushed back his coarse fair hair and wondered what he'd been dreaming about. It might have been . . . but no, he couldn't remember. Especially with Hani moaning on and on.

'For pit's sake, Rago's not that bad,' he snapped, for he felt as if he'd lost track of an important line of thought.

Hani was so surprised he actually did shut up. Everyone always moaned about Rago's lessons: it was a sort of compliment, really, because although Rago was the oldest person in the House of Truth he was still as sharp and spiky as a prickmouse. In any case, Rago had been a pockle player with United in his boyhood, and for that Hani would forgive Rago anything, even telling Hani he was a complete moron during every single weather-lore lesson they'd ever had.

Well, as far as weather-lore was concerned, that was fair enough. Hani *was* a complete moron.

Nian pushed off his cover, rubbed the sleep out of his eyes, yawned until his jaw cracked, and put his brain tentatively into forward mode.

Inner House. Morning.

Monday.

8

The sun was oozing steadily higher over the Plain of Hasiris. Already Rik's wet shirt was drying and stiffening into creases.

Rik stepped forward into the shadow of the Monument, which was built on stones where ghosts had used to sing.

And kept on walking.

The black stone of the Monument seemed to be radiating cold. That was so weird and impossible that Rik felt compelled to trudge round the corner of the Monument, out of the shadow, to make sure the sun was still working.

The newly-discovered door was on that side. It was flanked by stout columns which had been gouged deep with vicious zigzags. The sun slanted along it, so that the black stone of the door gleamed with a pearly sheen, green and purple, like the inside of a ornyx shell.

Rik looked back at the rows of tents. There was still no one else moving, and he suddenly felt so frustrated that he went up to the door and thumped his hand on it. It wasn't *fair*. The natives had wanted him when he was small and could fit through windows and help

'Uncle' Moram out with his security business. Rik had tried so hard to help 'Uncle' Moram by being extra quiet, when he was naturally not quiet at all. Oh yes, the natives had wanted him then, when he was useful.

Rik stood by the door to the Monument, and felt really angry. It was a waste that he couldn't be friends with Rolan and Aranna. Such a *waste*. Mater and Pater had always told him that he was lucky to live in a much nicer house than 'Auntie' Marle's—but Rik had always thought they were wrong. Rik's house was bigger and brighter and quieter, true: but there was no nice cluttery mess in Rik's house, and no one ever laughed out loud, and there was no . . . no *risk*, no *adventure*.

But now Rik was shut out of all that native stuff. Rolan didn't want him around, and Aranna had never even been allowed to visit Rik's house because . . . but neither Mater nor Pater had ever quite put that into words.

Oh, but Rik had had such happy times in the Native Quarter. Happy times with Aranna and Rolan, and also happy times with 'Uncle' Moram, probing into keyholes with things like spindly crochet hooks.

You mustn't tell anyone, now, 'Uncle' Moram would say, smiling, ruffling Rik's hair. *If anyone knows I'm a security chief then I won't be able to check out their locks properly, will I? It has to be our secret, little sootyface.*

And Rik had thought 'Uncle' Moram had appreciated him. He really had. 'Uncle' Moram had been so exciting: blustery and red in the face and cheerful. Not at all like the sort of security men you got at home, who just stood about in uniforms looking bored and suspicious. Rik had loved helping 'Uncle' Moram, but 'Uncle' Moram had just been out for what he could get. You couldn't trust any of these natives as far as you could . . .

. . . *hang on* . . .

Rik stood dumbfounded in the red sunlight as lots of what he'd thought he knew suddenly turned itself upside down.

Security business?

Security business??

Climbing through small windows and taking things . . .

Rik found himself gaping in sheer amazement as things rearranged themselves in his mind. Good grief, he had opened dozens of safes for 'Uncle' Moram. (*The courts are kinder to duns*: of course they were, of course they were.)

I must have stolen hundreds of talsworth of stuff, thought Rik, between wonder and a marvellous shivery, fearful delight.

However had it taken this long to realize what had been going on?

What an idiot he had been. What an *idiot*.

Rik stood in the dawn of the plain of Hasiris, and realized with utter amazement that he was a thief. A housebreaker. A picker of locks.

And suddenly Rik found himself looking at the Monument in a new way: as if he'd never seen it before. At the great blocks of greasy-looking stone.

The sun was shining right in Rik's eyes. It gave the

carved pictures on the Monument sharp dark edges on the side nearest him and feathered them away invisibly on the other.

Rik, the safe-breaker, turned back to the door and began to look for a lock.

He smiled as he searched, wondering how many shops and businesses he'd robbed in his time. Good grief, if the police ever got hold of his fingerprints he'd probably be implicated in a hundred robberies.

Rik ran his hands over the sheeny door.

If there was going to be a keyhole, it would be about . . . *here*.

Rik's fingers could feel nothing, so he went over the smooth stone of the door again with the edges of his nails. In the end he did feel something click, though it happened under a nail on the wrong hand. It took a while to work out just where the edge of the door was. And so the lock . . .

Rik pushed hard with his thumb at a likely spot, but nothing seemed to yield. He pushed harder. Nothing. And nothing. And nothing, anywhere.

Rik stood back, discouraged. He thought back to his days with 'Uncle' Moram. Sometimes, he'd learned, safes had trick sides. You could spend hours trying to pick the lock, but the lock wasn't in the door at all. The real lock was somewhere else, and might even be opened by a simple push-catch.

From the rows of tents Rik heard, clear but far away, the clatter of the first breakfast saucepan. Aranna would be getting up, combing out her black whisk of hair. He hadn't got long before he was discovered.

Where would someone put a keyhole?

No. Wrong question. Where would someone *not* put a keyhole?

Too high to reach? Or . . . *not on the door at all*?

That was it.

Rik turned his attention to the great gouged grooves in the pillars. Now he thought about it, the carving here was much coarser than anywhere else. Why would it be like that, except to hide something? Here was a place where the stone had crumbled. If he cleared away the clogged-up bits of sand . . .

Yes. Yes!

Rik looked round hastily for a piece of wire, and saw that there were wire ties round some of the bales which had been brought up ready for the blowing open of the door later on in the day. Rik, possessed of a passionate haste, scrambled over and untwisted a couple, straightened them, and bent over the ends. They were a bit flimsy, but they might do.

He inserted two pieces of wire into the keyhole, and then made himself stop until his breathing and heart-beat had slowed down. He had to be still.

Now.

He went carefully, listening for the tiny click of a tumbler falling. He felt one go almost straight away. The second cost him several attempts, but then three went one after the other, and along the sprung wire Rik felt a quiver which meant the lock was free.

And then the sun went out.

9

'Reeklet's got ever so cheerful lately,' remarked Gow, on their way to lessons. Through the door that led to the Outer House the boys could see Reeklet skipping joyfully back to the Outer House with the boys' breakfast tray.

Alin frowned.

'*Cheerful?* Didn't you hear him ranting and cursing yesterday after Emmec conjured up that drain-rat in his leggings?'

Emmec grinned.

'Reeklet nearly caught me, too,' he said, ruefully. 'If he hadn't tripped over that log we'd left in the corridor to practise our weight-lifting, and gone head-first into the floor bucket, I reckon I'd have been a goner.'

Alin smiled quietly and rubbed his arms where his biceps were just beginning to make an appearance.

'He shouldn't have been running in the corridor,' he said, virtuously. 'And it serves him right for coming into the Inner House, where he's not allowed.'

Hani hesitated with his hand on the schoolroom door.

'Nian,' he said, 'you know we've got Rago for weather-lore . . . '

'Oh, all right, all right,' said Nian, still irritable. 'If Rago asks you to do anything I'll help you out a bit.'

Hani grinned his thanks.

'You only need help me just a bit,' he said. 'Rago's never going to believe I can actually do anything properly, but if you could just make it so he doesn't spatter me all over in lethally disgusting spit and make me stay in Thinking all afternoon, that'd be brilliant.'

Nian didn't mind helping out, really: Hani couldn't help being so utterly useless at school work. Hani did have powers, sure enough, but they were odd sideways sorts of things that Nian was sure would be extremely useful. At some point. For something or other.

'Are you all right?' Derig asked Nian, quietly. 'Only you seem a bit . . . on edge.'

Nian pushed aside his bad temper and forced himself to stop scowling.

'I'm fine,' he said, though still rather shortly. 'Yes, it's all right, Hani, I'll make sure you're only slightly short of useless. I'll just help enough to stop you making it rain dogs' pee all over the schoolroom like you did last week. You don't want to be kept in this afternoon and miss seeing Alin's incredible fluke at pockle, whatever you do.'

He suddenly became aware that everyone was staring at him.

'My what?' asked Alin, puzzled.

Nian stopped short, and tried to work out what he'd been talking about. He'd been talking about an incredible shot that had involved a hayfinch . . .

. . . but that must be nonsense. Nian was the Truth

Sayer, but he couldn't tell the future, except for things that had their seeds in the present. He could predict the weather, because it was only a question of looking to see which way the clouds were coming; but as for what was going to happen in the afternoon's pockle game . . .

'I must have been dreaming,' said Nian, at last, disconcerted.

Alin nodded.

'I should think so too,' he said. 'I'll have you know my brilliance at pockle is pure skill.'

Derig had opened his mouth to say something when a cracked voice sounded from round the curve of the corridor.

'Well, are you ready? Because I am willing to give up an extra hour or so of my time this afternoon to complete our lesson, if need be.'

They all ran. By the time Rago poked his suspicious nose round the schoolroom door, the boys might have been sitting on their mats in quiet Thought for hours, except for the fact that they were all breathing fast.

Rik fell backwards and backwards and backwards. He fell further than the level of the ground, and this was such a surprise that he'd only just got as far as limb-kicking panic when he thudded into the ground. The impact hurt so much that he lay, amazed, for quite a long time, until he realized he'd stopped breathing. So he heaved in a huge gulp of air, found his lungs filled with throat-clogging dust, and gasped and coughed and coughed and half rolled over and sneezed tears of coughing and dust and bewilderment. And then, once he'd finished doing that, he wiped his eyes on the shoulder of his shirt (he'd lost his hat) and tried to work out what on earth had happened.

It wasn't quite dark where he was, though he couldn't see any obvious source of light. There was certainly no sign of the door or hatch he'd fallen through (a booby trap, it must have been, blast it). But the whole place was shining very very faintly in a gluey sort of way, as if the stone had been traversed by a million million snails.

That thought was enough to get him to his feet. He pushed himself up and his hands felt, not the rounded crunching of snail shells, but gritty sand. He took a couple of cautious steps forward and heard the familiar-but-never-before-noticed sound of the ashy sand of the plains of Hasiris giving way under his leather soles.

He peered through the almost-darkness. He couldn't see far, but there was certainly a snail-trail glistening wall on every side of him.

So what did he do? Did he panic, or did he keep hoping there was a really really obvious way out?

The place smelled of cold stone and mildew, but his eyes were getting a bit more adjusted to the dimness, now. And . . . yes, over there was a rectangle of utter darkness where there was perhaps no wall.

Rik walked cautiously towards it. He walked so carefully that when he tripped up an invisible step he only sprawled quite gently up the rest of a stairway.

Rik looked up, his heart thumping hard. The steps went up into darkness.

Rik started to climb, feeling his way. Once he put his hand down on something that scuttled away, and he nearly screamed.

The smell of the place changed as he climbed. The damp smell of mildew changed into the dry smell of . . . of what? Of flour, perhaps: of something dusty, anyway.

The dust was everywhere. It was so fine it kept getting up his nose, however softly he stepped. He was making the effort to slow his breathing when something went *cheep!* above him, and Rik jumped violently.

No. It was no good panicking. He had to keep calm. He had to keep calm.

Rik could feel the fear just a little way away, just behind him, ready to ram a sack down over his head and send him lashing out and falling and crashing and bumping back down the stairs onto the sand again.

But he wasn't going to panic. No. Whatever had happened when he'd arrived in this place, he had definitely fallen. So he was going to go slowly and carefully up the steps, and in the end he was going to get out.

The light increased a little as he climbed, but so slowly that he didn't realize how much he could see until he was halfway up the steps. Everything here was as grey as smoke, and the air that surrounded Rik felt smoky, too. The dust wasn't thick enough to make him cough, but it was bad enough to dry out his mouth.

He was thirsty. What if there was no way out? In another hour he would be parched, and in another few hours . . .

. . . but he was going to get out. Of course he was. And he would not think anything else until he had explored the whole place.

Hey! he thought, suddenly. *I'm in the Monument! Brilliant, or what?*

Rik went more determinedly up the last few steps and found himself on a flagstoned floor.

That was wrong, somehow—but he didn't have time to work out why because he was staring all round him.

Staring and staring and staring.

10

'Humph!' said the Lord Rago, at last, after a fraught couple of hours which the boys had spent trying to persuade a small cloud to rain into an egg cup. 'I suppose we have made a *small* amount of progress. Though, you, boy, are still a moron of the most determined sort!'

Hani bowed, resigned.

'Yes, Lord,' he said. 'Sorry, Lord.'

Rago slewed a skewering glare round the rest of them, and they held their breaths; but then he said, grudgingly, 'Very well. You may go.'

Nian was the smallest of the boys, and the youngest. Generally this caused him no trouble at all, partly because the others were a cheerful bunch, and partly because having the power to blow up the entire House earned him a lot of respect. But at break times, when they were all trying to get out of the door at once, he never had a chance. Gow barged him out of the way like the great blundering marsh-ox that he was, and bashed Nian quite painfully against the doorframe.

'*Oi!*' protested Nian, clutching his arm, which hurt quite amazingly. 'Can't you ever look where you're bogging going, you great lump of ox-grot?!'

Gow, who was actually the calmest and most scholarly of the boys, looked round in some surprise.

'Sorry, Nian,' he said. 'I didn't mean—'

'—yes, but you keep on bogging *doing* it, don't you?' snapped Nian, the bruise pulsing painfully through all the other identical bruises that Gow had given him over these last days. 'Can't you ever learn to look where you're grotting going?'

Gow looked a bit confused.

'I didn't know I'd done it before,' he said. 'I didn't really hurt you, did I, Nian?'

Nian rubbed the place tenderly, and winced.

'And it's in exactly the same place,' he went on. 'Honestly—oh, never *mind*!'

It was raining. The gutters were rushing and gurgling.

'No pockle this break,' said Hani, mournfully. 'Struth, what a day: weather-lore with Rago, and then a wet break. *And* it's only Monday. Hey, shall we play with my catapult?'

'We'll go somewhere out of the way and practise our pockle skills,' said Alin, leading the way along the corridor so they could make a racket without disturbing the Lords. 'Put that bogging thing away, Hani, you'll get us banned from the garden for a week.'

'*Are* you all right, Nian?' asked Gow, in a pause while the others were making a human pyramid to get their pine-cone pock down from where it had got lodged in the rafters of a long-abandoned storeroom.

'Oh, I'm fine, really,' said Nian, who'd mostly recovered his temper. 'It's just that you caught me right in the same place as yesterday, and it really hurt.'

Gow looked puzzled.

'I really didn't know I'd hurt you before today,' he said. 'You didn't say anything.'

'It was yesterday, at break,' Nian reminded him. 'It happened in just the same way. You barged into me when we were trying to get out of the door.'

Gow gave him an odd look.

'But we didn't have break, yesterday,' he pointed out. 'Yesterday was Sunday. We went out onto the mountain. You remember. We went swimming up at the waterfall.'

Nian blinked. Of course they had. He remembered that. But . . .

'Sorry,' he said, at last. 'Sorry, Gow. I think I must be going a bit mad. I thought . . . '

Gow was viewing him with some concern when there was a clatter and a load of thumping and yelling as the boys' pyramid collapsed. Nian jumped to catch the pock as it fell.

'Perhaps you've been dreaming,' Gow suggested.

Nian wondered. His feeling that this had happened before did seem a little bit like a dream, he supposed. But there was something about it that was different. Instead of being a real memory of something unreal, which was what a remembered dream was, this felt more like an *un*real memory of something which had really happened.

But that was nonsense: what on earth was an unreal memory?

Hani disentangled himself from the others with a cackle of delight.

68

'Nian's been dreaming about Gow!' he sang out, gleefully. 'Hey, you lot! *Nian's been dreaming—*'

And Nian was obliged, out of a sense of simple justice and good taste, to use his powers to stick Hani firmly against the white stones of the wall and bend a drainpipe in through a window so that it gushed cold water over the bits of Hani which weren't sheltered by his enormous ears.

The whole of the room in which Rik found himself was smothered under layer upon layer of dust, softening the edges of everything like fine grey snow. Rik stood and breathed air that could not have been breathed for centuries: millennia, perhaps.

He took a step forward and the dust, drier here than below, erupted in a hundred soft little clouds. He stopped abruptly, afraid the dust would mushroom up and choke him.

The room he found himself in was perhaps twenty feet square. Round the walls were rows of . . . desks?

Rik walked across the room very, very softly, with the dust compressing under his feet like a carpet, but without any spring to it. The desk-like things were studded with buttons or catches. They reminded him of . . . yes, they were like the biggest radio set in the world, or like the control panel of a plane. Yes, he felt pretty sure it was something like that. The walls all around the room contained something like a huge control panel.

But radios and planes had only been invented about

69

fifty years ago, and everything in the Monument must be over a thousand years old.

It was mad, but Rik couldn't help but remember Professor Hallam's spacemen.

Every movement Rik made was stirring up ghostly fingers of dust. Unless this was a dream (and this place surely *smelled* too real to be a dream), then he really must be right inside the Monument.

He suddenly found himself grinning with triumph and excitement. *Inside the Monument*, which Professor Hallam had been trying to get into for decades.

Rik looked round the room again. There was enough light from the slightly glowing walls to show him the dark rectangles of several doorways, and also a place where a large piece of the wall had crumbled away to leave an opening into complete darkness.

Now Rik came to think about it, there was something about the sound of his breathing which told him that the whole place was a labyrinth of stone rooms and stairways and crumbled walls.

It was cold in that place, but Rik's blood was running hot with excitement. This place was of great, colossal, mind-shattering archaeological importance. He was the first person to get inside for hundreds and hundreds of years, and he knew that nothing must be touched except after the most lengthy, careful study, and then only by a great expert, in a mask, with a fine brush. *This is it*, he thought. *I've got a place in history, now, for ever.*

And then he thought: *I can't wait to tell Aranna.*

He stretched out his hand and wiped a great fan-shaped swathe of dust off the nearest cupboard-top.

And there was a sound as if ten thousand bees had stirred out of their slumber, and a bright light flicked fiercely into life.

His first reaction was to crouch, like a sandhare in the shadow of a hawk. He put up his hands to protect his eyes from the clean green light as around him more and more lights began to come on, and machines quivered or coughed or whirred into life. He squatted, almost too excited and scared to breathe, as tiny hills of dust rose and burst and subsided, and the noises settled to a steady hum.

But nothing happened that actually hurt or exploded, so after a while, cautiously, he raised his head.

The dust on the radio-cupboards was studded with points of light. Green, red, blue, some winking, some constant. In one place there was a rectangle the size of an exercise book that was glowing with a faint dust-muted light.

Rik, curious, went over to it too quickly, so that the dust swirled up and made his dry mouth even drier (how long before I get really thirsty? he thought: but finding out what was under that rectangle of glowing dust was more urgent even than worrying about that).

Impatiently, he swept away a lawn of dust. The thing he revealed, set into the top of the desk, was a little like a window.

He stared at it. At first it was blank and only a little

71

lighter than the grey dust all round him, but then . . . yes, something in there was moving. There were faint grey lines stirring in the depths.

Unless . . .

. . . panic clutched at Rik's throat. Those grey lines— they weren't an image in the window, they were . . .

Rik flung himself round. On the wall behind him, which had been reflected in the window, something was happening. The charcoal of the stone was beginning to show a pattern.

It was like watching a body float up from the depths of a lake: a man's body, tall, bulky, grey, but with fiercely gleaming eyes.

And then, all in an instant, the figure's foot came right out of the wall. And then its hand did, too, raised threateningly, holding something glinting and sharp and held ready to stab. And suddenly the steely figure, powerful, grim, eyes burning, was striding across the floor towards Rik.

And Rik, with his back to the desk and the steelmen advancing, had nowhere to turn.

11

Snerk, the House of Truth's Tarhun cook, was probably the filthiest person ever to don an apron. Even worse than that, he was probably the filthiest member of the *Tarhun*. The nameless things that jumped or were pushed into his vast age-grimed cauldron in Snerk's quest for the Ultimate Eating Experience should have been enough to turn the most iron-stomached person faint with indigestion. But Snerk was a genius, and that was all there was to it. Everything that came out of his kitchen woke up every possible taste bud and sent it cavorting about in rapturous abandon.

'Mm, rutnips!' said Alin, sniffing at his dinner bowl. 'Fantastic! With green gravy, too.'

Nian pulled his bowl towards him. He liked rutnips, and Snerk's were superb, of course. But he had a sort of feeling he could have done with a change.

Derig picked up his spoon—and then put it back down again.

'We do seem to be having rutnips rather a lot,' he said. And it was so unusual for Derig to get even that near complaining, that everyone took proper notice.

Emmec was looking at him as if he were mad.

'What are you talking about?' he demanded. 'These are first of the year.'

'Best thing about the autumn, rutnips,' announced Alin. 'Mind you, they won't be at their best until they've had the snows on them.'

Derig blinked.

'But . . . we've had them loads,' he said. 'We had them yesterday—and didn't we have them the day before, too? Perhaps poor Snerk's not feeling very well. He did look a bit fed up this morning when I saw him out in the garden searching through his slug traps.'

'Caterpillar stew, yesterday,' said Gow, through a large mouthful of green gravy. 'And the day before it was . . .'

' . . . boiled mole pudding and sweetroot chips,' put in Emmec, helpfully. 'I knew we were having boiled puddings because I saw old Snerk out without his socks on. And we had a big cake, too, because it was Saturday.'

'Not that I was allowed any,' sighed Hani. 'Just because I knocked a titchy bit of the Lord Grodan's eyebrow off. It's not easy aiming a catapult in here when all the walls in this place are curved.'

'You got cake,' pointed out Emmec. 'We all shared.'

Nian sat there with a curious over-lapping feeling in his head. He was the Truth Sayer, so usually he knew exactly what was real and what wasn't: but this time he somehow agreed with Derig, but also with the others, too. These rutnips were definitely the first of the season; but he was also sure he'd been eating them day after day after day until he was thoroughly fed up with them.

He took a bite of rutnip and immediately spat it out again.

'Ergh!' he said. 'These are *revolting*!'

Everyone stopped chewing and stared at him.

'Nothing wrong with these,' said Alin.

'They're fine,' agreed Emmec. Gow and Hani just carried on shovelling up large mouthfuls.

Only Derig, wry-faced, put his spoon down quietly beside his bowl.

He and Nian restricted themselves to chunks of the really rather stale bread.

'Grandy said *what*?'

Tan hunched his shoulders defensively.

'She kept going on and on as if it was the end of the world,' he said.

Nian was having the same feeling he'd had with the stew. This had happened before. Except that it couldn't possibly have done.

'Grandy's not one to make a fuss about nothing,' was all he said. 'Did she say anything else about the cobbles?'

'I don't think so,' said Tan. 'Not that I could understand, anyway.'

Nian made a face. Grandy's hearing was so sharp that she could hear the rocks grinding together inside the mountains, so she probably knew what she was talking about. Anyway, what she was saying chimed in with the feelings he'd been having all day. If something were going wrong with . . . well, with *time*, he supposed . . .

75

. . . but what could do that?

Nian didn't bother trying to work it out. He wasn't like Gow, who could sit and think things through until he'd put together a whole chain of reasoning. Nian's brain didn't work that way.

'Perhaps Grandy can hear what's going on better from where she is,' he said. 'You know, I think I'd better go and have a look in the abyss between the worlds to see if anything's happening.'

'In the what?' asked Tan, who was looking too exhausted to be impressed, as if he'd been travelling for weeks on end, instead of days.

'The abyss between the worlds,' repeated Nian. And he suddenly knew it was the right thing to do. Something out there was causing trouble, and he had to find out who or what it was.

'And I'm setting off first thing tomorrow morning,' he said.

Rik opened his eyes. Everything was almost completely dark, and for a moment he wondered where he was.

And then he heard the humming above his head.

The Monument. He was in the Monument. There had been a tall steely figure with a knife . . .

Rik forced himself to sit up. His mouth was bone dry (he shuddered: he didn't want to think about bones) and his brain felt like a throbbing lump of lead inside his skull (bones again . . .).

There was a *clunk* and a *thrrrrrick* and the faint lights which studded the room changed configuration.

That steelman must have been a dream. Rik shuddered again, remembering the blazing hatred in its eyes. Yes, it must have been a dream, because the steelman had been carrying a knife raised to stab, and Rik wasn't hurt.

Phew, what a dream, though. It wasn't surprising that Rik, stuck in the Monument, should dream about a steelman from one of Aranna's stories. They were certainly the stuff of nightmares, what with their swelling and maddening plague that the stories said had come, through the ghost voices of the Monument, from beyond the sky.

The desks were humming like radio valves. Rik reached out tentatively and touched a red glow. It felt warm, and when he took his finger away the red glowed more brightly.

And then he heard a different noise, behind him.

He turned.

There in the middle of the room, the almost-black room, glimmering, was another steelman.

Rik would have screamed if he'd dared. This man was hugely swollen. His shoulders were packed with muscle, and his features were hardly visible amidst his crusty skin.

Here was a steelman, someone with the plague that made you go mad.

A ghost, thought Rik, his heart in his throat. *Only a ghost.*

The steelman turned his head. His eyes were steel, glowing, and what Rik could see of the steelman's features showed that he had been a native.

Rik held his breath.

The steelman's eyes looked straight into Rik's for a moment; but then the steelman turned and walked swiftly away across the felted dust and into the black hole where the wall was crumbled away.

Rik did shout then, though what came from his mouth was little more than a croak. He stood and gasped with terror and relief. The steelman had gone: but what had it been? Had it been some sort of a projection, like a film at the cinema? Or really a ghost? Or was he going mad?

If they blow their way through the door they'll probably bring the whole tower down, whispered a voice inside Rik's head. *You're going to die in here.*

And that threw him into such a fit of fear that he threw himself, stumbling, across the room after the steelman. He staggered up onto the pile of loose rock where the wall had fallen.

And then before he knew what was happening he'd tripped, and he was falling through the hole in the wall.

Down and down and down . . .

. . . jagged rock, sand, and black black nothing . . .

. . . and down and down . . .

12

'My friends!'

The mild voice from the doorway stopped the boys as they tumbled and barged along the corridor, free from Rago's weather-lore lesson at last.

The old man who was regarding them must have been nearly as old as the Lord Rago, but the Lord Tarq had none of Rago's irritable energy. Instead, he was frail: Nian, looking at him, was washed through with sudden shock at how very frail he was. Tarq was supporting himself on the frame of the doorway, and when Nian checked him with his powers he found that the old man was shining with white weakness.

'My friends,' the Lord Tarq repeated, courteously. 'Perhaps you could continue your exercise somewhere else? This is a day of fasting and retreat for me.'

'Sorry, Lord,' the boys mumbled as they shuffled off.

But Nian stayed behind.

'You're not well, Lord,' he said, really anxious. 'You're very weak.'

'No, no,' Tarq replied. 'I have just been fasting, that's all.'

'I think you need to eat something, Lord,' said Nian,

for Tarq's hand was shaking slightly with the effort of standing.

But the old man shook his head.

'Thank you, my friend, but I am very used to fasting. It will do me no harm.'

Nian didn't want to keep Tarq standing any longer. He waited until Tarq was safely back on his mat.

'Lord!'

'My friend?'

'Does it seem to you as if things are going . . . round and round?'

Tarq, smiling, shook his head.

'No, no. I'm not dizzy, Truth Sayer. In any case, you know, I am only a little man, and would not have far to fall.'

But that hadn't been what Nian had meant.

'I keep having a feeling as if things have happened before,' he explained. 'As if today hasn't been the first time.'

Tarq eyed him kindly.

'As you live in the world, my friend, days will often come again,' he said. 'Age dissolves the edges of time. It is natural enough, and all part of the journey.'

Nian bowed. But as he left to go after the others he was feeling increasingly uneasy.

'Truth Sayer!'

Nian turned away from watching the course of Alin's wild shot.

'Has Tan arrived?' he asked.

The Tarhun blinked.

'My brother,' Nian went on, impatiently. 'Is he here?'

There was a wild burst of cheering and hooting from the other boys. Nian ignored it.

'Yes, Lord,' agreed Snorer. 'But I'm afraid . . . I'm sorry, Truth Sayer, but I'm afraid he's brought—'

'—news from home,' snapped Nian. 'Yes, all right. Hey, Snorer, ask one of the others to look after my flipper for me, will you?' and he jogged off the pockle ground towards the Strangers' Room in the Outer House.

. . . and down and down and down through lamp-starred darkness, tumbling and turning . . .

. . . and then there was a paling of the blackness, and a slight rising feeling, and Rik felt the ground under him. He had landed somewhere. Somewhere *else*. Not just somewhere else from the room of the steel ghosts, or even somewhere else from the Monument, but somewhere else from . . .

. . . Rik sat up and looked around.

Somewhere else from *everywhere*.

He was in a narrow valley. It was quite cold, and the whole place was grey with what might be either dawn or dusk. Over on the horizon was a jagged line of rocky hills, quite unlike the swelling mountains of home.

He looked round for the steelman, his heart beating painfully, but there was no sign of anyone at all. There was no sign of anything he'd ever seen before. Even the rock in this place was white and rough, nothing like the red rock that lay beneath the ashy sand of the plain of Hasiris.

This wasn't the plain, then—not even the plain of the past, when the steelmen had lived. So where on earth . . .

And then, with a shaft of silver light, the sun rose.

That sun was a little pale thing. There wasn't much air here (that was why he was panting and panting, even though he'd been frozen with awe and amazement ever since he'd arrived) and the sun cast ice-sharp shadows. The sun rose, surely faster than it should have done, and showed him . . .

. . . *nothing*.

Really nothing. Not even a plant, or clutch of bare branches, or a building, or any sign that he was not alone in this whole valley.

The word *alone* chimed inside him like a gong.

Yes, he was alone. His whole world had somehow been swept away (no, he had fallen out of it) and here he was in a cold white desert under a little sun.

Out of the corner of his eye he glimpsed a patch of movement, but when he jerked his head round to look it was only a cloud.

There was no wind down here (*could* there be a wind, when there was so little air?) but there must be a gale up there, for the cloud, as green as florikale, was steaming across the sky trailing a spiderchute of rain.

The rain fell on Rik and drenched him. It was warm and tasted metallic, but Rik didn't care about that. He cupped his hands up to it and drank and drank and drank.

The storm passed as suddenly as it had come, leaving the cracked little valley glittering with pools. Rik drank from them, too, though the pool water was more bitter even than the rain.

At last he sat up, gasping from drinking, and from the thin air. He didn't know where in the world he was, except that he was almost certain he couldn't be *in the world* at all. But he wasn't thirsty. That was wonderful. He wasn't trapped in the dark with the steel ghosts, either.

Rik pushed himself to his feet. His clothes were wringing wet: he'd be able to suck the moisture from the material to give himself another drink whenever he wanted.

He looked round. He would have gone exploring, except for his deep gut-feeling that there was nowhere to go. That this whole place was nothing but endless winding valleys of damp white rock.

Though as soon as he'd thought that, he noticed that just behind him was a small pile of chunks of black rock. They looked quite out of place in the valley; in fact, they looked very like the stuff the Monument was made of. It didn't look as if they'd been there very long.

Rik stepped forward to pick up one of the black bits of rock—and his foot went straight through the granular white rock and he staggered forward and fell again. He was falling and falling, right through the earth and into the lamp-starred darkness again, and then rising a little and . . .

. . . he came to a stop, had a split second to realize there was nothing under his feet, and then fell ten feet or so very sharply. He landed one-footed, stumbled a little, and came to a halt. He was still in almost total darkness, but under his feet was, not the soft dust of the Monument, or the rough rock of the white desert, but ashy sand.

Rik blinked round at the darkness. He seemed to be in some sort of a cave. Above his head was a jet black chimney going up into a rocky roof, and over there he could just make out the edge of a jumble of rocks.

And there, beyond that, was a faint glow of what looked like clear red ordinary daylight.

Rik stood and gasped with hope and relief. He had no idea where he'd just been, but as far as this world was concerned he seemed to have fallen through a hole in one of the walls in the Monument and landed in some sort of a cave underneath it. And here, at last, was what might be a way out to the plain.

Rik made his way hastily towards the light.

The floor of the cave was uneven, and in his hurry he caught his foot on some projection and went flying. He flung out his hands to save himself and landed almost full-length, a little winded, but not really hurt.

But now there was light and freedom ahead of him, flooding into the cave mouth, and nothing else mattered.

Rik reached out a hand to push himself up.

And then he froze for one long long moment of absolute and dreadful horror.

For the skin of his hands was sparkling slightly, as if it had been sprinkled with specks of steel.

13

Nian woke up on his mat in the pupil's room of the Inner House. Hani was complaining about Rago's weather-lore lesson.

Nian made a face, because he'd woken up with ever such an upside-down and inside-out puky sort of feeling.

Hani was still going on and *on*.

'Oh, shut up,' growled Nian. 'For grot's sake, it's only a *lesson*!'

The others all gave him bleary, startled looks.

'Get the whole thing into perspective, Hani!' said Emmec, in a rather good imitation of the Lord Caul at his most exasperated. 'How can you expect to follow the paths of Truth unless you get things into *perspective*!'

The other boys laughed, and Nian managed to grin and throw off most of his bad mood. He heaved his brain reluctantly into forward mode.

House of Truth. Morning.

Monday.

The steel specks on Rik's skin didn't rub off. Even

when he scratched some sparkling flakes off with his nails, it didn't help: the new skin underneath shone with a yet more steely sheen. It was not an effect of the light, either. Rik tried and tried to believe that, but the terrible knowledge of what it really was had blown itself up like a balloon in his throat and was half-suffocating him.

Not an effect of the light: an effect of the *plague*.

Rik could see right out of the cave from where he'd fallen. He lay blinking out across the plain to the humped mountains. There was nothing to stop him running down the hillside and into the camp. Oh, he wanted to do that so much. He'd go and tell Aranna, and Aranna would make it all right, just as she'd always done when he'd fallen over in the alleys of the Native Quarter and skinned his knees.

Maybe they could cure me, he thought.

But following that thought came another. *If other people catch this plague . . .*

This plague, which was real. This plague, which turned people into creatures like the steelman ghosts he'd seen. Which made you grow strong, grow mad, swell up, and die.

Rik looked down at the tents and found to his mingled horror and excitement that he could see through them, right through the faded heavy canvas.

There was Professor Hallam, bent over his notebooks.

And there was Rolan, splashing cold water over himself.

And there was Aranna, combing out her long whisk

of hair. Rik could see her plainly, even though she was right inside her tent.

If Rik went down to the camp, what would happen? What would happen to Rolan and Aranna, and even to Professor Hallam? Rik remembered Aranna's warm breath on his cheek as she whispered stories about bloated bodies and madness and fights to the death.

Grow strong, grow mad, swell up, and die.

It'd happened so quickly to him. They'd all catch it. All of them. The whole world, perhaps.

Rik lay for ages, looking at the camp.

Looking, and thinking about what would happen.

I'm only the work experience boy, he thought. *No one could blame me if I went down to the camp to get help*.

At last Rik got to his feet. Aranna was tying back her hair now. He stood there, watching her neat fingers. Watching her.

And then he turned back to the cave, walked back into the darkness, and climbed up the tumbled chimney of rock back into the ghostly greyness of the Monument.

'Mm, rutnips!' said Alin, sniffing at his dinner bowl. 'Fantastic. With green gravy, too.'

Nian pulled his bowl towards him without enthusiasm. Snerk was a brilliant cook, but, boggit, he could have done with a change.

Derig picked up his spoon, but then hesitated, and put it back down again.

'The first of the year!' said Gow, scooping up slimy gravy with relish.

Nian sat there with a curious double feeling spinning round inside him. Yes, these rutnips were definitely the first of the season; but somehow Nian was also sure that he'd been eating them day after day after day until he was sick of them. *Really* sick of them.

He speared one with his knife and took a bite: and then was nearly *literally* sick.

'*Pfffoi*,' he spat. 'These are *rank*!'

All around the table people were looking at him as if he were mad.

'Nothing wrong with these,' said Alin, stoutly.

'They're delicious,' agreed Emmec. 'Good old Snerk, he's a genius. You know, I bet he *will* find the Ultimate Eating Experience, one day.'

Hani had already gone back to shovelling up large mouthfuls.

Derig was eating, too, though cautiously. *He* didn't look as if he was enjoying the meal very much.

Nian tried some bread. It tasted nearly as mouldy as the stew. But Nian was hungry, so he ate it anyway.

The plague was changing Rik's body fast. Even in the small amount of time he'd been out of the Monument, it had changed him. He could see much better in the dark, now, for one thing: and he could see the steely ghosts very easily. The ghosts were everywhere, shining with the sickly glow of coffin-beetles, crowds upon crowds of them. Each moment of their time in the

Monument had been recorded separately, but Rik found that there were ways of tuning his eyes so he could follow the ghosts along a narrow line of time so he could make sense of what they were doing.

When he could do that, he found he could hear the ghosts, as well as see them.

And then he began to understand exactly what had happened to the pale-skinned people of the Monument of Hasiris.

The stocky sandy-haired boy sitting on the bench in the Strangers' Room looked up, rather wearily, as Nian entered.

'What's happened?' demanded Nian, though he knew.

Tan shifted uncomfortably in his seat.

'It's Grandy,' he told Nian, shamefaced. 'She's started . . . talking.'

Nian pushed away his feeling of inevitability.

'Grandy keeps saying the paths of the worlds have gone bumpy, or something,' Tan went on. 'Mother, she says Grandy must be ill. And, I'll tell you what, Nian, I think I might be going down with something myself. My legs feel as if they've just climbed a *dozen* mountains.'

Nian felt as if *he'd* spent a whole week in a sort of strangely skew-whiff and difficult dullness. Of . . . of *Mondayness*. As if everything had happened lots of times before, but as if each time they came round they were more lop-sided and worrying and deeply deeply *boring*.

Nian did his best to ignore the sounds from the garden of Reeklet's joyful singing, and wondered what on earth Grandy expected him to do about all this. Go back home with Tan?

No, it would take a week just to get home, and he'd had enough. Really, really enough. Whatever was going on (which was nothing, really, that was the most annoying thing) he'd had enough of it.

Nian looked at Tan.

And found him fast asleep.

Nian left Tan slumped in an uncomfortable-looking and exhausted sleep against the cold wall and went out. He'd had enough of this. He was going to go into the abyss between the worlds and find out what was going on. And he was going to do it *now*.

14

Rik's skin was shining all over, now. That helped him see, because he cast light as he walked, instead of shadow.

The lights on the control-panel cupboards had all winked out. A valve must have gone, or something, for there had been a burst of dry crackling and a smell of burning dust, and then everything had puttered into silence. Even the shivery static that had been prickling the hair on Rik's arms had died away.

Rik, secure in the light from his steel skin, walked easily from room to room through the throng of ghosts that had been recorded on the black stone of the Monument. Sometimes he'd look at them in slightly the wrong way and see a sort of fan of steel shadows, each of them from a different moment of time, like an architect's drawing of a dome.

Rik's mind had gone very sharp and clear. He'd felt something like this when he'd been sickening for duck-pox, but this was much better. With almost every moment he was becoming sharper, cleverer, able to see more and more.

Rik could hear every voice from the history of the

Monument, too. They were all sounding at once, but also somehow singly, insistently. Yes, by some skill he could hear a thousand conversations going on at once and follow them all. His mind was strong. He could see, could *hear*, a year of history in one single flash of insight.

The steelmen had been like Rik: shining, and clever. They could move things with their minds. (Useful, that was—you could stand behind a stone wall and send out weapons to fight for you. Very clever, and very efficient).

Rik could do that, too, now. He hadn't tried it, but he knew he could if he wanted to. *Knew* it.

Rik could feel the exhilaration that came with having the plague inside him. It made his blood run fast and hot. He could feel the excitement of learning, of seeing more and more things.

The story of the Monument was simple and glorious. Rik could watch it, recorded in the spider-thin traces of the steelmen that stalked across the black stone.

(It was the steel Rik could see, he realized: those who were not strong had perished without trace. Rik spread out his own steel fingers and knew that his movement had been registered for ever in the black stone.)

The voices were there in the stone, too, layer upon layer.

Look, the steelmen had said, constantly, pointing steel sparkling fingers. *Look, Look! Before we were scarcely more than maggots, and now . . .*

At first they were pointing at the secrets of the world

around them—but these were mostly things Rik had seen already through microscopes or telescopes.

But later the eyes of the steelmen had grown stronger still, and then they could see yet further. Further than the stars. Further than . . .

Look, they kept saying. *We can do anything. There is nothing and no one who can stop us.*

Rik's mind accelerated and accelerated to take it all in. A year of history in a few moments, and a year more after that.

The steelmen's minds grew until they burst; and then, overtaken by madness, they fought. Rik heard the clash of weapons, and the last whimpers of the vanquished, and the shouts of triumph that grew to screams of joy and terror at things that Rik could not yet see.

Rik's hands were all steel, now: when he moved (though he did not need to move, for he could summon anything with a smallest twitch of his mind) his skin scraped against itself with a faint whispering.

He would not be afraid of the steelmen because they were long gone. There was no need to be afraid, even though their screams and fear and hatred were tearing the air all around him.

Rik listened to the whispering of the steelmen. There were years of speech, but Rik could slice through layer upon layer, through a year, a month, a day, to the very moment when a voice, rising high and triumphant above the clamour of voices that echoed round the Monument, screamed:

I can see further!

93

And Rik used his new plague-strength, and found he could see further, too.

The Lord Tarq was sitting on his mat, his skin stretched over his thin bones in steep shadowy ridges.

Nian went and sat down in front of him.

'I'm going into the abyss between the worlds,' he said.

Tarq smiled, though he looked very weary.

'Is it necessary, my friend?' he asked.

'I don't know,' admitted Nian. 'I won't know that until I get there.'

Tarq nodded, a little lurchingly, as if his head was heavy on his neck; and Nian was struck with fear.

'You're not well,' he said.

'I am feeling my age,' Tarq told him, gently. 'Sometimes there seem to have been a great many days.'

'Yes,' said Nian. 'That's how I feel, too.'

He got up; but when he turned in the doorway to make his bow the old man's fragility shocked him afresh.

'Perhaps you should eat, Lord,' he said.

'Yes,' agreed Tarq. 'And I shall, tomorrow.'

Nian hesitated. For the Lords, missing a day's food was a tonic. Tarq was old, but he should not be nearly as weak as this.

Nian called up a pulse of power to give some strength to the old man—but it skidded off Tarq as if his skin were as slippery as an eel's.

'My friend, you must not waste your strength on me,'

Tarq said, quietly. 'For who knows what challenges you may face if you are leaving the world?'

'Then will you eat?' asked Nian. 'I know you can easily fast for ages, but I think something's gone wrong with . . . ' But he didn't know what had gone wrong with what.

'I promise that tomorrow I shall make a hearty breakfast,' said Tarq.

And Nian told himself he must be content with that.

Nian tiptoed carefully to the door to the library and slipped a note underneath it. Firn the librarian wasn't a bad old stick, but he would probably want Nian to write him an account of everything in triplicate.

Nian went and got himself some biscuits from his box, but unfortunately the Lord Caul caught Nian sneaking along the corridor with his pockets full and a scarf round his neck (to make him feel slightly less guilty about dodging the Lord Firn, who was slightly mad about people going out without scarves).

'So?' Caul asked, having looked Nian up and down and guessed too much.

Nian made a hasty attempt at scooping together an explanation. Caul had a teacherly habit of pouncing on woolliness of thought, and Nian's thought-processes at the moment were as woolly as a whole flock of mouldy sheep.

'I'm going into the abyss between the worlds,' he explained. 'And I'm going to look at . . . stuff.'

Caul raised an eyebrow.

'Any reason?' he asked.

Nian had been afraid Caul was going to ask that.

'I'm not sure,' he admitted. 'I can't track it down. But I think there is *something*. Something I can't see from here.'

Caul grunted.

'Something apart from the fact that you feel like a holiday?' he asked, rather sarcastically, which wasn't like him. But then he sighed. 'Mind you, perhaps that's enough. You know, I feel as if I've been teaching non-stop for weeks, and it's only Monday. In fact, everyone seems a bit . . . well, restless, I suppose. Dissatisfied. Even Snerk seems to have given up trying out new ingredients: I saw a slime bug fly right past his nose just now, and he didn't even taste it. Quite honestly, Nian, I feel tempted to give myself a break and come with you. Have you told anyone else you're going?'

'I told the Lord Tarq,' said Nian. 'And I put a note under the library door for the Lord Firn.'

'Hm. Well, that's something. But, Nian, don't you think you'd be better to wait until tomorrow morning, when you've had a good night's rest?'

One half of Nian agreed; but the other half was filled with weariness and bafflement and a sort of horror at the thought of waiting even a moment longer.

'It does seem a pity I shan't be here when my brother arrives,' he began—but then broke off, puzzled. What in the name of *Truth* had made him say that? Tan was here already, slumped snoring against the white wall of the Strangers' Room.

Caul was watching him curiously.

'Everything's . . . strange,' said Nian, slowly. He tried once again to catch hold of what was going on,

96

but it was like trying to catch a greased hoglet: as soon as he so much as touched it, it slipped out of his grasp. 'But I think . . . I *think* I really do need to go now, straight away, Caul.'

Caul went to say something, and then seemed to change his mind.

'Well, if anyone knows, you will,' he said. 'Have you got everything you need?'

'I doubt it,' said Nian, ruefully, for the worlds were infinitely varied, and he might need snow shoes, a hunk of meat to distract a charging tiger, or his own supply of oxygen. 'I've got a scarf,' he volunteered, weakly.

And Caul smiled, a little grimly, but stood aside to let him pass.

Rik, in the darkness of the Monument which was no longer dark to him, pushed his mind past the crowds of steelmen ghosts which were thronging round the hole in the wall which led down to the cave and the plains, but which had also somehow tipped him into the white desert world.

Rik's mind was still getting more powerful. He could follow each ghost's speech along its own slice of time; he could even see what the ghosts had been looking at through the hole in the wall. There had been a tunnel there which had stretched out from the Monument . . .

. . . *past the sky*.

Rik could see it all. Professor Hallam called himself a scholar, but Rik's mind was so powerful now that

Professor Hallam's was puny, a maggot-brain, compared with Rik. And so was Rolan, for that matter. And as for Aranna . . .

An image of her whisking horse tail of hair flicked through Rik's mind, but he ignored it. He turned his eyes back to the bright tunnel which in the steelmen's day had stretched from the Monument all the way to another world.

The tunnel had led to a tree-shaded place, starred with flowers and bright with running water. Rik looked along the tunnel and found himself filled with longing, even though he knew that what he was looking at was long ago, back in the time of the steelmen ghosts.

Some steelmen had made their way down the tunnel—Rik could see them walking about in the shade of the trees—but most of the steelmen were still in the Monument, huddled together in a great ghostly mass and obscuring Rik's view.

All these steelmen were long dead and shrivelled to dust, of course, though he could still see their native features, and their voices still crackled the air in Rik's ears.

We have found ourselves a paradise, called the steelmen gleefully from the new world at the end of the sky-tunnel.

Yes, someone answered from the crowd clustered by the hole in the wall. *But you must return at once, or you will infect that world with the plague, too.*

The sky-tunnel was long beyond measuring, but Rik's strong eyes could see right to the end of it. He could see the far-away flash of a steelman's teeth as he answered.

This is no plague, you fools! We are growing, changing. We are becoming something new and strong. This is a great gift which has come to us.

The reply from the crowd in the Monument sounded close in Rik's ears.

A gift, yes, but a deadly one. Remember what happened to Fallan. And Halad, and Gant.

They were weak to start with. They could not cope with the changing. Did you not see their hands shaking?

Yes, we saw. And we can see your hands, too, my friends. The madness will surely take you, soon. Come back, my friends.

Rik's own hands were steady. He held them out in front of him. They were steely and shining, but steady.

Come back? When you have sealed up the doors to the Monument so that no one can leave? Would you have us die in the darkness like cave-crabs?

No, my friends, like heroes. We will die in here together, and the plague will spread no further, and we will save our world.

Rik, watching, saw something strange happen then. The steelmen in the bright world at the end of the tunnel staggered, as if the earth had shuddered under their feet.

What was that? called someone, sharply.

Rik looked with his new strong sight, and found he could see further still—even further than the world at the end of the tunnel. Not into space, exactly, but actually outside what he'd always thought was reality and into a place where spiked golden spheres turned each other like the cogs of a clock.

See? demanded a voice from the crowd in the Monument, a voice that had failed a millennium before. *The tunnel between our worlds is stopping them from turning as they should: as they must.*

Rik felt a sharp juddering through the soles of his feet, even though he knew it was not real, but something that had happened a millennium ago.

Amongst the throng of steelmen by the hole in the wall, steel faces were turned to each other in horror.

Here it comes again. The tunnel is stopping our worlds from turning: but they must *turn.*

Between the two forces, the worlds will be torn apart!

What can we do?

Everyone must return to the Monument. Then the tunnel will close and the worlds will be free to turn again.

A steelman burst out of the crowd in the Monument and raced down the tunnel that led to the bright other world.

Come back! he was shouting. *Come back, or the worlds will perish!*

Many eyes turned towards him from the green place at the far end of the tunnel, and they were steely and shining and poisonous as mercury.

The running man staggered as their gaze hit him. And then he fell, shuddered, and was still, one hand flung forward to clutch the acid-green grass of that other world.

This is the end, said someone, quietly.

That was the last thing anyone in the Monument said.

Rik felt (or perhaps only saw) a mounting vibration and then a series of great jolts. They were so fierce they jarred his bones, even though they were not happening in the present, but long long ago. Beside the bright water at the end of the tunnel Rik saw the steelmen tossed up by a great spout which burst through a crack in the ground: only it was not grey water that sprang up, but bright searing fire. The steelmen were jerking and screaming with voices harsh and shrill like crag-swallows.

The Monument was bucking and rearing under Rik's feet (though it was still, too, so still that not a mote of dust was stirring) and it was hard to see any more. Rik felt a great lurching and for a moment he was terribly afraid the whole building was going to be tipped over to shatter into pieces with him inside it. He saw the steelmen at the end of the tunnel flung far into the air, and, under them, the trees writhing as if they were fighting to be free of the earth . . .

. . . and then Rik had lost it. The whole vision. It was gone, and he was in darkness again.

Breathless, he used his strong eyes to catch the rest of the story.

There it was.

There it was, though not quite where—no, not quite *when*—Rik had left it.

When?

15

Grandy had been right. Nian knew it the moment he stepped out of the world and into the abyss between the worlds. Before, he'd fallen breath-takingly fast: this time his fall was much slower, as if the nothingness of the abyss had grown thicker (which must be nonsense: how could *nothing* be *anything*?). Nian fell, quite gently, for several seconds, and then he found himself coming to a stop, but without being anywhere at all. It was the oddest feeling, to be bobbing about in the cold nothing, surrounded by the tiny pin-points of the worlds. It might even have been fun if there'd been any air to breathe (not that he needed to breathe, here, but it was unsettling not to be doing it). Nian tried scooping at the no-air with his arms as if he were swimming. This moved him a bit, but at that rate it was going to take him several million years to get anywhere; and so he gathered his powers to him. *Move*, he told himself. *Move—fast!*

That worked almost too well. There were a confused couple of seconds when things like fireflies catapulted themselves past his ear holes, but then he managed to catch enough of a glimpse of one to realize what it was.

World, said his brain, but much too late. *That was a world!*

It took Nian a while to work out how to apply some brakes. He whizzed past the next three worlds far too fast to do anything about it, but the next time a lantern-like world came along he sort of grabbed at it and swung himself round into fast and dizzying orbit.

The world he was whirling round was an unusually dim one, but, as Nian hadn't a clue what he was looking for, one world was probably as good as any other. Nian waited until he'd slowed down a bit, and then he allowed that world to draw him in. He fell down a long way and then swooped up again as gradually the blackness of the abyss paled and he entered this other world.

And then he was there, breathing and breathing.

He was outside. That was actually quite surprising, because before he'd always ended up in buildings when he'd gone to other worlds. The place where a world touched the abyss tended to be so peculiar it ended up sacred—and people had a habit of building walls round sacred places.

But here . . . Nian looked round. The place was all damp white rock. There was no sign of life at all: not a lizard or a fly: not even a blade of grass.

Nian pushed his powers into the air of the place, searching for another mind. But there was nothing. Nothing at all. In this whole world, there was not one single other living thing.

Well? Well, he would have to try another world, then, because a world without life wasn't going to tell him very much, whatever was happening to Time.

Nian turned back to try to find the place where he'd arrived from the abyss; but just as he was stamping round experimentally, he saw something which made him snatch his foot back.

It was a footprint.

Nian squatted down to make sure it wasn't just a natural depression in the ground. But no, it was certainly a footprint: he could make out the marks of the nails in the soles of the shoes, and the crease of white mud where the heel had skidded a bit.

But it was ridiculous that there should be a footprint here. This world—he checked again—yes, this world had *no one at all* living on it. If there ever had been anyone here, it must have been hundreds of years ago because he couldn't even pick up a trace of so much as a ghost, or an echo of a voice . . . just a faint buzz that might have belonged to a swarm of large but long-extinct flies.

But this footprint (no, it was not his own, it was too long, and the heel was the wrong shape) could not be more than a few days old.

Which was impossible.

Nearly impossible: for here it was.

Nian had one last look round. He hadn't taken any notice of it before, but beside the footprint there was a heap of chips of black rock which looked quite unlike anything else in this valley. He checked them out. Yes, they shouldn't be here at all: they came from some other place entirely. In fact, they came from some other *world*.

Nian scooped them up, filling his pockets and,

reluctantly, putting the remainder down the front of his tunic where they felt knobbly and cold. There weren't enough of these rocks to stick two worlds together and cause serious damage, but there might be enough to put grit in the system (pretty much literally, as it happened) and make the worlds turn a bit bumpily.

Hm. Enough to *cobble the paths of the worlds*, perhaps? Could the thing Grandy had been worrying about really be caused by nothing more than this?

There were thick green clouds streaming over the ridge, even though down here there was no breeze at all. Nian was going to get drenched if he stayed much longer, and he had no intention of walking the worlds soaked to the skin. He stepped carefully over the almost impossible footprint and into the abyss.

This time he fell so fast that the lantern-worlds zipped past him in shooting blurs. It was as if his coming had sort of stretched the abyss, and now it was snapping itself back into shape again. That probably meant that Nian was being sucked back to the House of Truth again, and he wasn't ready to go back there.

Nian made himself some sort of invisible power-wings which braked his progress and brought him to a stop.

Nian hung in the abyss and wondered what to do. He did try to find a trace of the owner of that footprint, but he'd come so far so fast it would have taken a major effort to sense anything. Annoying. The footprint, as well as the black stones, was a sign that something very odd must have happened—and he'd been looking for something odd.

Nian emptied his pockets of the chunks of black

stone, and then flipped himself upside down and shook out the chunks that were down his front.

Then he did the only thing he could think of. He looked round for the nearest world, and with a small kick of his powers he sent himself towards it.

Rik's body was much bulkier than it had been. His shoulders had the muscles of a man. His mind was stronger, too, running clear and fast.

Rik held out his hands. They were steady, for now. The plague was making him strong, but he knew that soon it would make him mad and then it would kill him.

How long would that take? How long, before he didn't know what was real? It was difficult, already, with these visions of the past rising before him. Layer upon layer of time, slice upon slice of it.

And, incredibly, that wasn't the worst of it. At three o'clock that afternoon Professor Hallam was going to blow open the door to the Monument. He and Rolan and Aranna and the others would find a living steelman waiting for them in the darkness. Professor Hallam would probably try to kill it.

That wouldn't be easy, because Rik was strong. Rik's death would come, he was afraid, at the expense of many of their little lives. But even if Rik gave himself up, let them kill him, he would very soon be avenged.

For as soon as the doors to the Monument were open the soft dry dust would mushroom out into the light of the world. Out on the breeze, choking and spreading. There would be a glorious crimson sunset over the city, and then the dust would settle down into the windows and doors and lungs of every living creature in the place.

And the plague would go with it.

It would be the end.

The end of everything.

16

Nian rose up into the new world, found his head being forced up into a ceiling that was only a few spans high, and ended up on his hands and knees inside some sort of narrow twiggy tube.

It *smelt* revolting—like a mixture of old pee and bad breath.

Nian blinked along the tube. At the far end there was a large hairy thing. It looked like a pile of rugs, but . . .

Nian turned on his powers to have a better look, and then winced. There was a big hairy *something* curled up in a pile of grass in a round chamber at the end of the basketwork tube. It was no more than six paces away from him. It was making growling noises which Nian hoped very much were snores.

Nian stayed very still, with every nerve alert to jump backwards into the abyss should the big hairy thing pounce, and sent out his powers to see what sort of a place this world was.

Well, there was plenty of life here, anyway: millions of living things within a few reaches. Nian refined his search a little and discovered that most of the living things were what he would have called midges, except that they were as long as his thumb and had huge poisoned jaws that could have pierced ox-hide.

Nian began to see why the Big Hairy Thing had built itself a densely-woven nest. He pushed his powers very cautiously towards it. The Big Hairy Thing had a thick pelt and a thick hide (very sensible with all those giant midges about) and tucked under its webbed paws were span-long fangs of orange ivory and a small brain which could detect the heat of an animal's heart-beat from half a grohl away.

Well, at least it was asleep. Nian squirmed quietly round to face the mouth of the tube. He was careful not to let any part of himself go too near the several million huge salivating midges which were hanging round just outside.

The great beast behind him was still grunting. It was a bit like a web-footed bear, only more vicious and inclined to suffocate its prey with one blast of its rank breath—so it was more like a cross between a giant beaver and the Lord Rago, really.

Nian grinned to himself, and tried searching for anything that was out of place—or out of *time*.

The trouble was, that other worlds were such, well, *other* sorts of places that it was hard to know when something had gone peculiar, especially when you'd only just arrived, and your knowledge was restricted to one giant basketwork nest. That giant beaver, or whatever it was, seemed to have been asleep for several months, which was odd; but then some of the animals in Nian's world slept all through the whole winter, too.

And those big midges . . . they'd all hatched out only that morning after a long dormant period while their soft maggoty bodies had developed their netted wings and armour-plated skin and huge and powerful eyes. That, too, was odd, but normal.

Except . . . there was something *thin* about those midges. Not physically thin, of course, because they were encased in armour-plating, but . . .

A midge's brain was too small for actual thought, but the urge for *blood* was pulsing through their little heads in a whine that was . . . oh, it was so difficult to pin down . . . the noise seemed to be split into a series of echoes, somehow.

The brain of the midge Nian was watching suddenly stopped doing anything. Nian got a swift impression of falling, but darkness intervened before the creature hit the ground.

Nian was more annoyed than anything. These midges only lived a matter of hours, so it wasn't really surprising that one should drop dead just as he was looking at it. But it was still irritating.

Outside a rapid pattering had started. Rain, Nian assumed, although it didn't sound quite like rain did in his world. It didn't sound . . . well, it didn't really sound that *wet*. Nian crawled cautiously a little further towards the green light that shone in from outside.

Something fell into the woven edge of the nest and bounced and skittered along almost as far as Nian's hand.

A midge.

It was clad in shiny grey plates, and its legs were

spiked with luminous green hairs. It was astonishingly beautiful: but it was dead.

And here, bouncing shallowly along the basketwork tube opening to the nest, was another; and yet another.

That was what the noise was, Nian realized suddenly: not rain, but the falling of thousands of dying midges.

There was hardly room for anything in Nian's mind but amazement, but then behind him, through his wonder, Nian became aware of something else: it was a hunger, the massive ravening hunger of a beast which hadn't fed for months. Of an ability to sense the heat of an animal's heartbeat at a distance of a . . .

. . . oh bogging grotting *pits*!

Nian hastily squirmed himself back round.

The eyes of the great beast were shining at him, green as poison. It had settled itself into a crouch, ready to spring, and there was enough power in its jaws to crunch Nian up like a hay-apple.

Nian's instincts were screaming at him to run, *run*! But the only way he could get away from the giant beaver was by throwing backwards into the rain of stinging midges, and that would take him away from the opening to the abyss.

The great beast curled back its black lips to show its fangs and Nian found himself roaring as loud as he could as he tried to grab together the lunatic courage to throw himself back towards the beast.

It sprang, and Nian dived along the floor of the tube, his hands stretched out for the opening to the passageway out of the world.

He was halfway through when he felt the beast's hot breath on his legs—and then it had caught him. Nian howled and kicked violently, and suddenly found himself shooting into the blessed darkness of the abyss. He was missing the back of one of his shoes, but the beaver-beast's great fangs had done no more than scrape his heel.

Nian let the abyss take him a long way before he thought of stopping. When he did, he spent all of half a second wondering whether to go back for the bit of shoe he'd lost. The Lords were always terribly anxious about things being left in the wrong world.

Nian found himself laughing, slightly hysterically.

They must be joking.

He went on his way hastily through the inky abyss.

Rik was watching the death of the steelmen yet again. The earthquakes had happened because the worlds were being held back from turning. And then . . .

. . . each time the story cut off abruptly, and each time the slice of Time that Rik was following broke off with it.

What was happening?

Rik watched it again. Time seemed to . . .

Rik raised his heavy head.

That was it. That was what was happening. The worlds could not turn while the steelmen were in the wrong world. This put the whole system under pressure. But when the earthquake had thrown the steelmen off that wrong world then the tunnel joining the worlds had dissolved and all the worlds were set free to turn again.

And the sudden release of pressure was causing a whiplash effect which was jolting everything backwards. Everything. Even *Time*.

Rik's arms were massive, now, like a boxer's, and his brain was running swift and true.

If someone was in the wrong world too long then the whole system of the worlds came under pressure.

But if someone went into the wrong world and waited until just the right moment before stepping back again, then he'd create a whiplash effect—and Time would be snapped backwards.

Rik breathed air into his deep chest.

The doors of the Monument were being blown open this afternoon.

But if he went into the white desert world and waited until just the right moment before returning, he could make Time snap backwards.

And if he could do that, he could make it so that this afternoon never arrived.

17

Nian put out his power-wings and brought himself to a stop. The abyss hung all around him, dark and lantern-starred.

The trouble with visiting other worlds, he realized—apart from being torn limb from limb by monsters—was that unless he knew what a world was *supposed* to be like, then he wasn't going to be able to tell if anything was wrong.

Well, there were a couple of other worlds he knew quite well. He'd visit one of them, then.

He thought about it for a millisecond and then decided to go for the one that wasn't ruled by a homicidal maniac.

He sent his powers into the abyss, searching for a world where white clouds swirled above a vivid blue sea.

There. There it was, glowing.

He fixed his powers onto it and hurtled himself forward as fast as he could.

'*Nian!*'

The room was the right sort of size, and the boy sitting behind the frame of barrels and pan-lids had the right colour hair, but apart from that everything in the room looked different. Nian took a quick step forward to make sure he wouldn't fall backwards out of the world again and looked round.

The orange-haired boy's face was split into a wide grin of delight.

'*Fantastic!*' he exclaimed. 'It's you! I'd almost given up on you. Hey, you look different. Fatter. Which is good, obviously, I mean, you're not fat as such, no way, but you were practically *skeletal* before. So. You sorted out all those old monk-people all right, then?'

Nian found himself grinning back. He'd forgotten how refreshing it was to be with someone who had no responsibilities for anything whatsoever.

'Yes, I sorted them out,' he said. Jacob's language was still there in his head, he discovered, waiting to be used. 'I took their powers away.'

'Wow! Was there a fight?' asked Jacob, agog.

Nian laughed at the memory of it.

'Yes. A big fight. Half the House fell down.'

'Brilliant! Brilliant! I knew you would. Cor, Nian, I wish I'd seen it.'

Nian looked round. Someone had painted the room turquoise and dyed the curtains to match Jacob's hair. It was . . . different.

'Is everything all right here?' he asked.

Jacob waggled his orange head good-humouredly.

'Could be worse, I suppose,' he admitted. 'I mean, I hardly see sister Robyn now she's got her own room,

115

so that's good. And Dad's working at the Health Food shop. Mum found him this long velvet wizardy coat in Oxfam, and now everyone thinks he's the Sage of Essex. He's grown a beard and everything. And I've got my drum kit, obviously.'

Nian viewed the frame of barrels and discs with interest. Yes, now Jacob mentioned it, Nian could see it was actually an apparatus for making noise on a really colossal scale.

'I'm in a band,' said Jacob, grinning blissfully. 'We're playing at Kelly Bagshott's thirteenth birthday party tomorrow. For *money*!'

There was a light of fervour in Jacob's eyes that quite startled Nian, because generally Jacob was so laid back he was in danger of falling over.

'We're not bad, either,' Jacob went on. 'We were practising today, and I was teaching everyone this song I wrote. Well, it was mostly stolen from another world—I can still hear them just faintly, I think it's because you left your beetle behind you when you went home last time—and we all got the tune in, like, about *five minutes*. It was incredible. It was as if we already knew it. We usually have to go over songs loads and loads of times. It was as if we were sort of reading each other's minds, you know?'

Nian knew, but he was surprised Jacob did, because Jacob generally had all the mind-reading abilities of a hibernating hombat. But still, this was the sort of thing that had been happening in the House of Truth. People behaving out of character, and things seeming familiar before they'd happened. Yes, that was it.

Someone came thumping down the stairs and a tall dark-haired girl flounced in.

'Jake,' she began, bossily, 'don't forget it's your turn to do the—*Nian!*'

Nian put his fingertips on his heart and bowed. 'The day is nicer for seeing your eyes,' he said, grinning again. This was the usual greeting to strangers in Nian's world, but it had got him into quite serious trouble when he'd tried to use it last time he was here. The girl let out a shriek of outrage and pleasure.

'You got away!' she exclaimed.

'Yeah,' said Jacob. 'There was this gigantic fight, and—'

His sister Robyn ignored him.

'Oh, thank goodness!' she said. 'I've been worrying about that giant beaver thing all—'

'—*what?*' said Jacob.

'—*beaver?*' echoed Nian.

Jacob was looking at Robyn as if she'd gone mad. 'Did you just mention a *beaver?*' he asked.

'How did you know about that?' demanded Nian.

Robyn's ice-blue eyes stared from one to the other of them, puzzled.

'You told me, didn't you?' she said, disconcerted. 'A giant beaver. With orange fangs . . .'

Her voice trailed away.

'She's gone bats,' said Jacob, rather pleased. 'Hey, you haven't been at Dad's tablets, have you?'

Robyn swung round on him.

'Living with you is enough to drive *anyone* bats,' she snapped. 'What with your constant clattering about on that blasted drum kit, and your *perpetual* caterwauling whenever you hear someone through that blessed beetle. Not to mention your *compulsively* puerile behaviour.'

'Well, what's wrong with puerile?' asked Jacob, happily. 'Puerile is fun. Puerile is what life's supposed to be all about—unless you're Nian, when obviously there's a strong saving-the-universe element to it all— hey, Rob, what did one eye say to the other eye?'

Robyn clutched madly at her hair.

'Not *again*!' she howled. 'You keep on and on telling me that blasted joke that wasn't even funny to start with and it's *driving me mad*!'

'*A giant beaver?*' said Nian, again, very taken aback.

Jacob looked hurt.

'I've never told you that joke before,' he said. 'Steve only told it to me this afternoon, and I haven't seen you since then.'

Robyn stopping tearing her hair out. She looked suddenly doubtful.

'Yes you did,' she said. But she didn't sound sure.

'OK, then, what's the answer?' demanded Jacob. 'Tell me, then, know-all! If I keep telling you that same joke then *what's the answer*?'

A spasm passed over Robyn's face as if she'd just bitten into a sour hay-apple, but she recited, flatly: 'Between you and me, something smells.'

Nian let out a snigger, even though his brain was busy being puzzled about the beaver. The beaver thing was *weird*.

'How *did* you know about the giant beaver?' he

asked, again. 'That didn't even happen on this world!'

'You still never heard that joke from me,' said Jacob, a little accusingly. 'You must have heard it before.'

But Robyn was frowning at Nian.

'Did I mention a giant beaver?' she asked, vaguely.

Nian ran his hands through his hair. His own memory had got into such convolutions today that he wasn't all that sure any more what had happened and what was going to happen and what was just a dream.

His scarf was stifling him. He took it off and threw it down on a chair.

'This is why I've come,' he said, slowly. 'Things . . . the past and the future . . . seem to have got mixed up. I've been travelling round the worlds to try to find out what's going on.'

'Whoah!' said Jacob, pleased. 'Universal time-distortions. Cool!'

'Do you think it's serious?' asked Robyn.

'I've no idea,' Nian admitted. 'It might be. At least . . . it only just seems to have started happening today: but then *today* feels as if it's been going on for ages and ages.'

'Cool!' said Jacob, again, and threw one of his drumsticks up in the air and caught it again without looking at it.

Robyn did a double-take.

'Hey, when did you learn to do that?' she demanded.

Jacob looked at the stick in his hand as if he was fairly surprised himself.

'Just this morning,' he said. 'Brilliant, eh?'

Robyn began to look worried.

'Look, this is all *way* too weird,' she said. 'I mean, the giant beaver and the joke were bad enough, but Jacob being able to do something stylish is just crazy. Really *weird*.'

Nian nodded, seriously.

'And whatever is happening, it is affecting many worlds,' he said. 'You were right, Robyn, about the giant beaver.'

Robyn didn't seem to know whether she was pleased about that or not.

'Well, at least I've not started inventing beavers,' she said. 'But something powerful enough to overcome Jacob's habitual dorkiness . . . well, that's really *scary*. So what are you going to do about it, Nian?'

Nian shrugged.

'Haven't a clue,' he admitted. 'Well, I suppose I *have* got a clue, now, if you're getting glimpses of the future, and other worlds, and stuff. Time seems to have wrapped itself in knots and be leaking from one strand to another. I'd better go back to the abyss between the worlds and see if I can pick up some sort of a trail of something that's out of place. Or out of *Time*.'

Jacob gave a cry of disappointment.

'But I thought you'd come for a proper visit!' he protested. 'I thought you'd be able to come to the party and hear the band and do some magic and stuff. Come on, Nian! Mum'll be home in a minute, and she'd love to see you. You could stay to tea. And after that we'll go out and hang round the shops. It'll be a riot!'

But Nian shook his head.

'I'd like to,' he said, apologetically. 'I'd really, really like to. But this . . . I don't like it. It feels dangerous. I'd best get on.'

He took a step back towards the fireplace.

'Well, come back soon, OK?' called Jacob, after him.

'Yes, come back soon. I need your help to keep Jacob . . . ' called Robyn.

But the rest of whatever she was going to say was lost as Nian fell into the abyss.

18

Rik stood in the white desert world once more, waiting. It was important not to wait too long: if he set off a big earthquake then it would shake his own world, too, and might tip the great leaning mass of the Monument over into ruin and set the plague free.

But Rik had done this many times, now. He had let himself fall down through the hole in the wall of the Monument to this white desert world, and he had waited here.

Rik's mind was strong and clear. He was alert for the exact moment when the worlds were quivering, straining to turn; and then he would step back into his own world and set Time springing backwards.

Rik stood and breathed in the thin air of the white desert world. Time was moving backwards and forwards in the worlds, but the plague was constantly progressing through his body. The skin of his hands was crusting like tree bark, and his head was being forced down by the sheer mass of muscles at the back of his neck.

He didn't know how long he'd be able to go on. Each time the worlds sprang back they turned not quite so far, not quite so violently. It seemed as if the whole mechanism, as if Time itself, was slowing down.

That couldn't go on for ever.

But he would go on while he could.

Nian found himself being sucked down fast into the abyss. He kicked himself sideways and found that the sucking current only existed along quite a narrow path.

He hung, bobbing gently in the nothingness, and the worlds hung around him, separate, but invisibly linked together. There were hundreds of them, and, too far away to see, there might be thousands, millions, more. How did he find the one particular world where all this trouble was being generated?

He called on his powers to search the vastness of the abyss. But the abyss was empty . . . nothing, nothing, nothing . . . hang on! What was that?

It was only a faint trail of grey, but it stretched far, far across the abyss. In fact, now Nian looked, he found there was a similar faint trail behind him. Yes, these grey trails marked the paths of his own journeys through the abyss. That was Jacob's world at the end of that grey trail, and Nian was pretty sure that far, far over there was the old trail which, if he were mad enough to follow it, would lead him to the world of the magistra of the Mirelands.

Well, that was useful: now he'd worked out that, he would jolly well make sure he avoided it.

Nian looked out across the abyss to further and yet

further shining worlds, and noticed that the furthest ones over there looked a bit odd. Perhaps it was the distance which was distorting them, but they seemed to be swimming a little, as the suns of Nian's own world did sometimes when they were sinking into a haze.

Nian wiped his sleeve across his eyes, but it didn't stop those far-away worlds shimmering. In fact, those nearer worlds were shimmering, too, now.

Nian had no idea what was happening, but it was rushing towards him at the speed of . . .

. . . Nian just had time to shield his head with his arms before the thing hit him. It was so huge that it had rolled him over and had flung him past countless worlds before he even had time to be afraid, hurtling him along so fast that even his thoughts got squashed into bursts of nonsense.

On and on and on . . . his eyes must have stopped working, too, because all he could see were vague humps of colour. He had a go at putting out some powers to brake his progress, but even that slight movement was enough to send him spinning, fast. Very fast. Over and over and head over heels over head over . . .

. . . and *swoooosh!* A bright fuzzy flame zipped past and he must have just brushed it because a searing pain scraped along his leg and then he was free again and the pain had been left far behind him and he was . . .

. . . *back!*

Back.

Back floating in the calm abyss, with the lanterns of the worlds hanging round him. Nian somersaulted dizzily four more times before he realized that he could stop himself.

He hung in the middle of nothing and waited for his brain and body to connect themselves up again. Then Nian went round and collected up his thoughts, which wasn't easy, as some of them were rather a long way away.

But yes, his memory seemed to be working fine. He'd just come from Jacob's world, and before that he'd been in the world of the giant beaver, and before that he'd set out from the House of Truth.

There, behind him, was the thin ribbon of his trail which must lead all the way back to Jacob's world. Nian watched it twisting and looping in the most nauseating way. He followed it with his eyes until it disappeared into a woolly distance.

And then, quite suddenly, he remembered laying down his scarf in Jacob's front room and then going off and leaving it there.

But surely that couldn't have caused all this upheaval. Not just one woolly scarf? Could it?

Nian didn't really think so, but he supposed he'd better go and make sure.

He set off back along the trail, trying not to think about what that enormous . . . *thing* . . . might have done to Jacob's blue-green world.

19

The boy sitting at the drum-kit was alive. He even had all his limbs attached. Nian heaved a great sigh of relief.

'Are you all right?' he asked.

The orange-haired boy looked up, and his face split into a wide grin of delight.

'Nian! Fantastic!' he crowed. 'It's you! I'd almost given up on you. Hey, you're looking good. Fatter. Which is good, obviously, I mean, you're not actually fat, no way, but you were practically *skeletal* before. Did you sort out those old monk-people all right?'

Nian rubbed his hand up and down across his face in the hope that something would start making sense at some point.

'You don't remember,' he said, more or less to himself.

Jacob grinned, threw a drumstick casually up in the air, put out his hand without looking and missed it. It fell with a clatter and a ping right down between his knees and onto the floor.

Jacob didn't seem very surprised. He knelt down to try to disentangle it from the struts of his drum kit.

'Probably not,' he agreed. 'I never remember anything. I've got a memory like a . . . er . . . thingy.'

This was a joke, but Nian's brain was whimpering too pathetically for him to feel much like laughing.

'But look, you *don't* remember, do you?' he asked. 'You don't remember me coming here earlier.'

Jacob sat himself up cautiously. His hair was tangled up into a bonfire of orange.

'Of course I do. You came last year and we raided a police station and saved the worlds. Even I couldn't forget that.'

He yawned.

'Sorry, Nian, but I'm not really awake, yet, I'm never at my best in the morning. You're so . . . energetic.'

Morning? But it had been the afternoon just a few minutes ago. Nian was sure it had been . . . or was he? He tried to remember. Had someone said something?

You can stay to tea.

Yes, Jacob had said that. But now . . .

'Is it really morning?' Nian asked, truly disconcerted.

Jacob flicked his drumstick into the air, put out a casual hand, and dropped it again.

'Of course it is. It's no big deal, is it? We have one every day round here. Don't you?'

'Yes,' said Nian, his mind doing loop-the-loops. 'But not usually at teatime.'

'What?'

Nian was thinking. Perhaps he'd been in the abyss longer than he'd thought. It'd only seemed like a couple of minutes, but the abyss was a weird place, and perhaps Time didn't really exist in the same way once you were in it. Well, it couldn't do, or else he'd have suffocated. There was no air in the abyss, in fact nothing at all, only faintly glistening trails that marked his progress through it.

He remembered something else, and looked round.

'What happened to my scarf?' he asked.

Jacob shrugged, bewildered.

'*I* don't know,' he said. 'I can never even find my own stuff. Where did you leave it?'

Nian was blinking at the stuffed empty chair beside him, his mind still chasing itself round and round.

'Hey, Nian,' said Jacob, weaving himself carefully through the bits of his drum-kit again to retrieve his drumstick. 'I'm in a band, now. We're going to play at Kelly Bagshott's thirteenth birthday party tomorrow. For money!'

And at that the circles in Nian's brain chased themselves smaller and smaller into a small explosion.

'Tomorrow?' he echoed. 'The party's tomorrow? *Still?*'

Jacob grinned good-naturedly.

'Yep. Hey, why don't you stay here tonight and come with us? I can soon clear all the stuff off the spare bunk. There's going to be loads of people at the party, and we're going to play some fantastic stuff I've nicked from other worlds. Hey, you could turn all the Coke to alcopops, that'd be just so brilliant! And, hey, Nian, is there any way you could do something to Aston's vocal chords to make it so he can actually sing? Because we only let him in the band because his dad's a plumber.'

Nian was hardly listening. He was finally realizing what had been happening. That great wave in the abyss had been . . . well, not Time, exactly, but something which had pushed Time backwards. So that now Nian had returned to Jacob's front room several hours before he'd arrived in the first place.

He opened his mouth to explain: but that would have been exceedingly tricky even in his own language, even if he'd actually understood it.

He looked at the stuffed chair where he'd left his scarf and wondered where on earth his scarf was now. What might happen to something you'd left in the past but which was now in the future?

Oh *struth*, his brain hurt! What the grotting pits was going on? And what the *bog* was he supposed to do about it?

'So,' said Jacob, happily, playing a neat twiddle and a couple of thumps on various bits of his drum kit, 'have you come for just a visit, or are the worlds falling to pieces again?'

Nian couldn't think how he'd come to forget just how infuriatingly relaxed Jacob was.

'The worlds are falling to bits again,' he said, curtly. 'Something is making Time go backwards.'

Jacob made a *duh?* face.

'Backwards? What do you mean? Hey, I'm not getting younger, am I? Because if you think I'm going to go through a whole year of having Mrs Brown for English again . . . '

Nian waved all that away impatiently.

'No,' he said. 'Not. But I think . . . I *think* we are

129

having the same piece of Time again and again, perhaps. Many times. Yes, that explains much. It even explains Robyn and the beaver.'

Jacob's chin and eyebrows were now as far apart as he could get them.

'Robyn and the *beaver*?' he echoed, in a voice so incredulous it was nearly a hiccup. 'Nian, have you gone completely nuts or something? Because, I mean, that's absolutely fine, obviously, but it might just sort of help if I knew.'

Nian nodded absently, still thinking hard. There had to be some way of proving it, but . . .

'What did one eye say to the other eye?' he asked, suddenly.

Jacob shrugged.

'I don't know,' he said, still good-natured, but slightly warily. 'What *did* one eye say to the other eye?'

'Between you and me, something smells,' replied Nian.

Jacob's jaw dropped, and then he gave a delighted yelp.

'That's *rubbish*!' he exclaimed. 'That's the worst joke I've ever heard in *my entire life*. That's *beyond* pathetic!'

'Yes,' agreed Nian, still thinking about what was happening. The worlds were being sprung backwards in time, but, even worse, the process was doing damage as it happened. When Time went back, everything wasn't quite going with it. That was why (yes, *that* was why) people had memories (if they could be called memories) of things that hadn't happened yet.

Jacob started grinning.

'I can't wait to tell the band,' he said. 'What did one eye say to the other eye? Brilliant! Hey, I could tell that one at the party tomorrow. It'd be a brilliant chat-up line, that would. Girls can't get enough of guys who are really witty and all that. It said so in the August edition of Balls Up.'

Nian had been having little trouble with Jacob's English until then, but at least three distinct meanings collided colourfully and painfully at the end of Jacob's last sentence.

Nian shook the fireworks out of his head. He had more important things to think about. If time was being pushed backwards—and it was, it really was—then whatever was doing it had to be massively power-ful. Not just massively compared with Nian, but massively powerful compared with . . .

. . . compared with the whole abyss and every world that hung within it. About as much more powerful than him, as he was more powerful than . . . Jacob's chat-up lines.

Nian stood still, with that realization creeping icily through his insides. He enjoyed a fight. He enjoyed pitting his wits against something stronger than he was. But this time (this Time) it would be like trying to push a mountain over, or pull back the tide.

'So,' said Jacob, conversationally, throwing his drumstick up in the air and missing it again. 'Is there some big bad guy who's tampering with Time Itself for his own evil purposes?'

'I don't know,' said Nian, still shocked.

Jacob bent down to try to retrieve his drumstick, and let out a howl.

'Ouch! Ow! Puch!' He came up again, affronted and scarlet-faced and clutching his nose. 'I god a wingnud ride ub my nosdril,' he proclaimed, woefully. 'Hey, it's really *sore*, too. Really *really* sore. You wouldn'd have thord . . . '

'It's probably still sore from last time,' said Nian, remembering his own bruised arm.

'Frob . . . hey, bud you don'd thig I mayg a *habid* of shoving thigs ub my nosdrils, do you?'

Nian waved that away irritably. He had to *think*, hard, and having Jacob wittering on and on was enough to drive anyone demented.

'You *will have made* a habit of it,' he said. 'You will have done it every day for . . . '

How long? Was there anything to help him work that out? Was there anything to prove that Nian's whole life hadn't been a constant re-running of that particular day?

Well, he wasn't a new-born baby, so there must have been a time when Time was going forward. *This* day might have been flicked back a hundred times, but it couldn't have been doing it for ever.

Jacob was still massaging his nose with the greatest tenderness.

'Do you mean I'm faded to go od geddig thigs stug ub by nosdrils every day for ever?' he asked, plaintively. 'Because in thad case I'm nod sure life's goig to be worth livig.'

And suddenly a lot more things about today began

to make sense to Nian. Not just the memories that had been casting shadows over people, but other things, too. Tarq's being so very thin and frail, for one thing: if Time wasn't snapping back and rerunning the day quite completely, then in some ways Tarq might not have eaten for weeks, or months or years . . . and then there was Tan, exhausted with climbing the Holy Mountain. He'd been doing it again and again and again. And Reeklet had been winning at cards every day until even his grand surliness turned to sunshine.

And here was Jacob, happy-go-lucky Jacob, suddenly saying that his life wasn't going to be worth living. He didn't mean it, of course. But one day, if things went on like this, he might come to mean it.

This couldn't go on. Time had to start going in a straight line again so they could get on to tomorrow. To Tuesday.

'I've got to go back into the abyss,' Nian murmured, half to himself. 'I've got to search through it until I find out why things have gone wrong. And then some-how, somehow, I've got to stop it.'

Jacob stopped massaging his nose for a moment.

'So what you're saying is that there's some almighty evil wizard who's taken control of the universe and is torturing us all to death by slow and painful inches,' he said.

Nian winced.

'It might not be an evil wizard,' he said, with as much hope as he could muster. 'It might be a . . . a wizard's evil sister. Or just something that's gone wrong with the way the worlds turn.'

'Oh, right,' said Jacob. 'So that'll just be the Laws of Physics you're going to have to change, then. Well, that's a relief.'

Nian repressed a strong urge to hit him.

'It's not funny,' he said, shortly.

Jacob put his drumsticks down, suddenly serious.

'No,' he said. 'No, it's really not, is it? Because if we never get as far as tomorrow, I'm never going to get to my party, am I? And it also means that any chance of you stopping the worlds from shaking themselves to bits is going to involve you getting into a fight with something very very big and clever and nasty and dangerous. Hey, Nian!'

'What?' said Nian.

Jacob's blue eyes were suddenly filled with hope.

'Can I come too?' he asked.

20

The Lord Caul shifted his feet clear of the worst of the seaweed, and took a deep steadying breath.

'Hani,' he said, with a certain dangerous calmness, 'you do understand what you're trying to do, don't you?'

Hani hung his head.

'Well . . . '

Caul took several more steadying breaths. He was generally an enthusiastic and fairly patient teacher, but now he seemed to be on the verge of a great explosion.

'I know we're trying to join our minds together. And I know it's so we get a better perspective on things,' Hani mumbled. 'But I still don't really . . . get it. Sorry, Lord.'

The other boys exchanged glances. Caul had never really lost his temper in a major way before, so they weren't sure what he might be going to do.

'It's nothing complicated,' said Derig, anxiously and helpfully. 'It's just to help us see things better, really.'

Hani nodded seriously; but his face was still both blank and apprehensive.

'I do keep trying,' he said. 'But however long I try it just doesn't . . . I think I'm just too stupid for all this.'

The others exchanged glances. Hani *was* stupid at some things; but he'd never seemed all that bothered about it before.

'Hey, Hani,' said Emmec, encouragingly. 'It's easy. Even an idiot like you could get this. It's like . . . do you remember how rubbish you were at pockle that time after Alin found you filling up his boots with porridge? You couldn't judge distances with your black eye all closed up.'

Hani nodded cautiously. He remembered that. The black eye had been fair enough, he was ready to admit: but not being able to play pockle properly had been *torture*.

'Well,' continued Emmec, patiently. 'This mind-joining stuff is just like that. You need two eyes to judge distances well, right? So if we join all our minds together then we get a brilliant view of everything because we get a sort-of all-round view.'

Hani looked from one to the other of them. Then he blinked.

'Is that all it is?' he asked, cautiously.

The Lord Caul heaved a huge sigh.

'That's all it is,' he said. 'Thank you, Emmec. You know, I feel as if I've spent *weeks* trying to get that simple fact into your head, Hani. All right. Nian, do you think you could persuade all this seaweed to go back to where it came from before we get asphyxiated?'

There was no answer.

'Hey,' said Alin, looking round. 'Where the . . . hey, where's Nian gone?'

'Not out of the door,' said Gow, very puzzled. 'We'd have seen him.'

'This is impossible,' muttered the Lord Caul, looking round wildly. 'Quite impossible. He was here a moment ago. Hani, make up for having dumped seaweed all over the room and use your powers to find him, will you?'

Hani was a liability in lessons, but he could always find anything straight away.

Except, on this occasion, the Truth Sayer.

'He's nowhere,' he said, blankly. 'I know he was here a moment ago, but now . . . I don't think . . . I don't think he's anywhere at all *in the whole world*.'

'But look,' argued Jacob, 'you'd be better off to take me with you. Then there'll be two of us who know what's going on. And, I mean, all the best heroes have a side-kick. I bet I'd be quite good at all the screaming and asking very obvious questions and all that. I'll even wear a miniskirt, if you like.'

Nian shuddered slightly.

'I do *not* like,' he said, curtly.

Jacob shrugged good-naturedly.

'That's cool. But anyway, if it's true that Time keeps springing backwards then I can do anything I like and it won't matter, will it? Even if I *die* I'll spring up again as good as new tomorrow.'

That was typical Jacob nonsense.

'Not if you are in the abyss,' pointed out Nian. 'I

137

don't think there *is* any Time in the abyss. Not ordinary sort of Time, anyway. When I was there Time carried on in a straight line and did not go back even though Time did everywhere else. That's how I found out what was happening.'

'Hey, I'll tell you something else,' said Jacob, suddenly. 'If you go back to the House of Truth—to anywhere in your world—then I bet Time will snap closed again and *you* won't remember anything, either.'

Nian looked at him, blinking. That might even be true. That was worrying—but what was even more worrying was that *Jacob* had worked it out.

Nian had thought he was just getting his head round this Time business, but if Jacob started being intelligent then things were obviously even more complicated than he'd thought.

'What made you say that?' he asked, annoyed, and even slightly nervous.

Jacob shrugged.

'Well, it's pretty standard Sci-Fi stuff, isn't it?' he said. 'All that sort of thing's been done hundreds of times.'

'Has it? What's Sci-Fi?'

Jacob looked at Nian as if he was being slow.

'People in films . . . television . . . stories,' he explained. 'Not in real life, obviously. None of it would ever happen in real life.'

Nian was relieved. Jacob hadn't really got any more idea what was going on than he had. Jacob was still himself. But still . . .

'This *is* real life,' Nian said, grimly.

* * *

Each time Rik returned from the white desert he was newly aware of how the plague was progressing through his body. The muscles of his arms were strong enough to pull himself up the rock wall and back into the Monument easily, now.

His mind was more powerful, too. He could see right through the black stone of the Monument walls, even through the mountains. He could see everything. He could see out and out beyond the sea, beyond the world.

In the plain below him the little creatures were making their way to the door of the Monument. They had scraped it clear of the sand, and now they planned to open it.

Rik smiled to himself. They would not succeed. There were twenty ways he could stop them . . .

. . . but no.

NO!

Rik clasped his heavy head in his hands, gasping with horror. He didn't want to hurt them. He *didn't*— but the plague which was strengthening Rik's body was weakening his mind. He knew it, though sometimes it was hard to remember.

Rik stood and very carefully took hold of his mind. His own thoughts could still squirm their way through as long as he concentrated, though it took a lot of energy, and as often as not his thoughts ran out of strength before they reached their destination.

He didn't know how long he would be able to hang on.

Rik pushed his thoughts through the tangle of steel in his brain. The white desert—going back to the white desert and waiting there until the worlds were under pressure, and . . .

Yes. That was what he must do. Again. He had done it a dozen times before, but each time the effect was weaker. Time jerked back, but not so far. Rik was almost sure that the whole universe was gently slowing down. To start with, the whiplash effect had been strong enough to put the world back to the morning again, so the creatures on the plain—the *people*—had to start their slow creeping towards the door from the beginning.

If they got to the door then that would be the beginning of the end of the world. The beginning of the end of Aranna, who was his friend.

Rik went to the hole in the wall of the Monument and let his heavy body fall down towards the white desert once more. The entrance to the passageway hung in space, now, since the earthquake had tipped the Monument forwards, moving the walls and floors. Each time Rik returned to his own world he fell down into the cave below and had to use his ever-more powerful body to climb back up the rocky cave wall into the Monument again.

Rik knew he could not keep doing this for much longer. It was becoming harder and harder to remember what he should do. It was becoming harder and harder to remember that the others mattered.

He called a picture of Aranna to his mind. She was little compared with everything he could see, but in his mind she shone like a diamond, valuable and bright.

It wouldn't be long before she and the little people arrived and opened the door and let hell loose in the world.

But Rik would prevent it this time.

And next time, perhaps.

21

Nian, about to step from Jacob's front room into the abyss, halted with one foot in the air.

'Look,' he said, 'if you get killed it's all your own fault, all right?'

Jacob nodded good-humouredly.

'No worries,' he said. 'Anyway, it's one of those no-lose situations, isn't it? Unless this Time-thing gets sorted out then I'm doomed to go through today again and again. So I'm pretty much dead already, aren't I?'

Nian sniffed dubiously.

'And *that's* only if I don't pop up again here tomorrow,' Jacob went on. 'I mean *the next today*—as good as new. And I bet I would.'

Nian tried to work that out, but his brain immediately started disintegrating with the complexity of it all, so he gave up.

'And, after all, I was only going to spend my life working in the Health Shop,' mused Jacob. 'Which is fine, obviously. In a nothing sort of a way.'

Nian held out his hand.

'We must stay together,' he said.

Jacob looked a bit surprised, but he put his hand in Nian's own.

'We aren't likely to get separated, though, are we?' Jacob asked. 'When I was in the abyss before I just sort of got sucked towards your world. Won't it be the same?'

'Yes, but it would probably suck us to the world of the giant homicidal beaver,' said Nian. 'Which,' he admitted, 'would solve all our problems in two mouthfuls. I shall make my own passage, and take you with me.'

'OK,' said Jacob, with cheerful unconcern. 'How will you know where to go?'

Nian wished he knew. He wished he knew *anything*. Struth, he'd only noticed the Time wave because he'd been in the abyss when it had happened. What would happen if he was on another world when everything went back next time? Would he lose his memory? He could hardly fail to notice he was suddenly on a different world. Could he?

Nian groaned to himself. It was bad enough having world-shaking powers, without being required to be a grotting genius, as well.

He led Jacob forward a swift step and let the abyss take them.

Nian kicked himself out of the current which was taking him and Jacob . . . wherever . . . and looked out across the abyss, looking for a trail joining the worlds which he hadn't made himself.

He saw to his absolute horror that those furthest worlds over there were shimmering in an odd way.

Oh no, come *on*, he thought, savagely. There couldn't be another Time-wave starting up! Not so soon!

Jacob was hanging tightly on to Nian's hand and gazing around, grinning inanely. Nian, hopelessly, tried to blink away the shimmering, and wished, really *wished*, that he had time to enjoy this.

Across the abyss that closer world was shimmering, now, and that one, and the disturbance was rushing towards them at the speed of . . .

. . . Nian hardly had time to panic before the thing hit him. It was so huge and fast it had rolled him over and squashed his thoughts into nonsense before he knew what was happening.

And he'd lost something. He didn't know what, but it was something terribly terribly important. He was being tossed over and over and on and on. He tried putting out some powers to brake himself, but that just sent him spinning, fast. Over and over, head over heels over head over . . .

. . . and then he was . . . *back*!

Back.

Nian somersaulted four more times before he could even think about stopping himself, but he was back, back in the still abyss, with the worlds turning round him.

He hung in the middle of nothing while his brain connected itself. Yes, he'd just come from Jacob's . . .

Nian's heart lurched.

Jacob?

Oh struth, *Jacob*!

Nian turned round hastily in the nothingness of the abyss, round and under and over in a frantic searching eel-wriggle: but he was alone.

That meant Jacob was out there, somewhere, in all the hugeness of the abyss. He might have been sucked into a world, or be drifting helplessly, or be smashed to pieces by the great wave of Time that had swatted even Nian away like a fly.

Nian turned himself round urgently, again and again, looking for the merest snail-smear trail across the abyss which might be all that was left of Jacob Rush. Nian didn't know when he'd lost Jacob, but it had probably been just about as soon as the wave hit them.

All right. All right: then that was why there was no Jacob-trail from here, then. Jacob's trail would lead off from where the wave had hit them. Jacob might even have got knocked straight back into his front room and be safely practising his drums without knowing that anything had happened.

Nian flung himself back along his looping trail. He could travel faster than anyone on his world could measure, but he forced himself to keep to a pace where he'd be able to spot the faint trail of whatever was left of Jacob.

Even so, he nearly missed it, dizzy as he was from having to follow every wild curl and hiccuping loop of his trail, round and under and through, while keeping a look-out all round for . . .

. . . there! There it was, zigzagging and tumbling.

Nian followed it with his eyes. It twisted and dodged about but then, a million million grohls away (though Nian rather thought that the abyss wasn't the sort of place to have distances, at all) Jacob's trail smoothed out into a long shallow parabola, a faint trace of milkiness through the rich blackness of the abyss.

Nian gathered his strength and swooped along it at incredible speed.

Rik landed on the floor of the cave, panting. He hit it harder every time he came back from the white desert world, because each time he was heavier. How long could he go on?

Below him on the plain were the rows of tents. Professor Hallam's, Rolan's, Aranna's.

Rik turned away from all that and raised a massive arm to begin his climb back up into the Monument.

He'd done it before, and he'd do it again. And again, and again, alone in the darkness.

It was the only way that Aranna and the others could keep on living.

Nian saw the lantern world that lay at the end of Jacob's flight some time (though Time, like distance, did really seem to belong here) before he reached it. He was in too much of a hurry to notice much about it, but there was something about the shape . . .

. . . but here he was, rising through the darkness.

Nian waited until the ground was firm under his feet

and then looked round. Yes, there were the jagged hills and coarse white rock: this was the white desert world he'd visited earlier.

And there, breathing and alive where there was no other living thing at all, was Jacob.

Jacob grinned.

'Hi,' he said. 'Nian the Truth Sayer, I presume. Right. Well, I suppose this means I'm alive, then.'

22

Nian sat himself down on a bit of the damp rock of the white desert world. He felt vastly relieved, and rather sorry for himself.

'So,' said Jacob. 'This is another world.'

'Yes.'

Jacob looked around.

'Yeah. All rock and green sky. You can really tell it's another world, can't you. I mean, it looks like a *Star Trek* set.'

Nian pushed his powers rather wearily into the air of the place. He had ended up here on two separate occasions, and perhaps that was more than a coincidence.

But there was still nothing here. Nothing at all. In this whole world there was not one single living thing apart from Nian and Jacob.

'I don't know what that wave-thing was,' said Jacob, happily, 'but I must have whizzed past at least a hundred other worlds before I slowed down and then got sort of sucked up here. Hey!' he grinned. 'I got a glimpse of this incredible belly-slapping band as I went past the last world. Fantastic!'

Nian was remembering more about this world. He

got up and went back to the exact place where he'd arrived from the abyss.

There were lots of footprints there, now: some of them had odd wavy patterns on the soles (they were Jacob's footprints, and those, over there, the ones with the heel missing, were his own), but there had certainly been another person here recently who'd walked backwards and forwards again and again.

Nian squatted down to make sure. Yes, these were the same footprints he'd seen here before.

But that was ridiculous. This world—Nian checked again—yes, this world had no one at all living on it. If there ever had been anyone here, it must have been ages ago.

But that couldn't be true, because none of these footprints crossing backwards and forwards were more than a day or two old.

As Nian looked around the desolate valley he realized something that hadn't struck him before. The whole valley floor was sodden with white mud, but the footprints centred on this tiny patch. Whoever had come here had not walked off to the north or the south or the east or the west. He had come *here* . . . and then gone home again.

Jacob picked up a bit of the rough white rock and crumbled it into tiny crystals between his fingers.

'I suppose this whole place isn't made of diamonds, is it?' he asked, hopefully.

Nian checked.

'No,' he said—and then found he didn't know the English word for what it was.

'It is made of . . . of stuff which is found by water and can be used to make small houses.'

Jacob sighed.

'Sand,' he said. 'That's what I thought. Still, it was worth a try. Ah well, I suppose I couldn't have taken anything home with me anyway, could I, because it would weaken the worlds and everything. Though I suppose quite a small fist-sized diamond wouldn't matter much. Hey, how much are diamonds worth?'

There were dark green clouds streaming over the ridge, even though down here there was no breeze at all. Nian shuddered suddenly.

'This place is wrong,' he said.

Jacob brushed the damp sand from his fingers.

'Oh, I don't know,' he said. 'It's a lot better than the first other world I visited. That was all dark, and everyone thought I was a hallucination. This is just . . . well, a sort of gulch. Possibly. If a gulch is what I think it is.'

English was really rather an awkward language, but *gulch* did seem quite a good word for this place. It was the sort of noise a worzel might make if it was being sick. In fact, the whole place did look as if it was made of worzel sick. Not that Nian had ever seen a worzel, obviously, let alone a poorly one. But this world seemed . . . Nian wasn't sure how to put it. Sort of . . .

'Do passageways into other worlds always end up in rubbish places?' asked Jacob. 'No, they can't do, because I've heard loads of other worlds from our front room, and there's usually plenty going on. Loads of just fantastic music.'

'Usually they are fantastic places,' Nian told him. 'If there are people on a world a place where the worlds touch will probably be a sacred place. But there are no people here.'

'No sign of life at all,' said Jacob. 'Except that . . . here, I bet I'm breathing out bacteria and stuff all over the place. Hey, I'm probably the new Adam—no I'm probably *God*. My bacteria will probably settle here and raise families and all that, and in another couple of million years . . . '

Nian shook his head.

'The bacteria you carry need you to live on,' he said. 'They will not survive here alone.'

'Really? Bummer.' But then Jacob brightened again.

'I'll tell you what though,' he said. 'I've got a really major verruca. If I take my shoe and sock off then some of the germy things will probably jump off. They'll probably be quite happy in one of these puddles—I mean, they love swimming pools and all that. Just think, in another few millions of years there'll be loads of them all over the valley, all evolved into sweet little hairy things bouncing up and down all over the place and wondering whether it might be a nice idea to invent mobile phones and pizzas and stuff. Brilliant!'

'That is not going to happen,' said Nian, suddenly.

Jacob gave him an odd look.

'I know,' he said. 'I was *joking*, Nian.'

Nian shook his head.

'It will not happen because it has happened before,' he said.

Jacob's mouth fell open in disbelief.

151

'There have been small hairy bouncy things here that invented mobile phones?'

Nian clenched his fists with annoyance. Jacob had always been like this, making light of important things, failing to understand what was happening.

'No,' he said. 'Verrucas.'

'What?'

'Things *like* verrucas,' Nian went on, for he could feel the echo of a whole web of life, now, through the soles of his feet. 'And trees and insects . . . and a thing like a garden. A big garden that went over all the hills. But then . . . '

'But then what? McDonald's? X-Boxes? Mars Bars?'

'But then there was a big explosion,' went on Nian, slowly, for the vibrations of it were still there in the stone under his feet. 'And the whole world . . . '

And suddenly Nian knew what was wrong with this world. This place was too *small*: it was only the remnant of what it had once been. This world had been torn to pieces, and most of it had been scattered into the abyss.

Nian could see the place as it had once been, now, green and bright and full of life. There had been a million shades of green, and dragonflies with faceted eyes like diamonds.

But then it had been ripped apart and everything living had been scoured from existence by earthquake and fire and roaring wind until all that was left was a damp desert of white rock inlaid with long puddles that reflected the cloudy sky.

Nian shivered suddenly. That was what happened

when people started getting into the wrong world. And someone *had* been getting into the wrong world, those footprints proved that. Nian couldn't be sure that this had anything to do with the Time disturbances, but it was all he had to go on.

'Jacob!'

Jacob came jogging back from where he'd been doing a little rock-climbing, leaving a long trail of muddy footprints behind him.

The other person who had been here had not been rock-climbing. He had come from his world and stayed for a while, and then gone home again. He had waited here in this empty valley; and then he (whoever he was) had returned.

Nian didn't understand that at all. What would keep drawing someone here? Was there something precious here, like the diamonds Jacob had been hoping for?

There was no end to the strangeness of other worlds: anything might be rare and precious there, even sand.

Jacob came up. He was a bit red in the face because the air here was very thin.

'Wipe your feet carefully,' said Nian.

'Are we going home?' asked Jacob, turning up his feet to look at the white mud that caked his great shoes.

'I don't think so,' answered Nian. 'We have to go and visit someone.'

'Who?' said Jacob, scraping his soles on the nearest bit of gritty rock.

'Someone dangerous,' said Nian, thoughtfully.

23

'This time we must not get separated,' said Nian, as they stood side by side on the edge of the abyss. 'I have bound us together with chains.'

'What?' asked Jacob. 'Come off it, Nian! Who do you think you are, a dungeon master?'

Jacob took a step forward, and then stumbled.

'Hey, you have, and all! You great wombat, Nian, I could have tripped over them and broken my neck!'

Wombat? Nian tried for half a moment to work out what wombats had to do with invisible chains that tied him and Jacob together; but quickly decided that he had too much on his mind to bother.

'I feel like a dog on a lead,' went on Jacob. 'Hey, what if we do get separated? I'll be all tied up.'

'The only way we'll get separated is if your arms and legs come off,' said Nian. 'Now, come on. I shall guide us.'

'Where are we going?'

But Nian didn't know.

'To find the person who has been here,' he said. 'Now. One—two—three—*jump*!'

They fell fast out of the pale light of that world and

into the black of the abyss. Nian kicked them free of the current. The chains worked well: Jacob was bobbing beside Nian, his red hair floating loosely around him as if he were under water. Nian looked around.

And there. There it was. A whole skein of trails reaching away across the abyss. Someone had come backwards and forwards at least a dozen times between the white desert and . . .

. . . and where?

Nian sent himself and Jacob into a swift hurtling dive along the path of the silken trails.

The silken trail ended at what seemed to be a perfectly ordinary lantern-world, and Nian let the world draw him and Jacob in. It seemed to be night-time in that world because there was no paling of the blackness of the abyss, even when they came to a stop. Nian was just getting his balance (which was oddly difficult in the pitch darkness) when he suddenly found himself dropping about fifteen spans and crashing down onto a rock floor.

As if that wasn't bad enough, a split second later something big and knobbly fell on top of him.

Nian rubbed his arm, which had got bashed yet again—and then twigged that nearly all the howling and groaning that was going on wasn't actually him.

'Are you all right?' Nian asked.

'Er . . . dunno,' admitted Jacob. 'Hang on! *Ouch!* Well, mostly. For someone who's been yanked feet-first halfway across the universe and then fallen about three metres down onto a stone floor, I suppose so, yes.'

'Not halfway across the universe,' corrected Nian. 'Not far at all. From one world to the next. And you fell on *me*.'

Jacob seemed to be trying to work out where his feet were, so Nian helped by dissolving the chains that had tied them together.

'Well, I don't *think* any bits of me have actually snapped off,' said Jacob. 'Mind you, it's hard to be sure in here, it's as black as a panther's backside.'

Nian used his powers to have a look round. From the musty dampness and chill of the place he guessed they were underground.

'We're probably in a cellar,' said Jacob, his voice echoing coldly off the walls. 'Nian, is there anything in here? Barrels of wine, or treasure or stuff?'

'No,' said Nian. 'There is nothing, here. I do not think there has ever been anything much here.'

'Ah well. Just my luck. You know, I keep hoping I'll end up on a world where the floor is strewn with diamonds and naked girls, but so far I haven't found anywhere where they even have *food*.'

'I have been to a place with diamonds and all that,' said Nian. 'Only,' he admitted, 'without the *total* nakedness.'

In the darkness Nian felt the draught of Jacob's double-take. 'Really? Semi-clad girls? And diamonds? Cor, what did you . . . what were they like?'

'Homicidal,' said Nian, with a sigh. He sent his powers round the place again. 'Come. This way.'

'There's a way out?'

'There is a way out,' said Nian. 'Though,' he went on, thoughtfully, 'I do not know if we *want* out. Follow.'

Nian walked neatly along the flattest part of the narrow twisting floor. It was odd that this place, too, showed no signs of life, or ever having *had* much life.

'*Ow! Ow-ow-ow!*'

Nian waited while Jacob hopped and blundered about.

'Ow, Nian, I nearly cracked my skull on a knobbly bit on the wall, there!'

Nian wondered, not for the first time, why he'd agreed to let Jacob come with him. Jacob was a liability. He'd got very nearly no powers at all except for a slight ability to hear emanations from other worlds, particularly if they consisted of very loud thumpy music.

'Put your hand on my shoulders,' Nian told him.

'Fantastic, great,' muttered Jacob, waggling his hands about blindly. 'Nian, it's as black as a mole's navel in here. Where *are* your flipping shoulders?'

'Here. Here. Now come. There is no time to waste.'

Nian led the way round two or three bends. The place seemed to be some sort of a cave, although it didn't seem very old. Perhaps it had been cracked open by . . . not by people. By *something*.

'Daylight,' breathed Jacob warmly down his neck.

Another turn and the light was dazzling. Jacob took his hands off Nian's shoulders so he could shield his eyes from the glare.

157

'Whoa,' he breathed. 'Hey, Nian. This is a bit more like it!'

They were looking out across a dry plain of ashy sand. Down below them there were tents pitched in rows, and many long ditches; though this didn't look like an army, for all that.

'Look at the mountains!' murmured Jacob, in awe.

But they were small, far-away things, only faintly touched with snow. Nothing special. And here, on the plain . . . Nian searched the place. There were quite a lot of people. There were also dangle-flies and ticks and beetles, and several thousand lurking crack-scorpions, each as shiny as a grindlenut and as sharp as a needle. But that was more or less all.

'Wow,' Jacob was saying happily, beside him. 'Wow wow *wow*! It's a proper sandy desert. And tents. Hey, and listen! Can you hear that music?

Nian could hear it, *boinging* in the distance. He sniffed.

'I would not call it music,' he said.

'What? No, listen to that *beat*. I mean, wow. And . . . sheesh, Nian, this is *another world*!'

There were some people coming out of the largest tent. The leader was skinny and bent, though he was walking with such fierce purpose that he made the others seemed frail, like a column of woodmites following their queen.

Nian began to walk down towards the little procession and Jacob bounded along sideways beside him.

'What are we going to do?' he asked breathlessly.

Nian hadn't a clue.

158

'I don't know,' he said. 'I haven't a clue. But this place has something to do with what's been happening, I think.'

'Oh, right. So what are you going to say to all those people?'

'I don't know,' said Nian, again. 'I haven't a clue.'

'Oh. But then . . . '

Nian carried on making his way, skidding and clambering, down the rubbly side of the hill.

'We haven't got time to do nothing,' he said. 'That last time-wave happened much sooner than I'd thought it would. The next one might come at any time, and when it does we don't know what will happen. We might get transported back to our own worlds, or we might get our memories wiped.'

Jacob wrinkled up his freckly face.

'Hm,' he said. 'This has all gone a bit sci-fi and complicated for me. I never could get my head round all that Time stuff. I always skip those bits and go on to the next fight. Though,' he went on, almost thoughtfully, 'actually, on the whole I'm hoping I'm in one of those stories where there *isn't* a fight. Not against all that lot, anyway. Hey, though, Nian!'

'What?'

'This might have happened already.'

'What?'

'A Time-shift. If we're still here, but with our memories wiped, then . . . well, our memories will be wiped, won't they? And so we won't know if it's happened or not. We might have walked across this desert a million times already, and . . . whoa!'

They'd rounded a hillock, and there, to their right, was a great square black tower that was leaning precipitously over the plain.

'Whoa,' whispered Jacob, again, sobered. 'What on earth is *that*, Nian? It looks . . . it looks like the biggest tombstone in the universe.'

Nian sent his mind towards it, but he was met by a barrier so smooth and shiny and full of spite that he winced away from it.

'You know,' he said, slowly. 'I've got a horrible feeling that's exactly what it is.'

24

Jacob squinted up at the huge leaning bulk of the black tower.

'So is it full of bodies?' he asked Nian. 'You know, mummies? Or skeletons?'

Nian focused his powers on the great square tower again. The thing was old, and it had power: not really the sort of power that *did* things, exactly, but more the sort of power that . . . he wasn't sure how to describe it, but it was a sort of *pride*. The power to crush people, to make them feel small. Perhaps the power to make people feel too small to be brave enough to attack it. Yes, that was something near to it. Clever.

The stone of the tower was slippery, and hard to get his powers through, but he thought that . . . yes.

Nian turned back to Jacob.

'There's someone in there,' he said. 'At least . . . I don't think it's a person, exactly. But something with a mind.'

Jacob scratched his red head.

'So what is it, then? A super-intelligent machine, or a ravening sand-monster, or what?'

Nian tried to find out, but the walls of the tower

were really slithery and . . . well, Nian must be getting things wrong, because the thing in there seemed to be not entirely . . . not entirely *itself*, whatever that meant.

'If it's super-intelligent then we're in a lot of trouble,' said Nian. 'But it does seem a bit like a monster, I think. I think it might be very powerful.'

Jacob looked almost thoughtful.

'So . . . is this the bit where I scream and run away as fast as I can?'

Nian was concentrating on the tower. It had a door, but that hadn't been unlocked in centuries. So there must be another way in.

And yes. There it was. There was a way up from the cave where they'd arrived. Yes, that made sense: this tower looked just the sort of thing people built over the places where the worlds touched—and that cave hadn't seemed very old. This was probably a new way into the tower which had opened up quite recently.

'Or I could stay on guard,' suggested Jacob, hopefully.

Nian considered leaving Jacob somewhere safe: but decided that Jacob was too much of an idiot to leave unattended for a minute.

'I think this is the bit where you come into the dark tower to visit the monster,' he said, rather grimly.

'Hm. Right. Er . . . are you sure that's a better idea than going home and pretending none of this is happening?'

Nian honestly nearly thumped him.

'Don't you understand?' he demanded, rounding on

162

him. 'This isn't just a pleasure trip. There's something making time go backwards and forwards. It's affecting lots of worlds in lots of ways. It's colossal, and so far we haven't got a *clue* what's going on. I mean, look at this!'

He picked up a stone and threw it over-arm as far as he could. It arched through the air and fell with a *thunk!* into a sandy bit of soil.

Jacob gawped after it.

'What about it?' he asked.

'*I don't know*,' said Nian, clenching his hands in frustration. 'We can't see what's going on, can we, because we're in the middle of it. That stone might have been going twice as fast as it should have been, or zigzagging to and fro, but because we're in the same time as it is then we can't tell. Every single world in the universe might be dancing a jig for all we know, and we can't *tell*.'

'*Oh*,' said Jacob, dumbly. 'So . . . does it matter, then?'

Nian really really really wanted to thump him.

'*I don't know!*' he almost howled. 'Except yes. Yes, it does. Back in my world there's an old man called Tarq, and he's getting frailer and frailer. I think he'll die, soon. It's because in my world it's been a fasting day for him. Time isn't going back completely, you see; it's leaving trails behind it, and things are getting stuck in the grooves of that particular day. Do you see?'

Jacob sniffed dubiously. 'I suppose so,' he said. 'Sort of.'

'So I'm not here sight-seeing,' Nian went on, desperate

to make Jacob understand. 'I wish I was. I'm looking for someone or something that can stop the whole universe in its tracks.'

They walked together back up the sandy slope towards the cave.

'Nian!' said Jacob, after a while.

'What?'

'I suppose . . . I suppose this is quite serious, then.'

The sun was higher, now, and when they got to the cave the sun's red light was bumping in along the cave's rubbly floor.

And there, on a patch of sand, was a familiar footprint.

Jacob saw it too. He squatted down over it, his bony knees splayed around his orange shining head.

'This is the same as the prints in that white desert place,' he said.

He got up and placed one of his great hooves beside it. 'Hey, whoever this is, he's not that big,' he went on, with relief.

The footprint wasn't big, but Nian didn't think that meant very much. That looked like a boy's print, and the thing in the tower wasn't even *human*.

He opened his mouth to tell Jacob—and then decided not to bother.

Nian looked upwards into the darkness of the cave roof. Above him he could sense the almighty crushing weight of the tower.

But . . . hang on, there was no one inside it, now.

The whole tower . . . yes, the whole dark stone labyrinth was completely empty of life.

Nian turned to Jacob.

'There's no one up there. The thing that was in the tower has gone.'

Beside him, Nian felt Jacob perk up.

'I expect he's dropped dead,' said Jacob, happily. 'Great. So that's all right, then, we can go back home. Problem over.'

Nian shook his head.

'Of course he's not dead, he's just left—and he didn't come out this way, or we would have seen him. So he can only have left though the entrance to the abyss. We'll have to follow him there.'

Jacob began making noises like a pregnant hen.

'But . . . but . . . but . . . look, how can we do that? The entrance to the abyss is about four metres up in the air, remember?' he protested. 'We fell at least that much when we arrived here. And . . . hey, hang on! In that case, *how am I going to get home?*'

'We climb up into the tower,' said Nian, grimly. 'Come!'

'Climb? In the dark? Nian, come on, that's *dangerous*.'

Nian smiled to himself. It was almost worth going through this just to see Jacob taking something seriously, for once.

'There is some good news,' he told him.

'Really?'

'Yes. I think you're right. This incredibly powerful world-destroying monster probably *does* have quite small feet.'

The climb was easy for Nian, but it was a nightmare for Jacob in the pitch darkness. In the end Nian had to make Jacob's hand-holds glow so he could do it.

They stood at last, panting, on a ledge. The entrance to the passageway to the white desert hung in space a little way below them, invisible to Jacob.

'You want me just to step off?' Jacob asked, incredulously, gazing blindly down at the drop below him.

Nian took hold of his arm. He could sense the entrance to the abyss hovering like a huge ox-pat just one large stride in front of them.

'It's a big step straight forward,' said Nian. 'Ready?'

'I'm never going to get to that party unless I do this, am I?' said Jacob.

'Probably not,' agreed Nian.

Jacob shrugged.

'OK, then. Ready.'

Together they took a big step forward.

25

Nian knew he and Jacob were on the right track as soon as the white mud of the desert solidified under their feet. In this place, which had been empty, there was now a heart beating.

But there was no one to be seen.

'Hey,' said Jacob. 'There's no one here, after all! Ah well, never mind. In that case we might as well be getting back, then.'

Nian turned his powers carefully towards the place where he could sense the stranger. The stranger was large and strong, and Nian would almost have said *metallic*, except for that beating heart.

'Oh,' said Jacob, resigned, following Nian's gaze. 'He's over there, is he?'

'Just behind the ridge.'

'So what are you going to do? Send out a deadly ray to kill him before he realizes we're here?'

Nian hesitated. This was someone (or some*thing*?) with powers unlike anything he'd ever come across before. They weren't like his own, which moved with the worlds; but then they weren't like those of the Lords, which pushed against them, either.

167

'Go that way as quietly as you can,' Nian said to Jacob. 'Make your way round onto that far hill. When you're there, shout. With any luck he'll talk. And if he doesn't, he'll run away from you back to his own world.'

Jacob looked across the white crumbled valley. He hesitated.

'So . . . where will you be?'

'Out of sight.'

'I see,' said Jacob. 'Er . . . you'll be hiding behind a rock, then.'

Nian nodded.

'Be careful not to sound dangerous,' he said.

But Jacob still hesitated.

'Look, Nian, maybe you should go,' he suggested. 'You're not as tall as me. Less threatening. Cuter.'

Nian flung him a filthy look. Cute? If that word meant half what it seemed to mean . . .

'I do not wish to show myself to him because if he senses my great power he may panic and do something violent,' explained Nian, stiffly.

'Oh all right, all right,' said Jacob. 'I suppose I'm the expendable one. But I want a hero's funeral, OK?'

And he set off, loping away along the valley towards the slope that led up behind the ridge.

There was a large chalk-coloured outcrop of rock that Nian could hide behind, which would still give him a good view of the stranger. Nian pressed himself against it and watched the crumbled outline of the ridge, white against the pale green of the sky. Nothing happened for quite a while. Jacob was making his way up onto the higher slope behind it.

The surface of the long puddle beside him shivered a little, but that wasn't a mud-crab or an ooze-stinger in this dead world, but just a very small earthquake. The worlds were trying to turn, and the presence of the three of them here was stopping them.

Jacob had better hurry up, or there'd be bigger earthquakes, soon, and this world felt pretty fragile to start with.

Nian wondered again why that . . . that *thing* had been going backwards and forwards, tying the worlds together with the passageway he'd made, and then releasing them. Did he know that the worlds were straining to turn, pulling against each other, storing up power just like Hani's catapult did, and . . .

. . . and then, quite suddenly, Nian understood. He understood everything. Yes! If you went to the wrong world and waited until the worlds were pulling and straining to turn, and then you stepped back at just the right moment, then you might cause a spring-back effect just like with a catapult and everything would be jerked backwards. Yes, even *Time*.

That was it, that was it! And anyone could do it if they could get to another world. You wouldn't even have to be colossally powerful. In fact . . .

Jacob's head popped up against the green sky. Nian waved to him and pointed to the place where he could sense the metallic being who suddenly might not be the most powerful person in the worlds, after all.

Jacob gave Nian a thumbs-up. Nian was so outraged that he nearly threw a boulder at him—but realized just

169

in time that the gesture probably meant something different on Jacob's world.

Jacob cupped his hands round his mouth.

'Hello!' he shouted. His voice came down, sharp-edged in the thin air. 'Hi! I can *see* you!'

Then Jacob disappeared, moving noisily down the slope, again, giving the stranger every reason and opportunity to make a bolt for the passageway back out of the world.

Here was another tremor, a stronger one, that chopped the puddle beside Nian into little waves. The stranger had better start moving soon.

And there he was. Someone—something—was coming into sight.

It was hard to see the stranger against the white rock, but he seemed to be giving off little glints of light. Nian wondered for a moment if he was wearing some sort of armour: but the metal covering looked too flexible for that. Nian found himself wishing that the Tarhun Reeklet was there, for the vicious hairy brute knew everything there was to know about fabrics and needlework.

The figure wasn't any taller than Jacob, but it was bulky, with a powerful neck nearly as wide as its head and a chest which emerged in a wide V from its tight waist. Nian was reminded of the travelling wrestlers that performed in the villages at home.

The figure was heading straight for the passageway home. Nian ducked back out of sight. Once the thing was back in his right world then there would be time enough to find out why the *pits* it was messing about with the turning of the worlds.

Jacob came into view over the nearest ridge, the long shambling length of him a shock after the muscled bulk of the stranger.

Nian sent out his powers to search the heavy figure—and what he found sent him recoiling almost violently enough to send him slipping backwards onto the white mud. The man—thing—was hugely strong, and hugely powerful—and behind its powers was a vicious, power-crazed mind.

Its footsteps were shaking the ground as it ran, as unwieldy and unstoppable as a marsh-bull. Nian hastily withdrew his powers in case it detected them.

And then it reached the place where the passageway began, and with one massive stride it was gone.

Nian came out from behind the rock to meet Jacob.

'*Whoa!*' gasped Jacob, jogging up, his face red with running and his blue eyes bulging with awe. 'What *was* that thing? Sheesh, Nian, that really was a *monster.*'

Nian nodded, slowly.

'I've never seen anything like it,' he said. 'I've never even *heard* of anything quite like it. Boggit, Jacob, it was only partly made of flesh.'

Jacob pushed back his damp hair.

'It looked like a cross between the Oscar statuette and the Incredible Hulk,' he said. 'Hey, do I *really* want to be on the same world with even *one* of those things?'

'You do if you ever want to get to tomorrow,' said Nian, grimly, holding out a hand to him. 'We've got to get after him.'

Jacob sighed.

'And mind the flipping four metre drop,' he murmured to himself, as he stepped towards the particular patch of white mud that formed the entrance to the abyss.

26

Nian was prepared for the extra drop down to the cave floor from the end of the passageway through the abyss—but that didn't mean he hit the cave floor any more gently.

'Ow-ow-ow-ow-*ouch*!' someone was saying, as Nian tried to work out which part of himself had been jarred most painfully. 'Get *off* me, Nian!'

Nian rolled out of Jacob's way. Jacob was rotating his shoulder and making agonized faces.

'Sheesh, Nian, you landed right on me. You've practically crushed my shoulder bones to dogmeat.'

Nian was hastily using his powers to check round for the man. Yes, boggit, he was still close. Nian turned round in the darkness, searching for a glint of something that looked like extra hard and shiny iron. But he couldn't see anything, not even with his power vision.

Nian looked round again, very carefully. The cave was streaked with twisted shadows that might have concealed a whole army of iron men.

Nian got up cautiously, ready for anything. He was absolutely completely sure that the iron man was only just a few . . .

. . . and then there was a sound like ten tin trays crashing down on the floor and the cave was filled with bellowing.

Bellowing!

By the time Nian realized the person chasing after him wasn't the iron man, he was out of the cave and halfway down the sandy hill. Nian, weak with shock and relief, put his hands on his knees, and heaved in breath after breath.

Jacob, scarlet-faced and panting, wasn't far behind him. Jacob threw himself down onto the ground beside Nian.

'Whoa!' Jacob gasped. 'Boggit! Hey, Nian, it's lovely seeing you, and all that, but do you think I could go home, now? Because that thing back there nearly gave me a heart-attack. What *is* it?'

But for once Nian had no idea at all where the truth of that thing lay.

Jacob flopped over on his back, still panting.

'Well,' he said. 'I don't like to be negative, but that big steel glinty monster-thing has seen us, now, hasn't he. And he doesn't seem all that friendly. And he's also between us and the entrance to our passageway home.'

Nian nodded. There was nothing to say.

'So it's a good thing you're really strong,' Jacob went on, hopefully. 'I mean, if it got to the point where we *had* to go home, you could fight him so we could get through. Couldn't you?'

Nian thought about it.

'Couldn't you?' asked Jacob, again.

'That iron man has powers,' Nian said, slowly. 'It

isn't just that he's built like an ox, he has mind-powers a bit like mine, too.'

He straightened up. The sun of this world was large and fiery and was already beginning to redden his pale skin.

'I don't know if I can beat him,' he went on, seriously. 'But he's causing a lot of damage to the worlds, and he's blocking our way home. And so,' he went on, a little palely, 'I'm afraid I'm going to have to find out.'

'You know something, Nian?' said Jacob, wiping the sweat off his brow, as they trudged back towards the entrance to the cave. 'I know my world's really ordinary and boring and all that—but I was really looking forward to that party.'

Nian knew how he felt, because suddenly all he really wanted was to be at home. Really at home, with his family. Not doing anything special like a feast or the pig farrowing, just a bit of honest weeding and nothing to worry about except being late for supper.

Nian found he could almost smell supper: a big bowl of brown stew which had been tended most tenderly by Grandy for the long slow fragrant hours of a whole afternoon.

Grandy.

It was Grandy who'd started all this. She'd felt the trembling of her own world before he or the Lords, with all their wisdom, had known a thing about it. And Grandy had sent Tan to warn Nian, the Truth

175

Sayer, because anything to do with the turning of the worlds was his responsibility.

Nian sighed, and let all thought of home evaporate from his mind.

'This metal man must have a reason for what he's doing,' he said. 'Perhaps we could get him to tell us what it is. And then perhaps I could help him with whatever his problem is.'

Nian and Jacob walked on up the hill. Jacob's face was glowing red from the heat.

'Yeah. But he didn't seem that keen on talking, though, did he?' Jacob pointed out, reasonably enough. 'I mean, all that jumping down from the roof and screaming: he could have just said *hi*.'

'I wonder why he didn't follow us out of the cave,' said Nian. 'I mean, if he'd really wanted to tear our heads off then he would have done, wouldn't he?'

'It's probably because he looks like a spray-painted gorilla,' suggested Jacob. 'Must be a bit of a bummer, really. Unless you're a gorilla, perhaps. That might be quite cool. Those other people we saw all looked quite normal.'

'If he didn't want to be seen, then he could have stayed quietly where he was,' pointed out Nian. 'He didn't know I'd be able to sense him. He was trying to scare us off.'

'And succeeding,' said Jacob, feelingly. 'I'll probably wake up tomorrow with my hair dead white. I hope it's only my hair that's dead, that's all.'

Nian sighed. He suddenly realized he'd been wrong, as well as mad, to bring Jacob along. Jacob would have been safely at home if it hadn't been for Nian, not wandering the abyss on the trail of a vicious monster.

'We really do have to go into the Monument after him, Jacob,' said Nian, apologetically.

'Yeah, great,' said Jacob. 'Up into a dark ruin to look for a maniac. Hey, are you *sure* you wouldn't like someone to do sentry duty? Someone ought to be guarding the entrance, shouldn't they?'

'I honestly think you'll be safer if you stay with me,' said Nian. 'Sorry.'

Jacob walked on, musing.

'You still might not *have* to fight him,' he said. 'If you explain that you've come to help him . . . '

Nian wasn't sure that was why he'd come at all. If that monstrous thing was the only thing between him and stopping Time coming to an end . . .

'I could explain that I've come to put things back as they should be,' he agreed.

But he wasn't sure of anything.

'Look, Nian, are you *sure* I shouldn't wait here?' asked Jacob, at the cave-mouth. 'If anyone comes along I can . . . um . . . hide.'

Nian looked at him.

'Or I could make spooky ghost-type noises,' Jacob offered. 'That'd keep people away. And you don't want to have to deal with anyone else, as well as metal man, do you?'

Nian stepped into the cave, and Jacob, resigned, followed him.

'I can't see,' Jacob said, quite soon, his voice echoing off the walls.

Nian turned his head to hold out a guiding hand, but as he did he was aware of something big whizzing past his nose, and before he'd worked out what was going on Jacob had let out a howl and fallen over.

Nian flung himself down on the floor, realized that the missile, whatever it had been, had come from the crack in the roof which led up to the tower, and squirmed himself into as small a target a possible.

Jacob, beside him, was rolling about clutching his leg.

'My knee,' he gasped. 'It got hit!'

Nian, swearing, slammed up a wall of power to protect them from whatever the maniac in the roof might throw next. The missile had been a jagged lump of rock as large as Nian's head, and it had made a horrible mess of Jacob's knee. Nian slapped a sort of power strip round the joint to hold it still and grabbed Jacob under the armpits. It must have hurt Jacob to be dragged along, but he let Nian do it.

Nian got Jacob into the cover of a big chunk of rock and called on his powers. Jacob's skin was welling blood, and below that the joint had been bashed quite badly.

Nian called over a slice of the warm air from outside and wrapped it round Jacob like a blanket. Then he started to put Jacob's knee back together. It was fiddly and time-consuming, and he was all too aware that they were in danger of Time running out altogether.

It was no good. There wasn't time for this. Nian

wrapped the power-strip back round the wound and sat up.

'Does it hurt?' he asked.

Jacob's freckles were standing out against his white face, but he shrugged.

'Not too much.'

Nian hadn't got time to do anything other than believe him.

'It'll be fine in a couple of hours,' he said. 'But we haven't got time to wait. Come on.'

Jacob managed to pull himself awkwardly to his feet and limped painfully after Nian.

'Where is the metal man now?'

'He's gone a few rooms away. We'd better get after him.'

'I won't be able to climb,' said Jacob. 'I can't put any weight on my knee. It hurts.'

'Not as much as being pulled to pieces when the worlds end,' said Nian. He looked for footholds to start the climb up into the tower to find the great man-monster which lurked there.

'I wish I was home,' murmured Nian. The words came out of him all by themselves, and luckily in his own language.

'What?'

'Nothing,' said Nian, firmly. 'All right. I'll help you. You go first. Ready?'

And gritting his teeth he made a sudden effort and boosted Jacob up to his first foothold.

27

It had become very difficult for Rik to remember what he was doing.

At least, he knew he was in the Monument, of course. He knew that. But the hand that had snatched up the rock and hurled it at the intruders: it was certainly joined onto the arm that was joined onto his shoulder; but did that mean it had really been *he* who had thrown it?

Well, then, he must have done it for a good reason. Yes, of course he had, if only he could remember . . .

The plague. Yes, the plague. That was why. People had discovered him, and now they were coming to destroy him.

The plague.

He remembered, now.

The steel dust had built a maze of walls in his mind, and every one of Rik's thoughts had become an act of exploration: a new path. But now he remembered.

He had thrown the rock because those people wanted to come into the Monument. And he didn't want them to do that because . . . he wasn't sure why, but he knew it was desperately important:

desperately important because it involved Aranna, somehow.

He hadn't wanted to hurt those boys, but how could he have made them stay away, otherwise? He had tried frightening them.

But perhaps it didn't matter that he'd hurt them because those boys were small creatures, little more than . . . little more than . . .

. . . Rik could feel the steel, like oiled shutters, moving inexorably through his mind.

He hadn't hurt them enough, in any case, because they had still come. The boys. They were climbing up through the gap in the roof of the cave and now they were entering the Monument.

Rik watched them. He had not eaten for weeks (or since yesterday, depending on how you counted the passing of time) but he had stopped feeling hungry long ago. But now, as he watched the boys, Rik felt a sort of hunger. The boys were fair-skinned (natives, then) one slight and the other longer, thin and bony, with odd orange hair. No trace of the steely plague on either of them yet. Not yet. No match for Rik, then.

It was vital that neither of the boys left the Monument, ever. Rik couldn't really remember why, but he was certain it was important, just as he was certain it was something to do with Aranna.

The boys were stepping up onto the dusty floor of the Monument. They were both coughing and coughing as the dust rose up around them.

Rik listened as the boys spluttered and sneezed.

As the dust of the Monument entered deep, deep, deep into their lungs.

Nian spat out a mouthful of dust and wiped his streaming eyes on his sleeve. Jacob, beside him, was blowing disgusted raspberries.

'Is this *it*?' Jacob asked. 'But it's just all dark and mouldy-smelling! Why on earth would anyone want to hide up in this place?'

Nian was setting his powers searching through the black passageways of the tower. It was confusing, because although there was only one living being in the place apart from him and Jacob, the tower was full of movement. Nian used his powers to look at these moving things more closely, but they were only fragments of the past that had got recorded in the walls. Just ghosts. He ignored them. He was looking for something far more important. He was looking for . . . *there he was . . .*

There he was. The monster was on a higher floor than this, but not very far away. Nian scanned the monster carefully. Yes. He was no taller than Jacob, but muscled like one of the Tarhun.

Nian reached out his mind towards the iron figure. The monster's powers were fierce, and blunt—but at the same time there was something wrong about them, something . . . something *unfocused*.

Yes. That was it. These powers weren't really the monster's at all. They belonged to something else that was sort of twisted through it. In some ways the thing which owned the powers was easier to sense than the actual monster was, because the monster was . . . well, full of space, almost like a sponge.

Jacob sneezed violently.

'Hey, but what a place, eh? It's cold, it's thick with dust, and it's as black as a bat's armpits. You know, I don't want to be ungrateful, but I've almost given up on finding those naked girls.'

But Nian was so filled with curiosity about the monster and the steely powerful thing inside it that he hadn't attention to spare for Jacob. He was so curious he almost forgot to be afraid. The monster was along this way and round a corner and up some steps.

Nian went forward quickly and quietly, and Jacob, clutching the back of Nian's tunic with a firm and annoying hand, limped along behind him.

. . . and there! There, at last, up a flight of dusty steps and through an opening which had once perhaps contained a long-crumbled door, was the monster.

Its eyes were gleaming at them like iron through the dark.

28

If anything, the monster looked even bulkier and stronger than it had before. Nian edged softly sideways so the yawning blackness of the stairs was no longer behind him, and Jacob blundered along with him, still holding on tightly to Nian's tunic and wincing and limping whenever he put pressure on his knee.

Nian stood and readied himself to receive whatever the monster's massive body might be going to throw at him.

There was a long moment of waiting silence.

'*I can see him,*' Jacob whispered, distractingly. '*I can see his eyes.*'

Nian tensed himself to withstand an attack—but instead of springing at him, the monster jabbed forward a hugely muscled arm and a ray of stinging light shot out towards the boys. All Nian had time to do was to boost himself up towards the ceiling—and Jacob, clutching wildly at his tunic, went up with him.

The blast of power passed under Jacob's air-pedalling feet and hit the wall behind them with a sizzling sound and a smell of burning.

'Errrrk!' said Jacob, panicking altogether and losing his grip. '*Woomph!*'

Nian let himself drop, too, hitting the floor in a cloud of dust.

Jacob was rolling about on the floor clutching his knee, but Nian hadn't got any attention to spare for Jacob. He found he was crouching slightly, leaning forward, alert for anything. He didn't know what the monster had just fired at them, but that blast had been quite capable of blowing a hole right through the pair of them.

Jacob was massaging his knee and swearing quietly.

Below the monster's shining eyes, his iron lips had begun to move. And now a sound emerged. It creaked and twanged like a guy rope in the wind. But the word was clear enough.

Sorry, it said.

Jacob let out a sudden, distracting whinny of slightly hysterical laughter.

'It's true!' he said, almost sobbing. 'I thought it was just to make the stories work, but it's actually *true*!'

Nian stayed balanced tensely on his toes. Sorry? What for? For trying to kill them?

'English,' went on Jacob, managing with a dust-exploding wriggle to sit himself up. 'That thing speaks *English*.' Jacob stopped to cough a bit, and then went on. 'Honestly, I spend hours in French and German every week, and then in the end it's true, and everybody speaks English. Even in *another world*, people speak English!'

The shining eyes in the darkness blinked, slowly. The monster's back was swaying slightly with each breath, like a sick ox's did.

Was the monster ill? Nian ran a check through the huge body. No, it was hugely strong, except . . .

. . . there it was again, the twisted shadow inside its body that wasn't part of it at all.

Nian held out a hand that looked as fragile as a leaf in comparison with the monster's gleaming fist.

'Let me help you,' said Nian.

More slow words emerged creakily from the monster's lips.

'*Too late*,' it said. It sounded sad. '*I tried to stop you, but you still came. So it's too late.*'

Jacob blinked through what to him was almost total darkness.

'Too late for what?' he asked, nervously.

The monster ran a steely shining tongue along his lips.

'*Too late for you*,' he said, and he thrust his fist forwards in a mighty punch.

Nian was prepared for the attack, but this time the blast that shot from the monster's hand didn't go anywhere near them. Instead it hit the base of the wall beside their feet and suddenly huge chunks of stone were exploding round them. Nian was still trying to work out what the monster was trying to do when there was a great *crack!* and the whole wall shivered, bulged, and tumbled down in a great long rumbling roar of falling stones.

Nian flung up a wall of power over their heads to protect them as Jacob, not knowing it was there, threw himself down screaming with his arms over his head. Nian concentrated on trying not to breathe in too much of the cloud of bitter dust which puffed silently upwards round them.

By the time the stones had stopped falling, Nian realized what the monster had done.

'You've blocked our way out,' he said.

The monster's great head nodded slowly.

'*And the way in,*' it said.

'But why?' And this time he spoke to the metallic thing that dwelt inside its frame.

The monster's lips laughed, a harsh sound like a heron's cry.

'*Rik is still fighting,*' was the reply.

Nian, even more puzzled, looked very carefully at the monster. The metallic thing inside it was a curious twisty structure, and the monster's great body wasn't much more than the frame for it.

'Who's Rik?' Nian asked, fascinated. And then he looked again, and saw.

'You're just a boy,' Nian breathed, in pure cold horror. 'But—'

Rik's lips let out a scream of anguish or laughter, but all that followed was a sort of hiccuping hiss.

'Whoa!' muttered Jacob, from the floor. 'I hope I wake up soon, Nian. And I'll tell you what, I'm really glad all this is totally *totally* impossible.'

The boy—Rik, that was his name—was being split into a million pieces by the thing growing inside him; but Rik was still, just, alive.

'Rik,' said Nian. 'What is inside you?'

Nian held his breath, willing Rik to find the strength and words to answer. What was it, and why, why did he keep sending Time backwards?

Rik raised his head unsteadily. His steel bright eyes glared for a second, but then they dulled to brown, and suddenly it was as if someone was looking out from inside that great iron skull.

'*It is the plague*,' he whispered.

'Plague?' echoed Jacob, in a panic, trying to scramble up but forgetting his knee and ending up falling over with a clatter amongst the rubble of the wall. 'Ow! *Ow!* Nian! Did he just say *plague*?'

But Nian was too pierced with freezing horror to answer. Plague? But this was different from any disease he'd ever seen. It was sending trails of iron through more and more of the turnings of Rik's mind, but it wasn't making Rik physically weaker at all.

Rik's head sank back down with a sigh, and Nian could only just catch his next words.

'*It is too late*,' Rik whispered.

And Nian, lifting a hand to push his dusty hair back from his forehead, saw a shining movement in the darkness.

His hand was shimmering gently through the darkness with a faint iron glow.

29

Nian tried to scrape the sparkling flakes of iron off his skin, but his nails were as bright as the back of his hand.

'*It goes all through*,' whispered Rik, with a gasp. '*I tried and tried, but you can't rub it off. It goes all through.*'

Nian felt a new flare of terror, but he thrust it away.

'*I* can rub it away,' he said. 'I am the Truth Sayer, and—'

A squawk from Jacob distracted him mid-sentence. Jacob was holding his own bony fingers out in front of him, fingers spread. They glistened like the wings of a heron.

'But *I* can't have it!' protested Jacob. 'I've got to play with the band at the party tomorrow night. For money!'

'Don't worry,' said Nian, quickly, recovering himself. 'It's all right. I'll make the plague go away. And then . . . '

But suddenly he couldn't remember what then. It was daft, but he really couldn't remember . . .

'Nian!' said Jacob, incredulously. 'Well, go on, then!'

' . . . go on?'

Jacob's mouth gaped in horrified disbelief.

'Go on and *get rid of the plague*, what do you think?'

Of course. Of course. He would cure it by using his powers to cure them. Make him and Jacob strong again.

Except that they *were* strong, and getting stronger. The plague wasn't trying to damage them at all, it was trying to change them in some way that Nian couldn't quite understand. So how on earth did he cure something like that?

His hands had changed so quickly. They were almost completely the colour of iron, now. Nian held them up before his eyes. Through his skin, every tendon and bone shone. He flexed his fingers, fascinated by the smooth movement of the metallic joints.

Rik's hoarse voice sounded, a grunt of sudden effort.

'*They're here*,' he said.

From far away on the other side of the tower, softly, came the *thunk* of an axe. Jacob whirled round towards the place where the sound was coming from, but the others stayed still: neither Nian nor Rik needed to use their eyes to see what was happening.

'They're getting ready,' said Nian.

'Getting ready for what?' demanded Jacob, his voice high with exasperation and mounting panic.

'To open the door.'

'The door to this place?'

Nian didn't bother to answer. He could feel himself changing. He had always been full of power, but until now his powers had stayed quiet inside him until he'd needed them. But now he could feel himself strengthening, as if great girders were growing through his limbs.

It was a good feeling. It was a marvellous feeling.

'Nian!'

Jacob's face was right in front of Nian's, shouting.

'The plague. You've got to cure the plague, remember? You said you could do it. *Nian!*'

Rik's heavy body had sagged down until he was crouched on the floor. One of his fingers twitched, and then another, as if he were trying to push himself up again, but perhaps the effort of those two blasts of power had weakened him, because Rik didn't seem to have the strength to move the monster's mighty body very far. He fell down heavily onto his side, rolled a little—and then, shakily, he lifted a powerful arm.

Jacob squeaked and hopped behind Nian, but Rik's thoughts didn't seem to be focused on either of them. He was moving a thick iron forefinger, slowly, as if he were beckoning to someone. Even Jacob felt the pull of the power of that beckoning finger—but then the pulling feeling snapped away like released elastic, and Rik's hand was stabbing forwards, but still not in the direction of either of the boys.

Somewhere outside the tower there was a small bang which was followed by a much bigger one. The whole building lurched and the dust that cloaked the floor mushroomed up threateningly around them.

'What was *that*?' yelped Jacob, staggering and nearly falling flat on his face over some invisible rubble. 'Nian, *what the hell was that*?'

Jacob saw the flash of Nian's eyes through the darkness. (Or—Jacob took a great gulping breath of horror—had Nian's eyes already changed to the colour of steel?)

'There were men outside with explosives,' Nian said. His voice sounded just as usual, but he spoke in a steady, measured way that was not at all like his own. 'They were planning to blow open the door to the tower. Rik has set off the explosive. He's stopped them from getting in for the time being.'

Jacob stared in alarm from one to the other of them.

'There are *people* outside? But they might have helped us!' he almost howled.

Nian's steel eyes turned coldly on Jacob.

'They would have fought us,' he said. 'If they had entered the tower then they would have caught the plague. The plague would have made them strong and they would have fought me. They had to be stopped.'

'But . . . but . . . what about all the people? The explosion . . . '

Nian shrugged.

'They were only little people. Hardly more than maggots. But if they got powers then even I would not be safe.'

'Yes,' said Jacob, pleadingly, 'but . . . '

Now Rik was moving again. He was getting to his feet. There was no sign of weakness, now: whatever fight had been going on inside him must have ended. He moved smoothly, massively, like a great machine, and his eyes were glowing bright.

Jacob grabbed Nian's arm and found it as hard and unyielding as rock.

'Nian,' he said urgently. 'Look, Nian, we'd better get out of here! We need to find someone to help you. Help you get better. *Nian!*'

But Nian showed no sign of noticing Jacob.

Now, through the darkness, two pairs of steel eyes glowed.

Jacob was an optimist: in fact his sister Robyn always said that was one of the most annoying things about him (though she generally used the word *idiot* rather than *optimist*). But even to Jacob there was something about the glare of those two pairs of steel eyes which made all his insides dissolve sickeningly into mush. He stepped backwards, staggered painfully round some biggish slabs of broken stone, and hastily squirmed into what cover he could find in the dark.

Jacob was trapped in the wrong world, with at least one, and he was afraid, two, homicidal maniacs. As if that wasn't unlucky enough, one of the maniacs was his only available friend, Jacob himself was showing signs of having contracted a mind-destroying disease . . . oh, and his route home was blocked under tons of rubble, which meant the world was going to end.

'Bummer,' Jacob breathed, as he ducked down behind the biggest bit of stone he could find and watched his whole life flash before his eyes. That didn't take long.

Ah well, he thought, *I suppose nothing's gone seriously wrong until now.*

The two steel-eyed figures were standing facing each other, arms held clear of their sides like wrestlers before a bout. Rik was half a head taller than Nian, and looked infinitely stronger and heavier; but Jacob had seen Nian do things that were, frankly, terrifying. Jacob was pretty sure that Nian could bring the whole Monument down on their heads if he wanted to.

He just hoped that Nian really *didn't* want to; but now Nian had gone and caught this plague or whatever it was . . .

Rik wasn't much of a fighter. Even Jacob had warning from the tensing of Rik's massive shoulders that Rik was about to throw another stabbing blast of . . . whatever.

Nian, slighter and much faster, had plenty of time to duck. Luckily the blast went through the same gap as the last ray had, so all it did was explode a couple of square yards of the wall beyond.

Jacob, on the powdery floor, held his nose and tried not to breathe in too much of the exploded dust. He did this even though he knew it was a waste of time: Jacob's hands were covered in dust, and he'd caught the blasted plague already.

'Missed,' said Nian, evenly, teeth bared; and Jacob, wincing, wondered if winding Rik up was really the best thing to do.

Jacob didn't wonder long. Rik let out a thunderous bellow and swung his heavy body forward a pace, his arm raised high and every tendon and gleaming muscle ready to slam down on Nian's steel (steel?) head.

And Nian just stood there and waited. Had Nian gone so bonkers that he *wanted* his spine squashed half a metre shorter?

Rik's fist moved, and Jacob couldn't bear to watch. He turned his head away, every nerve screaming away from the dreadful crunch of shattered bone.

But instead of a *crunch*, there was a *clang*. And when Jacob peeked between his fingers he saw that Nian was untouched and Rik was reeling backwards.

Almost the worst thing about that horrible moment was that Jacob, incredibly, found that he understood what had happened. Nian had put up some sort of a shield, and Rik's huge fist had slammed into it.

Jacob shook his head to try to clear it of all this alien intelligence, but it was no good. With each moment that passed the room grew a little brighter to Jacob: and it wasn't just because the figures before him were shining more strongly (though they were), it was because Jacob's own eyes were able to see better through the dark. Good grief, he could even see the shield that Nian had put up: it was hazy, like a floating puddle of raw egg white, but at the same time he knew (*knew*) it was stronger than plate iron.

That was so weird and horrible that Jacob clenched his eyes as tightly shut as he could.

And found to his even greater horror that *he could still see*.

Jacob, wildly, opened one eye as a sort of compromise. Rik was bending down in a smooth-as-machinery sort of way to grasp the ends of a great fallen block of stone. He lifted it, grunting like a weight-lifter, first up to his chest and then up again, high above his head.

Nian smiled scornfully, ducked under Rik's elbow, and gave Rik a shove from the back.

Rik had to step forward, or the slab would have fallen on his head—but because of all the rubble he had to do a little dance to find somewhere to put his feet. By the time he'd regained his balance Nian was raising his own steel-glistening hand.

Jacob knew that Nian was powerful, but even so he was shocked by what Nian did next. Jacob was shocked by the ever-so-casual way Nian clicked his fingers, and even more shocked by what that little click of the fingers did.

Something like a streak of lightning spat out from Nian's hand. It hit Rik in the chest as he was turning back to face them, still with the great slab of stone held at arm's length above his head.

There was a blinding flash, and a massive *crack!* and then a smell like acid. The massive figure of Rik jerked once, then again. And then it fell.

The slab of stone fell with him. It landed across Rik's great back, rocked backwards and forwards once or twice, and then was still.

And Rik lay, just as still, beneath it.

30

Jacob was too horrified even to breathe. He stood, seeing impossibly through the blackness, as the dust swirled and danced and settled all round him.

'What have you done?' he asked Nian, weakly.

Nian was breathing fast, but he looked cool. Poised. He seemed so unaffected by what had happened that Jacob had to glance down to check that Rik was really lying (injured? dead?) on the floor.

'I can see things,' Nian said.

Nian was holding his head as if he was concentrating absolutely on something. His face was almost completely steel, now, and there was something about the look of it that sent shivers down Jacob's back.

'What . . . what can you see?' Jacob breathed, but without being sure he wanted to know.

But now Nian's face was changing again. Suddenly, he looked afraid; and when he spoke again his voice was hurried; harried, almost.

'I can see so far,' he muttered. 'There is so much . . . further and further. Oh, there is so *much*!'

Jacob wavered. Nian was scaring him horribly. He

moved to put a reassuring hand on Nian's arm, but then didn't quite dare touch him.

'Nian, we need to get some help,' Jacob said. 'We're not well.'

'No!' snapped Nian. 'No, you don't understand. I'm not ill at all. It's not a disease. I'm better than I've ever been. I'm stronger. I'm changing. And *I can see so much*.'

Nian put his steel hands up to his temples as if he were trying to keep the pressure of all that knowledge from exploding his skull.

'I can see so much,' he whispered again. 'Jacob! Jacob, there are colours. Everywhere, there are colours. You've no idea.'

Then, in a tight, strained voice:

'Jacob, my head! It keeps going on and I can't . . . I can't . . . I can't . . . '

He was swaying, now, still with his steel hands pressed against his steel temples. And then he stumbled and Jacob instinctively caught hold of him to steady him.

'Help me,' whispered Nian. 'Jacob, help me!'

Nian's arm was as hard as the metallic shine of his skin, which was vibrating faintly, as if it were charged with electricity.

'What can I do?' asked Jacob, foolishly. But Nian's head was nodding forward as if he were about to pass out.

'*Nian!*' said Jacob, bracing himself for the sudden drag of Nian's weight on his bad knee if Nian lost consciousness. 'Nian, what should I do? What should I *do?*'

Nian's knees buckled. He was much heavier than Jacob was expecting, and Jacob couldn't hold him. They both ended up in a tangle of limbs amidst the soft dust.

Nian spoke in the barest thread of a whisper.

'I'm nearly gone,' he said. 'I don't know . . . just a minute! Who are you? Who are you?'

Jacob, panic-stricken, extricated himself and scrambled to his feet. Rik was lying still and might be dead, and Nian was in a state where he might do anything.

'What do I do now?' muttered Jacob. 'Oh, what do I do *now*?'

Jacob had always worked on the assumption that things worked out all right in the end, but now he suddenly realized that he'd been wrong all the time. It was just that until now he'd always been able to leave things to other people to work out.

But there was no one to help him now.

Jacob looked left and right through the transparent blackness of the tower. He could see further, too, now: he could see the kerfuffle on the other side of the great door. Several people had been hurt when Rik had set off the explosives: there was a young fair man over there, desperately searching through the rubble and calling *Aranna! Aranna!*

Jacob flinched, and looked away. If Nian had been in his right mind then he could have healed them all, but as it was . . .

Nian was still breathing. This plague or whatever it was seemed to be affecting them all differently:

199

Nian hadn't grown any bigger, but his mind had been affected almost at once. Rik must have held onto his mind much longer than Nian. As far as Jacob could tell his own mind was as much all right as it had ever been; but for how long would that carry on?

What *could* he do?

They needed a cure; but if Nian couldn't cure this blasted plague, then who could?

There were doctors in Jacob's own world who could practically work miracles. Antibiotics were brilliant, and there were X-rays and stuff—you could even get coloured plaster-casts, now.

But Jacob's mind was filled with a new, sharp intelligence that showed him things he'd never have thought of by himself. If Jacob took Nian back to Earth and the doctors couldn't do anything . . .

I might end up wiping out the whole planet, Jacob thought. *And I can't do that. Not before the band have played Las Vegas.*

He looked round. Rik wasn't moving. Jacob sort of hoped he was all right, but mostly it was a relief that Rik was out of it, because Rik was a flaming homicidal maniac. Nian wasn't looking all that lively, either, and that was a bit of a relief, too, because Nian seemed to be following Rik along the same route. If it came to a fight between Jacob and Nian, then Jacob had had his chips and all that'd be left of him was a smear of ketchup.

Nian shifted a little, panting, his steel eyes focused on something that Jacob didn't even want to see. Jacob patted Nian's stone-hard arm.

'Don't worry,' he said foolishly. 'We'll soon get you sorted out.'

Nian's face looked stiff, as if the steel of the plague had frozen his muscles, but his lips moved a little.

'Tarq,' he murmured.

Tark? What on earth was a *tark*?

But . . . hang on. Jacob had come across that word tark before, hadn't he? Yeah, now he came to think about it, Jacob was almost certain that Tarq was the name of one of the spooky old Lords who lived in Nian's House of Truth. Yeah, Tarq. That was right.

Jacob scratched his nose to help himself think. Those old Lords in Nian's world had powers, of course, and he thought he remembered Nian, long ago, saying that they were healers. But could they heal this plague? Well, Jacob hadn't a clue, but, he had to face it, there was nowhere any better he knew of that he could take Nian.

But first they had to get out of this blasted tower.

Jacob clambered carefully over to the slabs of rock where Rik had blocked the staircase. The slabs were massive—far too heavy for Jacob to be able to shift them—but he forced his glistening fingers under the nearest chunk of rock and heaved, anyway.

It came up so suddenly that he overbalanced and ended up sprawled on his back. He'd lifted it as easily as if it'd been a piece of polystyrene.

Jacob found himself laughing madly. He was strong. Really strong: even his bashed knee was now as strong as steel.

He pushed himself to his feet and started picking up great slabs of stone and flinging them aside.

'Nian!'

Jacob laid a hand on Nian's arm and felt the buzzing electrical feeling running through him into his belly.

'I'm going to take you home,' Jacob said, earnestly. 'I've cleared the way to the steps, so we can get to the entrance to the abyss. I'll take you home and then Tarq can make you better. OK?'

Nian let Jacob help him up, but his face was so blank that Jacob was startled when Nian spoke.

'No others,' he said.

Jacob went through that a few times, but then gave up on trying to work out what Nian was going on about.

'No others what?'

'They would change too,' said Nian. 'The change would make them strong and then they would fight me.'

Jacob tried laughing, but the sound of it was so thin and peculiar in the old air of the tower that it frightened him.

'That's no problem,' he said. 'That lot have never had a chance against you, have they? No need to worry about that.'

Jacob wasn't sure if Nian had heard him, but Nian let himself be helped along towards the top of the black steps.

Jacob had thought there was nothing left in this place that could surprise him, but just as they'd got to the top of the steps he heard the last thing he had been expecting: the sound of footsteps coming along towards them.

Impossibly, he saw the girl before she came in sight: slight, dark-haired, with a ponytail which whisked and bounced behind her.

But where had she come from? The whole tower was locked up tight, apart from the crack in the rock that led down to the cave.

But Jacob's mind was working with disconcerting smoothness: he remembered Rik's steely beckoning finger, and the pulling sensation Jacob had felt just before Rik had detonated the explosives outside. Yes, that was what Rik had been doing: he'd been summoning this girl to him.

She'd got nearly to the top of the steps before she looked up. When she saw Jacob and Nian her face went white to the lips with terror.

'It's all right,' said Jacob, foolishly. 'Really, it's all right.'

But her eyes had gone past him to the great figure on the floor. To his swollen face that gleamed through the darkness.

'Rik?'

Jacob hesitated. But there was nothing he could do. He resettled his grip on Nian's steel-hard arm. If he didn't get Nian sorted out then Nian might go anywhere in his unstoppable Truth Sayerish way and spread the plague with him. If Jacob didn't get Nian sorted out soon then all their worlds were likely to start crumbling.

Jacob began to help Nian down the steps and

through the dark tower to the place where they could cast themselves into the entrance to the abyss.

Jacob fell down into the abyss and Nian fell with him. Nian's eyes looked blind, and yet Jacob knew that Nian was seeing far, far into the abyss. Jacob also knew (though he didn't know how) that if he'd looked around he himself would have seen much more than last time. He might even see a pattern traced out amongst all the little worlds of the abyss.

There was something about that thought that terrified the life out of him.

Jacob turned to speak to Nian, but found that his voice didn't work here. The abyss was vast and dark and empty, and no sound had ever existed there.

Jacob pulled himself round face to face with Nian. Nian's eyes were steely-blank, but Jacob mouthed, urgently: *home. You have to go home!* into his face.

Tarq, shouted Jacob, soundlessly, as they hung amongst the lanterns of the worlds. *Tarq will help you! Nian, home!*

Nian's shining eyes flashed out a ray that dazzled Jacob. And then Nian's lips moved, and Jacob found he could hear what Nian was saying close in his head even though his ears were ringing with the great silence of the universe.

Home? said Nian. *Tarq is not at home.*

And then he somersaulted neatly in the air like a racing swimmer, slipped easily out of Jacob's grasp, and kicked himself away.

Jacob made a wild lunge and just managed to catch hold of one of Nian's shoelaces as Nian zoomed away through the wide wide nothingness of the abyss.

Jacob had no idea where they were going. Some of the lantern-worlds they raced past looked pinker or bluer than the others, but Jacob couldn't tell if Nian was leading him towards Nian's own world or away from it.

But Nian seemed to know where he was going. His course was making a fine sweeping arc across the abyss. Jacob held on for grim life and tried not to think too much about the fact that there wasn't going to be any chance of breathing until they arrived.

He wasn't sure how long they travelled, accelerating, through the abyss; the little worlds grew long, and then dissolved into smears of colour as their speed increased. *It's a good job there's no air*, Jacob found himself thinking, *or else we'd be burning up*.

He spent several seconds marvelling at this piece of cleverness, but then got distracted by realizing that he could hear each world as it zipped past. There, on that world, there was a vast maze swarming with whistling chocolate hedgehogs; and that one there was dotted with turbo-charged shopping trolleys. Even though Jacob went past in a split second, somehow he found he could hear the clicks as their wheels crossed the cracks in the pavements: *clickety clickety CLICK cliiick click!*

Jacob would have liked to listen properly to that, but there were more worlds and more, every world full of pulsating or bouncing or clattering music.

Nian was going faster and faster. Jacob hung on grimly and hoped that Nian wouldn't change direction, because his fingers were beginning to slip along the soft leather of Nian's shoelace and the smallest thing might be enough to fling him off across the abyss and . . .

. . . hang on, it was getting a bit lighter. Did that mean they were nearly . . .

Jacob shot up through the ground, kicked his legs wildly, overbalanced, fell, rolled, and ended up mostly upside down against a large rectangular slab of rock.

He lay for a moment until the world had stopped spinning round him, and then he gently wriggled himself the right way up and looked round.

He'd not seen this place in daylight before, but the smell of crushed earth and plants brought back memories of an amazing night. Yes, there, just as Nian had described it, were two great ring-shaped walls, white and smooth as ice, and through the break in them was the misty greenness of a far-away valley and the swelling shoulders of mountains.

Jacob took a deep breath of the thin mountain air.

Nian had arrived back in his own world.

31

Nian was showing no signs of pleasure or relief at being home. He was standing quite still, his head cocked at a listening angle. Jacob listened too. The place where they were (the garden of the House of Truth: yes, that was right, the sacred garden) was deserted except for . . . well, there was a tiny owl inside that tree trunk over there, and a rat-thing just in the middle of that clump of . . .

. . . Jacob shook himself uneasily. How did he know that? That was crazy, bonkers, copper-bottomed round the *twist*.

But crazy or not, he knew he was right. He could hear the ticking of their tiny hearts. Jacob was surrounded by a million little lives—in the grass, in the trees, under the earth. His flesh crawled with all that life.

'Ignorance is bliss,' he said, out loud. But even as he said it more and more knowledge was crowding around him. He could feel the thirst of the trees as they sucked deep at the soil, and the shrivelling of the edges of their autumn leaves.

Jacob shook his head. *Ignorance was bliss*. He clenched his fists to keep out the clamour of the teeming garden and turned to Nian.

But Nian was not there.

'Hoi!' shouted Jacob, after his retreating figure. 'Where do you think you're going? Hang on! Nian, you idiot, you need help! Nian! Nian! *Don't go near anyone!*'

Nian must have heard his shout, for Jacob was certain that Nian could hear every tiny distinct piece of life on the whole mountain.

But Nian did not turn, or break his step.

Jacob started to run after Nian, and then stopped. Nian was heading for the outer of the two great ring-shaped houses, but it was the Inner House where the Lords who had healing powers lived. Jacob turned away from Nian and ran towards the great ice-cliff walls of the Inner House.

Jacob scanned the curved wall anxiously. He knew there was a door, but he had to search quite a long way, before he saw it. He jogged down a beaten path which soon joined a bigger one and ended at the door. It was tall and massive and locked.

Jacob, in his great hurry, raised a fist to thump on the door, but before he realized what he was doing his bunched fist had punched forward—and the next thing he knew he was extricating his hand from the grey splintered remains of the weather-bleached wood.

Jacob examined his hand with respect. His steel-striped skin showed no sign of damage, but, weirdly, his hand seemed to have started operating pretty much by itself. Jacob watched, fascinated, impressed, and rather scared, as the hands that were attached to his arms and were generally his own tore several large pieces of wood off the door, and then reached in and snapped the heavy beam that formed the latch as easily as a bread stick.

Jacob saw all this with a sort of appalled delight. It was utterly brilliant, but at the same time he couldn't help but realize that tearing the place's ancient door to bits wasn't the best way to ensure a friendly reception.

His feet stepped through the doorway and into the House of Truth.

There was a bristly doormat. It seemed a bit late for manners, but Jacob, hopefully, wiped his feet.

The House of Truth was quiet, but there was life in there. Jacob jogged cautiously along the gently curving corridor. He would have shouted out for help (though of course he'd have been shouting in the wrong language), but the House had been so very quiet for such a long time that the silence had assumed an almost solid quality. Jacob felt as if yelling would break something, and he'd already broken enough.

Jacob ran on, with his brain telling him things he shouldn't know. There was life here, but not much. There were a few old men, all on the small and thin and weedy side: surely they'd be no match for the immensely powerful thing that Nian had become.

And there—there, behind that door. There was a whole group of people. They didn't seem to be very big, but at least they were young and healthy.

Jacob came to a halt. His steel fist was bunching itself ready to punch itself through the door, but Jacob took control of it (he could still control it if he concentrated, though he didn't know for how long he'd be able to do so).

Controlling his hand carefully, he reached out and turned the handle of the door.

In the schoolroom the Lord Caul was at the most intricate point of explaining, yet again, the principles of the joining of minds.

'It takes a lot of courage, as well as trust,' he was saying. 'But when you can view something from everyone's perspective at once, then you can see the whole thing very exactly, and . . . '

He became aware that none of his pupils were listening to him. He was a little hurt, until he heard the rapid footsteps out in the corridor.

'Someone's in a hurry,' Caul observed.

The boys looked at each other.

'It might be Nian,' suggested Derig, hopefully.

Everyone's minds went out into the corridor to check.

'That's not Nian,' said Gow.

'That's nothing *like* Nian,' said Emmec. 'Too tall, for one thing. I'll tell you something, though: that person out there is *weird*.'

'It must be one of the Tarhun, I suppose,' said Hani.

'With a bucket on his head,' scoffed Alin, witheringly. 'Honestly, Hani, can't you tell that person out there is covered in some sort of metallic coating?'

Derig was sitting with his head on one side, as if listening.

210

'I think . . . I know that's not Nian . . . but I think Nian *is* here, now,' he said, puzzled. 'I don't mean out in the corridor, but not all that far away. Somewhere within the boundaries of the House. Yes, I'm almost sure he is.'

'Yeah,' said Hani. 'I think you're right. Except . . . actually, though, I'm not sure it *is* Nian, really.'

Caul compressed his lips.

'I hope Nian is back, and safely,' he said, rather grimly. 'Though what on earth Nian thought he was doing leaving the House like that—leaving the *world*, most probably—without even bothering to let anyone know where he was going—'

The door handle rattled.

'Yes?' said the Lord Caul, rather impatiently. 'What is it?'

And then the door opened and a figure stepped into the light. His hair was bright orange, which was weird enough, and his clothes were like nothing they'd ever seen: he wore dull blue leggings that went right down to his boots, and a violently coloured round-necked vest.

But it was his face that made them stare.

It was glowing with streaks of shining iron.

They all took one look and scrambled to their feet. The Lord Caul, nearest the door, took a step towards the stranger, but the boy put up a hand in warning.

'*Noh!*' he said. '*Dohnt kum enni klohssa!*'

His meaning was clear enough, even though none of the others could understand his words.

211

There was a dead silence, and then the Lord Caul raised his own hands, palms up, in a peaceful gesture.

'Can we help you, friend?' he asked, quietly.

But the iron boy only made a screwed-up confused sort of face.

'*Grate*,' he said. '*Ov corss, they orl speek sum forin langwidge. Now wot doo Ei doo?*'

'Great,' said Alin. 'He speaks some foreign language. Now what do we do?'

And then the strange boy, contorting his face in painful concentration, spoke again.

'Tarhun,' he said.

The others exchanged glances, and Hani sniggered.

'He's never come to join the Tarhun. It'd take three of him to make one of them.'

'Perhaps he's come to visit the Outer House, and taken the wrong turning,' suggested Derig, helpfully.

The bits of the boy's face that weren't iron had gone bright red with effort.

'House of Truth?' he said.

Alin pulled a face.

'He's got ever such a funny accent,' he observed. 'I've never heard anything like that, even in the city.'

'Perhaps he's from some really primitive desert tribe,' suggested Emmec. 'I've heard they paint their faces.'

But Gow shook his head.

'That's not paint,' he said. 'All that iron goes right through him. And I'll tell you something else: he's got powers. Really peculiar ones.'

The strange boy was making the strained sort of faces that Hani made when he was trying to do weather-lore.

212

Then he pointed a finger at his frankly hideous vest and said: *Jaycub*.

And at that everyone gasped in sudden realization.

'Jacob!' echoed Hani. 'It's Jacob! You know, Nian's friend from that world where fish have fingers!'

The strange boy nodded several times.

'Nian,' he echoed. Then he pulled his mouth downwards to make a sad face. 'Nian,' he said again, with dramatic gloom. '*Nian not well. Por Nian.*'

They stared at him, excited and curious and baffled.

'Hm,' said Caul. 'The Jacob Nian told us about did speak a strange language. But that Jacob didn't have powers. And Nian didn't mention any iron streaks, either.'

'Gow,' said Alin, 'you're an egghead. Can't you work out what he's going on about?'

Gow grimaced.

'I've been trying,' he said. 'But I don't know where to start. Don't forget that even Nian had trouble learning Jacob's language, and he's the Truth Sayer.'

The boy Jacob had started beckoning to them urgently, even though he was still holding up his other hand to stop them.

'Do you think that's some sort of sign-language?' asked Emmec, bewildered.

'He looks more as if he's directing wagons through the Grand Square,' said Alin, with scorn.

Derig took a careful step forward, and then another, and Jacob retreated just as carefully in front of him.

'I think he wants us to go with him,' said Derig. 'But he doesn't want us getting too close.'

'But why not?' asked Gow, fascinated.

The Lord Caul had been silent, searching Jacob with his powers, but now his thin face suddenly grew sharp with alarm.

'I think he's ill,' he said abruptly. 'Those iron streaks are new. I think it must be the result of some sort of disease. And those powers he's got aren't really his, either: they're new, as well.'

'A disease?' echoed Alin, stepping back. 'Then what on earth does Nian think he's doing bringing him here? And where *is* Nian?'

'Nian,' said Jacob, again, beckoning frantically. 'Nian!'

'All right,' said the Lord Caul. He sketched a careful arch-shape with his fingers. 'There. I've put Jacob inside a dome of power. I don't *think* anything is going to get out through that, not germs, anyway. So let's go with him, shall we, and see just what he wants.'

'Wow!' said Hani, with the deepest respect, when he saw the splintered remains of the garden door.

'Don't touch it!' snapped the Lord Caul. 'You might catch something!'

Hani snatched his hand back guiltily.

Emmec rubbed his knuckles with respect as he stepped carefully between the jagged bits of wood and out into the garden, but Jacob was beckoning again, and walking away from them.

'It's funny, but I still can't quite work out where Nian is,' said Derig, as they followed Jacob. 'Even though I'm sure he's not far away.'

There was a pause while they all tried to find him.

'Do you think he might be hiding inside a metal pipe or something?' asked Alin. 'Here, Hani, can't your dog-nose sniff Nian out?'

A fleeting look of intelligence passed across Hani's face. That meant he was using his powers. Even Hani didn't know how he did it, though he pretended it was all to do with the focusing powers of his big ears, but he possessed an almost miraculous ability to find things, as long as he didn't actually think about it too much.

'He's over . . . no, wait a minute, hang on, that can't be him. Hey, there's something really weird over in the Outer House, though. Something sort of . . . shiny.'

'Metallic,' suggested Alin.

'Iron,' said Emmec.

The boy Jacob might have guessed something of what they were saying, or perhaps he'd just thought of a new bit of sign-language. He started pointing to an iron streak on his hand, and said *Nian*. He repeated this several times.

Gow stared at him in dawning horror. 'Nian's got it, too!' he exclaimed. 'Nian's caught the disease that Jacob's got!'

'Yes,' said Alin, grimly. 'I can sense him, now: he's over in the Outer House, all shot through with iron.'

'Not actually iron,' said Gow, frowning tremendously.

'Well, some stuff that looks like it, anyway,' said Alin. 'Come on!'

But Jacob's signs to them to stop became quite frantic. Then with his other hand he jabbed a bony finger towards his temple and moved the tip of it round in rapid circles.

'What on earth is that supposed to mean?' asked Alin.

The Lord Caul pursed his lips.

'We should be able to sense Nian quite well from here, and work it out for ourselves,' he said.

There was a pause while they all tried.

'You know, it's odd,' said Gow. 'But I don't think Nian can really be ill at all. He seems stronger than ever, if anything.'

Jacob was pulling up wisps of his red hair and waggling his head from side to side and rolling his eyes, now.

Alin snorted.

'He looks like a complete idiot!'

'Oh!' said Derig, as if someone had just stabbed him with a pin. 'That's what it is! Nian's gone ill in his mind. Jacob's trying to warn us.'

'That Nian's gone *mad*?' asked Hani, incredulously. 'Come off it!'

The Lord Caul was looking even more alarmed than Derig.

'Yes, but if it's true . . . well, look what it's done to Jacob, who's normally quite powerless. If Jacob can punch his way through ironwood doors . . . '

Emmec whistled.

' . . . then whatever will Nian be like?' he finished up. 'Struth, Nian can pull walls down by *accident* as it is. If Nian's suddenly gone even stronger than that . . . '

'And if he's really mad . . . ' Gow's voice trailed off into appalled silence.

'His mind is unusual, to start with,' said the Lord Caul, very worried. 'I'd better go and call together all the power I can. You lot stay here, do you understand? Derig, you're the best at mind-listening, see if you can get inside Jacob's head and find out what the gr—what the goodness has been going on. Alin, you run to the Outer House. Don't approach Nian under any circumstances, just get as many of the Tarhun as you can out here into the garden away from him. Oh, and Alin!'

Alin looked back.

The Lord Caul's thin face was very grim.

'Tell them to seal the great door,' he said. 'No one is to leave the House of Truth under any circumstances whatsoever, do you understand? Thank Truth the House is closed to tourists on Mondays.'

The boys exchanged glances.

'But that means we're all stuck in here with this disease, whatever it is,' said Emmec.

But the Lord Caul was already hurrying back to the Inner House.

32

Nian was glad to be back to the sharp sunlight of his own world. He walked across the garden to the newly fitted door which gave access to the Outer House, and went through into the lumber-filled corridor. He sniffed. The whole building smelled most comfortably of ancient filth and soft decay.

Home. Home was where he needed to be while he was changing.

He strode determinedly along the corridor.

Jacob, slightly dizzy from a combination of his unaccustomed cleverness and Nian's world's low gravity, took hold of a tree branch for support and absent-mindedly crumbled it to dust. Whoops. He wiped the bits off onto his jeans and wished that his hands wouldn't keep doing things when he wasn't looking.

Well, at least that spooky monk-person had started running about doing stuff. That was good, probably—but Jacob did wish Nian hadn't taken himself off. This place was just so *quiet*. Jacob was surrounded by a deep wide silence that stretched out into the air around the Holy Mountain and right across the valley to the peaks beyond.

Phew, thought Jacob, this world was a big place. There, across the valley from the House of Truth were rolling green pastures, and he suddenly found, miraculously, that his eyes could zoom right in on them. He could see the gold pollen on the stamens of each single scarlet flower. There was a black fleck of a beetle climbing crazily through the thrusting forest at the centre of that one.

Jacob grinned, and flicked the stalk of the flower with half a thought, and the beetle was catapulted off the flower and over and over through the air which was itself full of minuscule bits of floating life. Over and over and . . .

Jacob twitched, and blinked, and came back to his own mind. Phew, that was weird. Really and truly *weird*. To be able to zoom in on one flower in one meadow twenty miles away . . .

But suddenly he was thirsty to see more, *hear* more. To hear that whole world, the whole circle of it. The possibilities were tickling the edges of his mind. If he tried he'd be able to hear the whistling of blue-haired desertmen and the mating howls of magenta swans and the swinging clatter of pearl-strung rope bridges.

Jacob found himself laughing at the nervous hooting of a very young gibbon who was trying to get up courage to pick up an orange frog. The look on its face reminded him of the time Dad had found a slug on the saddle of his bike.

But the thought of Dad, of home, snapped every-thing else away.

Hang about, Jacob thought. *I don't want to spend hours listening to monkeys. I want . . . I want . . .*

But it was oddly difficult to know what he wanted. His mind had never worked what you'd call smoothly, and now suddenly it was hard even to remember . . .

This is Nian's world, he thought, with an effort like trying to thread a needle. *This world . . .*

This world was full of people talking, singing, danc-ing. Suddenly Jacob found himself assaulted by a mul-titude of voices, too many voices for him to hear; loud, enormous, deafening.

He found himself sitting on the damp thin grass, his steel palms clasped to his steel ears. All around him were voices, voices, roaring and clattering and beating down on him. He wanted to flap them all away, but he knew with a cold and deadly certainty that there was some very good and some very terrible reason why he mustn't.

So he disconnected his ear drums; and the noise was snipped off as crisply as if with scissors.

Jacob stayed very still, with his hands still over his ears, and waited for his heart to stop thundering inside him.

Thud-thud-thud, it went. *Thud-thud-thud*, in a hasty galloping triple beat that Jacob's own heart had never, and should never, ever, have even thought about.

And Jacob suddenly realized that he was very very afraid.

Nian heard the mounting buzzing of the filth-flies with satisfaction. Yes, that meant he was approaching Snerk's kitchen. Tarhun Snerk was a cook of surpassing genius, but the spirit of untrammelled inspiration with which he approached his calling left no room for hygiene, and he generally worked surrounded by a busy cloud of enraptured flies. Snerk's kitchen was packed full of ingredients to be used in his quest for the Ultimate Eating Experience. A lot of them might not be generally considered to be edible (maggot purée, for example) but that didn't matter, because Nian didn't need food any more.

The great fat bulk of Snerk sat overflowing his chair, grunting softly as he pared his fingernails with a carving knife. Snerk was the only person in the world who might seriously be suspected of serving up a dish garnished with flaked fingernails, and if there was one thing the people of the House of Truth had learned, it was Never Ever to Ask. Snerk guarded his secrets with the utmost jealousy—and a meat cleaver—and, in any case, there was hardly anyone in the House who could understand a word he said.

Nian paused in the doorway and sniffed at the scents of rot and filth. He was here because he needed . . .

But then Snerk's kitchen was suddenly sliding away and Nian found himself looking at the room as if from a great height. Nian could see the ring of the mountains, with the Holy Mountain standing alone inside it, and further away the glittering restless sea, and further still a whole universe of world upon world upon world, each intricate and well-fashioned and full beyond measure.

Nian's iron eyes looked out and out and out . . .

'Murrrrrrr!' said a surly voice. 'Wodjawurrrrrrr?'

But Nian was seeing wonders beyond anything he'd ever dreamed of: groves of chiming lilies; the pearly sphere of an ant-library; a great city floating on a lake the colour of . . .

'Rrrryrrr?'

There was something huge and red and foetid in front of Nian. It was perhaps an insect of some kind—something too small to bother with, anyway.

Nian forgot everything. He even forgot that he was on his way home so he could change safely. He blew the insect-thing away, and its nest with it, and turned and walked calmly through the white stones of the corridor wall and back into the light of the garden of the House of Truth.

'Struth!' murmured Gow, softly.

The others were already spinning round towards the sound of the falling stones of the wall of the Outer House.

There was a long moment of utter horror.

'What the pits . . . ' began Emmec.

'Nian!' Derig exclaimed. 'It's Nian! He's walked through the wall!'

'Yeah,' said Hani. 'It's Nian. But . . . '

There was a commotion from behind them, and the Lord Rago's voice sounded from the direction of the wrecked door.

'More trouble!' he was saying. 'I knew it, I knew it! Once you let a parcel of boys loose in the House then there's going to be nothing else *but* trouble!'

The Lord Caul had summoned the Lords. There was the long sarcastic face of the Lord Grodan; even the Lord Firn had left his precious library. The sight of Nian brought the Lords to a halt, their dull white hair illuminated by the suns.

'Nian!' called Derig, anxiously. 'Nian, are you all right?'

The Lord Rago made a sound like an exasperated weasel.

'Idiot boy!' he muttered, enraged. '*Are you all right?* With half the Truth Sayer's body made of metal?'

'Not metal,' said Gow. He spoke under his breath, but the Lord Rago swung round his reptilian head to scowl at him.

'Metal, not metal . . . whatever it is, he's got himself into trouble again, I can see that. Typical of the Truth Sayer. No sense. He rushes off half-cocked on the slightest pretext without letting anyone know where he's going, and then turns up and expects us to sort everything out.'

The Lord Grodan narrowed his eyes suspiciously.

'And who is *that*?' he asked, gesturing towards the other steely figure, who was sitting on the ground half-obscured behind a tree trunk.

The Lord Rago squinted across the garden.

223

'*Another* boy?' he yelped, outraged. '*Another* boy? Why the place is swarming with the wretched creatures as it is!' He jabbed his face towards Jacob, sniffing with distaste. 'And he's half iron, too, like the Truth Sayer! As if one wasn't enough!'

'It's not actually—' began Gow, but bit off his words at the look Rago hurled at him.

There was a sound of tramping feet and a jostling crowd of red-clad figures carrying staves and cudgels appeared on the other side of the garden. They were led by Alin. The sight of Nian brought Alin to a sudden amazed halt and all the Tarhun behind him fell over each other.

The Truth Sayer showed no signs of having noticed any of them. His eyes were completely grey, with the dull sheen of a lake under a cloudy sky.

'Alin!' called the Lord Caul, urgently. 'Don't go any nearer to Nian. Bring the Tarhun round the other way, through the Inner House.'

Alin turned obediently, but the Lord Rago actually began jumping up and down with rage.

'The *Tarhun*? Through the *Inner House*? Now I have seen everything. The thought of that great rabble of idle sots—'

The Lord Grodan cut across his words.

'We cannot risk the Tarhun being infected,' he said. 'That illness of those boys, if it can be called an illness, is moving fast and affecting their minds.'

'Yes,' said Caul. 'It is making them stronger.'

'Stronger?' echoed the Lord Rago, in a tantrum. 'The Truth Sayer? *Stronger?* Why, the young idiot causes far too much trouble as it is, without his having any *more* power!'

The Lord Firn began bobbing gently up and down like an agitated owl.

'We must be sure to keep him away from the library,' he bleated. 'I've only just got the new louse-lore shelves filed and indexed.'

Derig had been standing very still, as if he were tuned in to something the others could not hear. Now he turned troubled eyes on the Lord Caul.

'Please, Lord,' he said. 'It's not just that Nian's stronger. He's . . . he's sort of seeing further, too.'

The Lord Grodan turned on him, scowling.

'You're interrupting a conference of the Lords of Truth, boy, to tell us that the Truth Sayer has *long sight*?'

Derig flushed painfully and ducked his head, but he managed to find courage to say:

'It's more as if . . . as if Nian can see bigger things.'

The Lord Rago snarled.

'Fool of a boy! As if one needs better eyesight to see large things! It's *small* things that are difficult to see, you young fool! Ah, you'll find that out once you get to my age. If you *do* get to my age. You youngsters are so lacking in sense I'm surprised you remember to keep breathing!'

'I think Derig means something more than that,' said the Lord Caul, seriously.

The Tarhun were making their way out through the smashed garden door, now.

Derig clenched his fists to help him speak.

'Nian . . . I think he can sort of see right across . . . well, everything,' he said. 'All the way to . . . I don't know. To the end of the universe, perhaps.'

'To the end of the universe,' repeated Gow, thoughtfully. 'What would you find there?'

Alin detached himself from the great hulks of the crowd of Tarhun and made his way up to the others.

'Snerk's been hurt,' he said.

'What?' snapped the Lord Grodan. 'How?'

Alin looked much younger than he usually did.

'It looks as if there was an explosion. He was blown right out through the kitchen wall. He nearly went over the precipice.'

Emmec shifted uneasily.

'He was probably trying to make firework curry again,' he suggested.

But Alin shook his head.

'There's a great big Snerk-shaped hole in the far wall: that's nowhere near his cauldron. It looks as if something exploded from the direction of the doorway. It's pretty much destroyed the whole kitchen.'

There was a groan of loss from the whole crowd. Snerk was a genius, the superlative cook, and the world would lose a great master without him.

'But Snerk himself?' asked the Lord Firn, anxiously. 'How badly is he hurt?'

'He's here, Lord!'

Snorer and Bulls-Eye stumbled forward. They were supporting a huge soot-encrusted figure between them. The great mass of blubber that must be Snerk was

226

black from head to toe, and his little head was hanging forwards limply on his great shoulders.

A gasp of dismay went all round the crowd.

But then Snerk lifted his head and opened one bloodshot fiery eye.

'Nurrrrrr,' he said, glowering. 'NurrrrrMurrrrrr! SCRAGim!'

33

They settled Snerk down as comfortably as possible with his back propped up against an anthill. It wasn't easy to be sure how badly injured he was, because of all his fat, but it wasn't long before he began to scrub round on the ground and experiment with ants sandwiched in bits of fungus, occasionally spiced with the odd mouselet dropping, or some ooze from a passing toad.

The others found themselves grouped in a council of war.

'Brilliant,' Snorer was muttering. 'So you're telling us the Truth Sayer's gone nuts. Does that mean we're going to have to take him out?'

'Jolly good, jolly good!' said Reeklet, beaming all round. 'Nice bit of fighty-fighty!'

But there was a swelling rumble of protest from the rest of the Tarhun. The Truth Sayer was only a slip of a lad, but he had power enough to blast the whole House to smithereens.

The Lord Caul cast an anxious glance at the slim distant figure whose face was now almost entirely grey.

'We don't want to harm him,' he said.

'No,' agreed the Lord Grodan, sharply. 'He's the Truth Sayer. He's too valuable to be damaged.'

Tarhun Bulls-Eye shifted himself on his great flat feet.

'Well, how about the other one?' he asked hopefully. 'The boy Jacob. He's going the same way as the Truth Sayer, isn't he? And from what I've seen of the little bogger when I was in his world—'

Everyone groaned. Bulls-Eye was always going on and *on* about his adventure on another world.

'—he thinks he's a right little comedian, he does. *He* might do anything.'

'We should have a sing-song,' suggested Reeklet, brightly. 'Keep our spirits up. *Bing bong booly-wooly-gooly-hooly* . . . '

His brother Tarhun rolled their eyes, but otherwise ignored him.

'If we all got together we could probably push that ironwood tree over on top of them,' suggested someone from near the back of the crowd.

The Lord Grodan snorted.

'Brilliant!' he snapped scathingly. 'So which bit of *we don't want to harm him* do you Tarhun not understand?'

The Lord Caul shook his head.

'Ten to one it *wouldn't* hurt Nian, anyway,' he said. 'Even Jacob's become extraordinarily strong. And they're both getting stronger by the minute.'

Snorer hunched his head between his great shoulders, his little eyes flickering with cunning.

'The Truth Sayer doesn't look as if he's noticing much,' he said. 'Perhaps we could steal over, grab him—gently—and then put him somewhere safe until your lordships could find a cure for him.'

'What ripping fun!' said Reeklet. 'Put him in the cellar and then creep away and slam the door on him!'

But a snarl of derision arose from the Tarhun ranks.

'Grab him?' Bulls-Eye muttered. 'The boy's diseased. And look at the speed it's taken hold. He's only been away since this morning, and already he's . . . well, it's horrible. Horrible. What if *we* catch it? And what if there *isn't* any cure? And what if he decides to serve us all like he served poor old Snerk?'

The Lord Firn bobbed and blinked and licked his lips.

'But surely the Truth Sayer wouldn't . . . '

The Lord Caul looked grim.

'I'm very much afraid that he might. Nian's getting more powerful, and seeing further, by the minute. He can probably see right across the abyss. Yes, I can see why he blasted Snerk away.'

The Lord Rago snorted.

'As if the doings of that idiot boy make any sense at all!' he muttered.

'I'm afraid they make perfect sense, Lord,' said the Lord Caul, deadly serious. 'Because if Nian has the whole universe in his mind, then we ourselves, and even the House of Truth, must seem just about as big and important to him as grains of dust.'

The Truth Sayer was standing looking like a statue of himself, the boy Jacob was *sitting* looking like a statue of himself, and Tarhun Snorer was pacing round and round in agitated circles.

'We're going to die,' he was muttering, again and again. 'We're all going to die!'

The Lord Grodan rubbed his chin.

'This is a very peculiar disease,' he said. 'In fact in some ways it doesn't seem to be a disease at all. More a sort of . . . growing.'

'And?' snapped the Lord Rago. 'Is it curable?'

'I've no idea,' replied the Lord Grodan.

'We could probably put an arrow through the Truth Sayer,' said Bulls-Eye; but Snorer turned on him in rage.

'Of course we can't put an arrow through him! An arrow would never get through that iron skin of his.'

'If there was just some way of getting through to Nian's proper mind . . . ' said Caul.

'If there was just some way of avoiding him throwing us all through the bogging walls,' muttered Bulls-Eye.

The Lord Firn wrung his ancient hands.

'What if the Truth Sayer *sneezes*?' he asked, plaintively. 'All those germs . . . '

The Lord Caul grasped at this as something he could do.

'I can put Nian inside a dome of power,' he said. 'I've already done that to Jacob. I don't suppose for a minute that it'll stop him doing anything he wants to do, but it should at least stop any of his germs getting through it.'

'Unless you go close to him, you're going to have to make a power-bridge all the way over to the Truth

Sayer to do that,' pointed out the Lord Grodan. 'There'd be a risk the disease might back-track along it and the infection get loose that way.'

Hani cleared his throat into the baffled silence which followed this remark.

'Lord,' he began diffidently. 'Look, I know this is probably really really stupid, because obviously I *am* really really stupid, and all that. But couldn't we send the dome over without a power-bridge if we had something to sort of throw it with? Like my catapult, perhaps?'

Hani extracted his catapult from down his tunic and looked hopefully at the Lords Caul and Grodan.

The Lord Grodan pursed his lips.

'It won't be easy to judge the distance,' he pointed out. 'But I suppose it could be tried.'

'Well, it can't do any harm,' said the Lord Caul. 'We'll have a go. Get ready, then, Hani.'

Caul, concentrating hard, sketched out a tiny invisible dome with his fingers, and Hani, stepping up beside him, put the sling of his catapult behind it and took careful aim.

It was a beautiful shot—perfectly judged, so that the dome stalled in the air above Nian's head, opened out like an expertly-flung net, and didn't so much fall on Nian as waft over him. No one watching dreamed for a moment that the Truth Sayer would even notice it.

But Nian did notice.

The Truth Sayer moved. Stiffly, he raised an iron arm, paused—and then swung it round in a backhanded slash . . .

. . . which uprooted every plant and tree in a great swathe of the garden and threw them, together with all the inhabitants of the House, backwards in a whirling confusion of screaming roots and howling voices, to land in a great ruinous heap against the long curved wall of the Inner House.

The Tarhun ended up at the bottom of the heap. That was lucky, really, because it meant that everyone else got a soft landing.

There was a long long moment when everyone's brains whirled dizzily and their ears rang with the echoes of cracking branches and the bellowing of out-raged and very surprised Tarhun.

After the bellowing came a lot of swearing (most of the Tarhun had travelled a great deal in their time, and so swearing was something at which they excelled), but before the Tarhun were even halfway through all their strongest words they remembered that the Lords of Truth were somewhere in that grotting heap with them.

Then there was silence again, broken only by the sound of several skittering mouselets, a dozen scrab-bling dung-rats, and an affronted least owl.

Hani opened his eyes, which he had screwed shut just before he'd smashed back to earth, and found to his surprise that he was still alive. Cautiously, he tried moving a hand, and found it worked. So did the other one. Emboldened, he started to wriggle himself free of all the branches that were on top of him.

'Ouch!' said someone. 'Watch where you're putting your great grotting feet, can't you?'

Hani twisted his head round and saw a patch of light brown hair that might have belonged to a marsh ox, but didn't.

'Emmec? Is that you?'

'What's left of me,' Emmec muttered. 'Just move your bogging feet, will you?'

'*Heer*,' said another voice, a foreign voice, right in his ear. '*Giv mee yoor hand!*'

But Hani took one look at Jacob's outstretched iron palm and decided to manage for himself. He wriggled himself precariously down the great heap over spiky branches and tangles of brambles until he landed on bare rock.

Hani looked round and whistled. A wedge of the garden had been blasted away right down to the rock of the mountain. At the pointed end of the wedge was a small lonely figure which might have been cast out of iron.

'No, I'm all right,' Emmec was saying, to Jacob, in a language Jacob wasn't going to be able to understand. 'I expect I'm covered in Nian's germs since he's just blown a hurricane at us, but I'd rather not touch you, if you don't mind.'

Behind Hani the huge heap of debris was beginning to shift a little, as if a giant mole was breaking free of the earth. Jacob picked up a tree with a trunk as thick as a Tarhun's waist and carried it casually out of the way. Hani, rather hopelessly, pulled a branch off the top of the pile.

No one was hurt. That was the most peculiar thing about the whole peculiar business. Well, Bulls-Eye had got quite badly scratched by a dung-rat, but that was only because he'd got worried about starving to death before he was dug out, and had grabbed the poor thing and tried to bite its head off. Even the Lords, the ancient, delicate Lords, even the Lord Firn, who looked as if a puff of wind could blow him away, was found, once he had been helped quivering from the wreckage, to be pale and wild-haired, but entirely in one piece.

The Tarhun, of course, had to wait until everyone on top of them was extricated before, with a great heaving and grunting like a mass of giant hogs, they gradually unwound themselves and unhooked themselves. They emerged red in the face and glowering (except for Reeklet, who was chuckling like a lunatic) but whole.

'Boy!' croaked the Lord Rago, with his collar all up under one ear and his backside slicked with mud. 'You! You, *boy*!'

Hani flinched.

'Sorry, Lord,' he mumbled. 'It was a really stupid idea about trying to use my catapult to send over the dome. Sorry.'

Rago hissed at him like a malevolent turtle.

'Fool of a boy! The catapult was an excellent idea! It's not your fault that the Truth Sayer's gone mad. But look at you, boy! You look as if you've been dancing through a briar patch. You're a disgrace to the House! All you boys are. Tidy yourselves up at once!'

Alin froze in the act of patting his hair back into place.

'What is it?' asked the Lord Caul, for the colour was draining from Alin's face until he was nearly as white as the wall behind him.

Alin had balled his hands into fists, but he was surrounded by people with powers and that didn't fool anyone. Alin knew it, too. He opened his hands again, slowly, and spread them out.

And then everyone could see.

Alin's hands were streaked and shining with the dull metallic sheen of iron.

34

Aranna gave a great gasp of horror and threw herself down on the dusty floor of the Monument beside the great body which lay there.

'Rik! *Rik!*'

Rik's eyelids were swollen, but through them Aranna could just see a glint of grey.

'*Aranna*,' he breathed.

Aranna blinked back tears of horror and pity. Rik's body was trapped under a huge slab of stone. He must be badly hurt—perhaps dying.

His lips were moving again. Aranna leaned down so she could catch the words.

'*Lift*,' he whispered. '*The stone . . . lift.*'

The slab was obviously going to be too heavy to move, but Aranna put her hands beneath it anyway. She couldn't let Rik die for want of trying.

But her first attempt shifted it, and the second pushed it clear. Aranna could hardly believe it as she wiped the steely dust from her hands and turned back to Rik. He was trying to speak again.

'*Move*,' he whispered. '*Through the wall. Show you.*'

She didn't understand.

'Through the wall?'

Rik managed to nod his great head a little.

'*Send back time*,' he said. '*Help me.*'

Aranna didn't understand. But she was strong, suddenly, so she could help him. Rik was a dun, and she was pale, but that didn't matter. It had never mattered, not really, not to her. He was Rik, and he was her best friend and always would be whatever Rolan and the others said. She would take him wherever he wanted to go.

She put her hands under Rik's arms and began to help him to his feet.

The boys and the Lords and the Tarhun stared at Alin's hands in shock and fear.

'What can we do?' whispered Derig.

'Do? We must reverse whatever this is, and quickly,' said the Lord Grodan.

'But where do we start?' asked the Lord Caul. 'This is a . . . a *process* we don't understand, from a place we cannot begin to imagine.'

Rago snorted.

'Well, we'd better start understanding it soon,' he snapped, displaying a hand that was beginning to sparkle slightly along the creases in his old skin. 'We are all infected, now. Presumably we will all end up like the Truth Sayer, will we? As iron statues?'

The Lord Firn trod uneasily from foot to foot. His wispy white hair was already developing a sinister metallic shine.

'Perhaps we should go inside,' he quavered. 'Into the House. We don't want to risk any chance of *rust*.'

'Tcha!' The Lord Rago showed an iron peg of a tooth in a sneer. 'There will be no rain today, Firn. And by the time the evening mists form we will be too far gone to care!'

Hani was viewing his own palms with a sort of fascinated disgust.

'It's moving really fast,' he said. 'And it's funny, I look as if I'm turning to iron, but I can still move my joints. Can all you lot?'

All around him the Lords and the boys tried wiggling their fingers.

But then Gow gasped.

'I can see my bones!' he said. 'Look, my hands have gone transparent! Look! Look at all the tendons and the joints!'

Alin gave Gow a sharp glance.

'No they haven't,' he said. 'They're just like mine: a bit silvery, but that's all. You're going mad, you are.'

Gow gave a great whooping gasp of horror and shut his eyes tight.

'That's right,' he whispered, ashen-faced. 'That's right. It happened to Nian and now it's happening to us. It's turning us mad.'

The Lord Grodan's face was grim.

'And very quickly,' he observed. 'How can we hope to understand this thing in time? This is like nothing I have ever seen. Not a disease as we understand it. I would have to think for days to have the slightest idea how to start.'

The Tarhun had been shuffling backwards unnoticed for a while, but now they drew attention to themselves because Bulls-Eye got his red leather bootlace tangled up in a fallen branch and only saved himself from falling over by pulling on Snorer's ponytail.

'Whoops-a-daisy!' said Reeklet, jovially; at which Snorer unballed the fist which he was about to smash into Bulls-Eye's face, grabbed Reeklet by the throat, and bellowed, '*Stop being so bogging cheerful!*' in his face.

The Lords and the boys turned, suddenly aware of the gap between them and the Tarhun.

'Where are you going?' demanded the Lord Caul, sharply.

Bulls-Eye tried to smile reassuringly, but from fifty piggy faces a hundred furtive eyes were flickering.

'Just about our duties, Lords,' said Bulls-Eye, with a greasy bow. 'If you Lords aren't feeling too well, then you'll need us to keep everything running smoothly, won't you?'

But then Jacob spoke. He spoke slowly, assembling a sentence word by word with an effort like someone building a wall.

'I think it too late,' he said, apologetically. His accent was barbarous, but everyone understood what he said.

The Tarhun all eyed him with bulgy-eyed amazement and horror.

'Jacob no lord,' Jacob explained, unnecessarily. 'Jacob . . . Jacob like Tarhun.'

There was a rumble from the ranks of the Tarhun, and someone muttered something about Jacob hardly making *lunch* for one of them.

Jacob looked as if he understood. He screwed up his face with the effort of finding words.

'No,' he said. 'Nian power—iron quick. Jacob no power—iron no quick.' And then Jacob blew out his lips in exasperation and went on, much more quickly. '*Hay, yoo havnt startid understanding inglish, yet, hav yoo? Beecoz* Eiv *beegun too understand wot* yor *saying. Itz the plaig, Ei think. Eim seeing mor and mor orl the teim, and sumteims Ei kan sort ov see yor thorts.*'

The Lord Grodan put a lean and shaky hand up to his forehead.

'Did any of you understand that?' he asked. 'Because it seemed to me—'

'I can understand him, too,' said Gow, quietly.

'And me,' said Alin.

Bulls-Eye began shaking his fat head over and over again.

'Oh no. Oh no no no. There's nothing wrong with me,' he growled.

'Nor me,' said Reeklet, brightly. 'So I think I'll be taking a nice little holiday!'

He took three steps away across the garden but then seemed to walk into an invisible wall. The *thunk* of it reached them quite clearly. Reeklet staggered back, cross-eyed, and sat down hard.

'None of you will leave the House until the plague is gone,' announced the Lord Grodan over the growl of anger which rose round the Tarhun's fat heads.

'But, Lord,' said Snorer, reasonably, 'keeping us all herded together will just make us all the more certain to catch it. You wouldn't want us to be ill, now, would you, Lord?'

Bulls-Eye spat challengingly on the bare rock.

'Could the Lords stop us if we walked out?' he asked. 'If we all charged out, now, all of us together?'

'Fools!'

The Lord Rago bared his ancient tooth contemptuously and spat out a word that none of them had heard before. At once a hum made itself heard from across the garden. It wasn't loud, but it had a menacing edge. People began to fidget and look around them.

'Tiger bees,' said Gow, suddenly. 'It's the colony from that hollow wine bush by the pockle ground. They've swarmed.'

The Lord Rago made a sound that might have been a laugh, had it been oiled and polished and not totally malevolent.

'You Tarhun will be all right as long as you don't move,' he cackled, his eyes shooting out darts of the nastiest sort of glee. 'Controlling a swarm of bees is very like controlling a cloud, you know. It'll be all right, I believe, as long as I keep up my concentration.'

The Tarhun froze at once: in a matter of seconds even their fat had stopped wobbling.

The buzzing of the bees got nearer and nearer.

'I'll hang them on that tree root,' said Rago, snickering. 'Then they'll be handy if I should want them.'

Into the silence that followed this remark there came a sound from the direction of the broken doorway. An

242

old man was emerging. He seemed to be having to concentrate on the precise balance of every step, as if his legs were threatening to fold beneath him.

A dozen voices called out.

'Tarq, I never thought to call Tarq!'

'Tarq, stay back!'

'The Truth Sayer has brought a plague upon us from another world!'

The Lord Tarq raised his head, and looked at the iron-streaked, angry, and frightened crowd.

'And where is the Truth Sayer, my friends?' he asked quietly.

'There!'

The Truth Sayer looked like a solid iron statue. It was hard to believe that it had ever been able to move.

'He can't even be breathing,' murmured Alin. 'Oh *struth* . . . '

Caul ran his hand through his gleaming hair. It made a faint scraping sound.

'If our powers are growing, what must his be like?' he asked. 'What can he see now?'

The answers came from the other Lords.

'Darkness.'

'And distance. Huge distance.'

The Lord Firn's voice rose in a wail.

'To him we are nothing but specks in the abyss of the worlds. Even my library, my precious library, is nothing, nothing, compared with the width of the worlds.'

But the Lord Tarq only smiled, and shook his head.

'My friends,' he said, gently. 'Surely you do not measure your worth in spans?'

'There are many ways of measuring, Tarq,' spat the Lord Rago, thrusting out his scrawny head. 'And I am growing. Yes, growing mightily. I shall soon have such great power—'

'—and so shall I,' put in the Lord Grodan, turning swiftly on him. 'Enough power to turn this mountain into the biggest firework the world has ever seen.'

Derig was breathing fast.

'Perhaps we should do it,' he said, white-lipped. 'If it would stop the plague spreading . . .'

But Tarq stood, as calm as moonfall.

'My friends, I am a little man,' he said. 'Small and thin and not strong in body or in power. And measured in time, indeed, nearly all my span is gone. And yet I am not so very small, I think.'

'Of course, Lord,' said Gow. 'But, you see, Nian's mind is full of such great things . . .'

The Lord Rago was never an attractive sight at the best of times, and now, with his skin as grey and wrinkled as a lizard's and his iron tooth gleaming in his black mouth, he looked like a troll from some dreadful tale.

'The boy is right! The boy is right!' he crowed. 'Oh yes, I can see a long way myself, now. Yes, further than I have ever seen before. This plague has given me a remarkable gift, indeed!'

And even the Lord Caul was nodding, nodding.

'Yes,' he said, wonderingly. 'Power as long as the worlds. It's a great weapon, you know. A truly *marvellous* weapon.'

Suddenly Caul's long heron-figure had something predatory about it.

'So much power,' he went on, turning eyes on the boys which were suddenly blank and grey. 'So *much* power.'

He held out his steely hands, gloating, and the boys watched, transfixed with horror. This was the Lord Caul—quiet, self-deprecating Caul.

'So what, I wonder, boys,' Caul went on, chillingly, 'should I use all my power *for*?'

35

The Tarhun had clustered themselves together, heads down, like oxen in the presence of a cloud-lynx. The boys found they had drawn together, too.

'Struth,' muttered Hani. 'The Lords are stark raving bonkers. What the grot are we going to do?'

'What the grot are *they* going to do?' said Alin. 'That's what's worrying me.'

'But none of them would . . . ' began Derig.

Gow shook his head.

'None of *them* would,' he said. 'But *they* aren't *them*, are they? Their minds are going; they're plague-people.'

'Just think,' said Emmec, shuddering. 'Rago's getting madder by the minute—and he was bonkers to start with.'

Hani shivered.

'I'll tell you what,' he said, seriously. 'Whatever he does, I bet he'll do it to me, first. He's never liked me ever since that time I set fire to his nose hair when I was trying to call up a storm in a tea bowl.'

'At least the Lord Tarq's still all right,' said Derig. 'Everyone respects him. If anyone can calm the Lords down, he can.'

'My Lords,' began Tarq, right on cue; but then his chin jerked forward as if something had punched him in the stomach, and his knees gave way, and suddenly he was on the ground, unmoving.

'Boggit!' said Alin. 'Who did that?'

'Rago,' said Gow, tersely.

'But why? Tarq's never done anyone any harm!'

'Because Rago's as mad as a scorched dung-rat. Hey, Emmec!' Gow barked, suddenly. 'Don't touch Tarq! Leave him alone!'

'But—'

'—if he catches your plague it won't help him, will it?'

Emmec hesitated, but came back to the other boys.

'Grodan's beginning to look as crazy as Rago,' he said, throwing an anxious glance over his shoulder to where the Lord Grodan was twitching his fingers and muttering to himself. 'And Caul looks ready to strangle the next person he lays eyes on.'

Jacob, who'd joined the other boys, cleared his throat.

'*Yoo noh sumthing?*' he said, oddly serious. '*Itz reelee grate beeing aybl too tare thingz too bitz with mei bare handz and too heer the rithms ov the werldz and orl that. But Eim still sorree Ei never got to play that gig.*'

Behind him, a small tree uprooted itself.

'Duck!' shouted Alin—and they all dived down flat on their faces to prevent themselves being decapitated as the tree flew through the air. It landed upside down on top of the Lord Firn, trapping him in a cage of branches.

247

A little way away the Lord Grodan let out a spine-chilling snicker of contempt.

Emmec raised his head.

'Anyone got any good ideas?' he asked. 'Because now would be a really good—'

'—wow!' said Alin, suddenly. 'Bog, I think the plague's just . . . *wow!* Hey, I can see so *far.*'

'Don't look!' said Gow, tightly.

'But you've no idea how—'

'Yes I have,' snapped Gow (Gow, who was quiet and clever and never ever snapped). 'But I'm still not looking.'

Hani clutched at his greying ears.

'Hey, yeah,' he said. 'So *that's* what Caul's been going on about in lessons. Hey, guess what, I think I may be going quite clever. It's cool, isn't it, being able to see how things work.'

Emmec suddenly gave a huge whooping gasp.

'Yes,' he breathed. 'I can see it, now. This is fantastic. You know, if I looked properly I'd be able to—'

'—don't!' said Gow, though his face, where it was not iron grey, was crimson with effort. 'Don't look, Emmec! If you look then your mind will get dragged further and further away from itself.'

Alin stared at Gow through ominously cloudy eyes.

'You're just jealous,' he said, accusingly. 'You're trying to stop us growing, trying to stop us seeing things so you'll end up the strongest and—'

The great bulk of the Tarhun Snorer loomed up behind Alin and a huge hand reached out for Alin's neck.

'No!' gasped Derig. 'There's no need. Really, Snorer. Alin's all right. Aren't you, Alin? You're all right.'

Alin stopped, and gulped, and clenched his fists.

'Yes, I think so. Yes. I'm fine.'

Snorer sniffed, unconvinced.

'You haven't been getting any urges to tear people's heads off and take over the world, then?'

Alin looked slightly shifty.

'Well, not more than usual,' he muttered.

Snorer peered down at the boys suspiciously.

'I suppose, if you're sure he won't be causing trouble then I'll leave him,' he agreed. 'But I'm wondering if I shouldn't serve the Lords with a little bit of strangulation. It won't be long before they start killing each other, at this rate. *And* the rest of us, too.'

'*Ei wont too goh hohm,*' said Jacob, suddenly. '*Ei noh Eiv waysted mohst ov mei leif, but if this orl werks owt and Ei get hohm, Eim gohing too . . . doo sumthing!*'

Snorer shook his great chops. He didn't understand Jacob's words, but the tone was clear enough.

'Now this here alien's getting agitated,' he said, grimly. 'The plague may come on slower in those of us without powers, but it still comes on, doesn't it? I never thought it would end like this, overtaken by some terrible creeping disease. I thought I'd die fighting, to tell you the truth.' He grinned, rather sadly. 'Yes, that was the way I always hoped to go, so I could make sure I didn't travel the wastes of death alone. But now—'

'—I can see the wastes of death,' said Gow, with a gulp. 'All scarlet and spiralled, like a spider's web.'

'No they're not, idiot,' said Alin, roughly. 'They're all in steps.'

'And blue, like beetles' wings,' put in Derig. 'It's strange, though,' he went on, thoughtfully. 'Because they didn't look like that before, when I was actually there.'

'*Blue?*' echoed Emmec, incredulously.

Hani sniggered.

'They're bonkers,' he said. 'I can see right across them. They're twirling squares, and sort of snot-coloured.'

They were all sitting up, now, and blinking at each other.

'Well, I know I'm right,' said Alin. 'I can see them.'

Gow looked round at the others.

'And so can we,' he said slowly. 'But we can't *all* be right. Can we?'

Jacob spoke, then.

'*Thayr leik perpl seeweed from heer,*' he said. '*But sort ov wobbling. In swing teim.*'

Hani gasped as if he'd sat down on a thorn.

'From *here*!' he exclaimed. 'That's what it is. It's like Caul's been teaching us. We're all seeing a long way—but from only our own direction. Everything's real, sure enough, everything's true—but we're only seeing a tiny slice of what's there, so it's sort of not true, at all.'

Gow slammed a metallic fist into his palm with completely uncharacteristic violence.

'Hani's got it!' he said. 'And I think he's got the solution, too. Look, we'll join our minds together—'

'—sounds like a grotting Hour of Thought,' muttered Alin.

'—and then we'll show Nian what we can all see, all of us together. He's a brilliant healer, we all know that, but I reckon he hasn't even thought about curing this plague because, as Grodan keeps saying, it isn't really a disease at all.'

'*Thatz reit*,' said Jacob. '*Neean corld it a chayng. Hee sed it woz mayking him stronga.*'

'Yes, and it is. But if we could just show him that the plague's fooled him—that what he's seeing is only a narrow slice of the Truth, then I reckon he'll do everything he can to get rid of it: to reverse the change inside him. He is the Truth Sayer, after all.'

Alin sniffed.

'But that means presenting Nian with all of our knowledge, and quite a lot of our powers,' he said, sourly. 'What if he goes totally mad and decides to wrench our powers away from us—and then kill everybody and take over the world?'

Emmec stared at him in amazement.

'What, *Nian*?' he asked; and Alin, rather unwillingly, subsided.

'Let's make a circle, then,' said Derig.

'I'll go and get some of the lads to stand round and shield you,' offered Snorer. 'The Lords are barking mad, and that old Rago is frightening enough at the best of times, if you ask me.'

He prowled away, and the boys quickly arranged themselves in a circle of Thought.

'Ready?' asked Gow, looking round.

'Ready,' said Derig, nervously licking his pale lips.

'Good luck, you lot,' said Emmec.

It was fortunate that the Lord Grodan chose that moment to launch an attack on the other Lords with a giant octopus-like mass of whipping brambles, because even the Tarhun, lumbering across the garden to form a wall of human blubber round the boys, could tell that something was happening. The air inside the boys' circle of Thought was dotted with tiny sparkling lights, and, as if that wasn't enough of a give-away, the Tarhun found their heads throbbing with somersaulting colours and mad rhythms.

The boys sat quietly facing each other. Nothing seemed to happen for a minute, except that the bits of Hani's face that were not cold iron went mauve with effort.

'I don't think I can—' he began.

'—oh yes you *can*!' snapped Gow, violently.

And now the circle of sparkling air between the boys was bulging upwards into a dome, and then something like a giant bud; and then it was splitting and opening.

Inside the ring of boys there was a leaping glow like white flames, now, as over the heads of the Tarhun huge arching petals spread out, translucent and throbbing with colour.

The boy Hani was having trouble catching his breath, but the others were as still as if they had turned to iron already.

Now the tips of the petals were dissolving, sending a glowing mist pouring downwards and spreading out until it lapped over the feet of the steely statue of the Truth Sayer.

Nian, the Truth Sayer, was riding a beam of light across the abyss. Fast, he was going, so fast, although it took no effort at all. He laughed with triumph. *He could see so much.*

And then, before he knew it, something had come at him across the abyss and bludgeoned into him so hard that it knocked him off course.

Outraged, he went to swipe the thing away, but before he could, something else came at him and knocked into him—and then something else—until he found himself tumbling and staggering through the abyss.

Nian, furious, tried to right himself, but things kept coming along and barging into him, until all the beautiful clarity of his passage through the abyss was ruined.

And now, with the shoving, came distracting voices. *Look*, they said. *Look, look, look, look, look, look!*

Nian didn't want to look. He wanted to get to the end of his journey, to assume his new form, but the voices teased at his mind, and he couldn't help it.

He looked, and there spread out before him was the whole of the abyss, a billion spinning worlds, and each world full of a million colours.

Nian tried to clear his mind so he could see his beam of light again, but this vision, this huge universe, filled his mind, cluttered it.

Nian wavered. He was supposed to be changing, growing new senses, moving to a new reality. But these voices . . .

Look! Look, look, look, look, look . . .

He was surrounded by a hundred *looks*. Their narrow beams shone across the abyss like prison bars, trapping him, anchoring him, weighing him down.

Look! Look! Look!

He didn't want to look, because looking would mean stepping back into the self he had been, and giving up all this glorious space and freedom.

Look!

Nian clenched his fists and screwed his eyes tight shut, but that didn't stop him seeing.

The choice between that simple hurtling distance and this crowded complicated universe tore at him. One would be marvellous and exciting and narrow and easy, and one would be difficult and complicated and true and load him with a huge responsibility for the rest of his life.

He cursed and cursed, and chose.

Snorer's mind was being battered by all the lights and noises the boys were somehow creating (struth, he was glad he was normal), so it wasn't easy to see the small figure of the Truth Sayer. But even so, Snorer was almost sure that something there was moving. Occasionally the golden boiling mist would shift a little, so he got a clearer view, and . . . yes. Yes, the boy was still iron-grey, but he'd started looking . . . softer, somehow: like a boy again, he supposed, instead of a statue.

And there. There. Snorer's head was still being bashed and dazzled by everything in the boys' minds, but through the metallic sheen to the Truth Sayer's hair was emerging the bleached-grass heron's-nest that he usually wore (scruffy little tyke, the Truth Sayer was, and no amount of nagging or combing or tidying made the slightest difference).

The boy Hani was beginning to look blue. Poor little bogger, he was trying his best but he hadn't got the brains of a hayfinch, that one.

And now the Truth Sayer was moving. He was rubbing his face with his hands, and shaking himself like a waking wolf. And then he looked up, and saw the boys in their intent circle, and frowned.

36

'Hey!' called Nian, to the other boys. 'What do you think you're doing all barging me about and shouting right in my ear holes like that? There I was,' he went on, indignantly, 'quietly changing into my adult form, and then you go and . . . '

Nian stopped and frowned, confused.

'Hang on,' he said. 'I'm not . . . no. I've never actually been a maggot, have I.'

The boys' concentration shattered. Hani flopped back onto the rock and lay there groaning, not with pain, exactly, but to make it clear to everyone how much effort he'd put into the whole business. The other boys sagged and panted.

Nian came over and stared at them.

'Are you lot all right?' he asked. 'Hey, just a minute! What am I doing here? Shouldn't I be in . . . '

'*Anutha werld?*' asked a voice.

Nian spun round.

'*Yair, anutha werld . . . Hay, Jaycub, wot ar yoo dooing heer?*'

The boy Jacob held up a pair of iron-striped bony hands.

'*Oh, the yooshul,*' he said. '*Sayving the wurldz. Oh, but Ei seem too hav picked up a littl tuch ov the playg, on the way.*'

Nian looked at Jacob's hands, and blinked, and then he looked round at the other boys.

'*Grot,*' he said, quite gently. '*Ei woz . . . oh bogging grot with antlers on. Jaycub, Ei am remembering rite, arnt Ei?*'

'*Dunno,*' said Jacob. '*Iz it sumthing abowt a hyooj black towa full ov dedlee dust and a boi hooz terned intoo a monsta?*'

Nian nodded, appalled.

Jacob sighed.

'*Dam,*' he said briefly. '*Then Ei suppohz Ei must bee remembring it rite az well.*'

'Nian,' said Alin, sharply. 'Stop gargling and *do* something, won't you? Because if you don't get this bogging plague out of my head I think I might go and do something regrettable, like hitting someone over the head with a wall.'

Nian opened his mouth, but before he could reply Emmec screeched *look out!* and a full-sized snowman zoomed towards them, its flint-chip teeth grinning wickedly below his rutnip nose.

The boys yelped and flung themselves down flat. The snowman landed right beside Hani's head in a soft explosion of snow which left him spluttering and sneezing.

Snorer ran through the swear words of several empires.

'You'd better see to the Lord Rago, first, Truth Sayer,' he said grimly. 'It looks as though he's got back all the weather-lore powers he's ever had, and then some. He'll be sending over a squadron of man-sized icicles, next, to spear us together like kebabs.'

Nian hastily scanned the garden.

The Lord Rago, chuckling nastily, was beckoning to a small black cloud on the horizon, and the Lord Firn was carefully folding a piece of hartskin into a dart with a tip as sharp as a thorn.

Nian didn't bother to find out what the rest were doing, because if daffy old Firn had got to the stage where he was making lethal weapons then there was no time at all to lose. Nian felt—not tired, exactly, but as if there was rather more space inside him than there should be—so it took a little time to pull his powers together. He concentrated on Firn, first, poor old Firn; on his shaking excited hands which were fashioning a dart which would have the power to fly cleanly into Bulls-Eye's great gut and out the other side again.

Nian focused his power carefully. The others had shown him what the plague did. This plague . . . it wasn't a disease, at all, which was one reason why he hadn't been able to work out how to cure it straight away. On some other world this had been the process which changed a crawling maggot into a steel-armoured midge. But in a man . . . well, whatever it was, it was clever. It had blinkered the Lord Firn so that his dithering had developed into a mighty and most un-Firn-like desire to rule.

The old man was snickering to himself as he used his iron nails to crease the hartskin into the sharpest possible point.

Nian could see what he had to do, now. This process did not belong inside people, so all he had to do was to turn things back to how they should be; and that was as natural to the Truth Sayer as breathing. The Lord Firn . . . *this* was what Firn was really like (which wasn't exactly what he *should* be, perhaps, but Nian didn't have to worry about that).

As Nian watched, Firn's busy fingers lost their deftness. He began to fumble at the piece of hartskin, and then to rock backwards and forwards in moist-eyed bewilderment.

There. That was right. Now it was just a matter of . . .

'*Watch out!*' screeched Emmec, and Nian found that everyone in the garden had thrown themselves down to the ground again.

Nian didn't have time to work out what was happening. He ducked instinctively and the dazzling light that was shooting towards his head hit his bad arm and knocked him flying. A second after Nian hit the ground, he discovered the thing had been hot. Nian's sleeve had a hole burnt through it, and under it his arm was boiled-pink, and stinging like mad.

Someone let out a cracked and scornful laugh, and Nian, furious, lashed out unthinkingly.

The Lord Rago made a noise like a constipated frog and fell over.

Nian scrambled to his feet, his teeth clenched against the pain, and looked around. The hummocks littered all over the ground like giant swamp-hogs were frightened members of the Tarhun (though one of the great brutes, strangely, seemed to be singing to himself), but over there the Lord Grodan's teeth were bared in a snarl. That was nothing unusual, but Grodan's grey hate-gleaming eyeballs were. Grodan was just pointing one grey hand towards Nian and . . .

. . . Nian focused his powers on that grey hand. It should not be as tense and knotted as a tree root, but calm and smooth, the hand of a man who had not done any physical work for decades. Grodan was a cold, sarcastic man, but he had a great talent for healing. Grodan should be . . .

. . . yes. Grodan should be like that.

All around Nian, the other boys heaved sighs of relief.

'Me next,' said Alin, stiffly.

Gow shook his head.

'The Lords—'

'—I know about the bogging Lords, you grotting moron!' snapped Alin, violently. 'But I've got a thing like a puffball growing in my head, and if someone doesn't get rid of it I'm going to . . . ' He paused, and swallowed, and then went on in a muttering whisper, ' . . . the thing is that I know what everyone else is thinking in their rotten hearts. I must keep myself safe, that's the thing. That's the—'

'—boggit!' said Snorer. 'Truth Sayer, I think he's going to—'

'I know, I know!' said Nian. He swivelled his Thoughts to Alin.

Alin . . . should be . . .

There. There he was. That was it.

Alin stood heaving in breath after breath after breath.

'Grot,' he said. 'Grot grot grot. All right, then. Fair enough. Perhaps I *won't* destroy everyone in a river of molten rock, after all.'

Derig went pale.

'Were you going to?' he asked, faintly.

Alin shrugged.

'Well, it seemed like a good idea at the time,' he admitted. 'All right, Nian. You'd better let us help you.'

It was easier after that. With Firn and Grodan and Alin definitely themselves again, Nian could rely on them to cover his back; and the Lord Grodan was not a bad healer, really, so he took care of Nian's scorched arm.

The plague did not survive long. As Nian looked into each mind it flinched and withered and died. It took no time at all with the Tarhun, who were hardly touched by it; and the boys saw it go with a few gasps and a shudder or two (except for Jacob, who, oddly, got hiccups); but the Lords swayed like trees in a high wind as the new powers the plague had given them were lost, lost, lost and dissolved into the thin pure air of the mountain of the House of Truth.

Nian left the unconscious Lord Rago until last, even though the old man's faintly twitching body was very far from decorative. The Lord Rago's case was actually quite interesting: the plague made people go mad, far-seeing, and paranoid—but that was so near to what the Lord Rago was like anyway that it was quite tricky to work out which bits were plague and which bits were actually the Lord Rago.

Even so, when Nian looked carefully, he found several streaks of something that was more golden than iron in the old man's constitution. Nian didn't like to pry too deeply, but it seemed possible that even the Lord Rago had some good in him. Somewhere.

37

Snorer rubbed his great blobby nose and sighed from the depths of his blubbery heart as Bulls-Eye and Reeklet carefully carried the Lord Tarq into the Inner House under the supervisory glower of the Lord Grodan.

'So it's back to normal, then,' he said. 'Boggit, Truth Sayer, I suppose it had to happen. But struth, me and the boys, we were just powering up for the biggest punch-up the world has ever seen.'

He sighed again, wistfully.

'Still,' he went on, brightening a little, 'the world's safe. I reckon that calls for a bit of a celebration, tonight, Lord.'

'So that's over,' said Emmec, with enormous relief. 'Grot, Nian, that was *scary*. You wouldn't believe the things I was beginning to think.'

'Yeah,' agreed Hani. 'Hey, it's odd, being clever, isn't it? I don't know how you can stand it, Gow. All those thoughts in your head all the time. It was driving me bonkers.'

'It was like . . . like flying on the fastest cloud in the worlds,' said Gow, wistfully. 'I could see so far. You know, I might sit here and think for a lifetime and not get as far as I did when I had the plague to help me, even though what I was seeing wasn't really any good at all.'

Jacob sighed, too.

'*Ei havnt the fayntist eideer wot enneewunz gohing on abowt,*' he said. '*And just for a mohment Ei reelee thort Ei woz getting the hang ov utha wurldz.*'

Alin grunted.

'What I want to know is where you got the grotting plague from, Nian,' he said.

Nian sat up in alarm.

'Oh grot,' he said. 'Oh grot oh grot oh grot!'

The Lord Rago, who had recovered annoyingly quickly, and was carefully sending the small black cloud back to the exact position it'd come from, gave Nian an evil look. But Nian's brain was connecting itself up really properly for the first time since the plague had descended upon him.

'Rik!' he exclaimed.

'Rik?' echoed Emmec. 'What's a *rik* when it's at home?'

Nian got to his feet.

'He's a boy, and I'm afraid he's about to set the plague loose on his own world,' said Nian, turning towards the statue which marked the beginning of the passageway out of the world. 'I must go back and—'

The Lords Rago, Caul, and Firn all put out arms and grabbed him.

'Don't you think that would be unwise?' Caul said.
'But—'

The Lord Firn shifted from foot to foot as if he was afraid he was going to wet himself.

'I'm sorry for the sufferings of that world,' he said, with what was really only technical sincerity. 'But think, Truth Sayer. If you were to contract the plague again . . .'

Nian shook his head.

'No,' he said. 'I know I might go berserk and do all sorts of things—though, actually, now I know what the thing is, I reckon I'll be able to dodge it—but it's even worse than that. Rik—I don't know if you've realized, but he's been moving time backwards. We've had a whole series of todays, of Mondays, one after the other. Rik's really ill—dying—and I've left him trapped under a big stone, but if he has a clear-headed moment then he just might manage to send time backwards again.'

Nian found himself surrounded by horrified faces. 'Do you mean we might have to live through today again?' Hani asked, appalled. 'Weather-lore with Rago, and then catching the plague and having to stop the Lords killing everyone? *Again?*'

The Lord Rago moved with a swiftness surprising in a man of his age.

'Don't just stand there, Truth Sayer,' he snapped, 'you're wasting time. Come along! Come along! *Quickly!*'

And he hastily led the way across the garden towards the square statue which marked the entrance to the abyss.

* * *

Nian threw a few ropes of thought round Jacob and together they jumped off the edge of the world.

They fell fast, but not fast enough for Nian. There was no telling what Rik was doing (he might be in the white desert, waiting . . .) and no way of telling how near the people outside the tower were to blowing open the great doors. Nian had managed to wipe out the plague in the House of Truth, but there the plague had been confined to one small garden. If the doors to the tower were opened and the plague-dust was blown out onto the wide winds of that world . . .

I wouldn't be able to stop it, Nian realized. He thought of the millions of people in that world, whose ways of life he couldn't begin to imagine.

He looked round hastily. There, faintly, traced across the abyss like a wind-arc strand of spider's silk, was the trail that led to Rik's world.

Nian hurtled himself along it.

'Oof!' said Jacob, falling over onto the floor of the cave under the tower. 'Ow, Nian, that drop always takes me by surprise.'

'Wait here,' said Nian. 'I won't be long.'

'OK. But hey, Nian! Nian!'

'Tell me later. I haven't got—'

'—you do know about the girl, don't you?'

Nian stopped with one arm reaching up to his first hand-hold. He blinked back through the darkness.

'Girl?'

'Yeah. She was in the tower. Rik summoned her, somehow, I think. She arrived just as I was helping you down to the passageway. You were pretty much out of it by then, so I thought you might not have noticed her.'

'All right. I'll look out for her,' said Nian, possessed of a desperate urgency.

'Yeah. I thought I'd better warn you. Oh, and Nian!'

'*What?*'

'They seemed to be pretty good friends.'

Nian froze for a split second with apprehension. If Rik had called someone into the tower to help him, then he might have managed to get back into the white desert; and in that case, Time might be about to snap back at any moment.

Nian turned and launched himself up the rough rock and into the glistening darkness of the tower.

Once Nian was inside the tower he could hear the people working just outside the door. What they were doing was so dangerous that Nian was tempted to blow the lot of them all away across the plain to the mountains; but he didn't dare stop even for that.

Nian hastened through the glistening snail-trail darkness which had endured for a thousand years. Every room was like every other, and Nian needed his powers to guide him.

He ran over the felted dust.

And there. *There* was something. Nian's mind twisted through the black doorway and over the dusty heap of great stone slabs that had once been a wall. The thing was still three rooms away, but he could sense it. There was a girl, yes, but there was also . . .

What exactly was it, this thing which had once been Rik? It was warm, or Nian might even have wondered if it was some outcrop of rock. Its skin was crusted, sharp-ridged, and the head (though there was not really a head, because the neck had swelled outwards and fissured into hot cracks like gills) seemed hardly to have any eyes or a nose or features at all.

The thing must have felt Nian's arrival, because it was snuffling round as if it were trying to scent something. Nian winced as the thing's mind touched his. The thing was both ice cold and violently hot, and the mind inside this . . . this mound of matter (for the limbs had grown into the body, or the body into the limbs, Nian could not tell which) was spiked like a fishing spear.

Nian's mind flinched away from the horror of that dreadful thing, but he ran forward through the doorway and over the heap of black slabs which were piled there.

And there, there, just a few feet from the entrance to the passageway to the white desert, crusted like old lava and yet tender as a maggot, was the thing which had once been Rik.

The girl was there, too, crouching beside a black-glistening wall. She was glowing faintly through the dark, but her body was still unswollen.

She looked up at Nian.

'He won't let me touch him any more,' she said. 'I did help him a little way, but then he forgot who I was. He won't let me touch him now.'

Nian looked at the thing, and his heart went cold with horror. The creature could hardly move: its great body could only just scrape its belly through the soft dust which had killed it.

Nian found himself confronted by two deep-set sparks of chilly light, and then the creature raised a flipper-like thing. There was a dreadful egg-splintering noise above Nian's head, and a spider's web of cracks spread out through the ceiling.

The ceiling held for perhaps three seconds, and Nian stood and gawped for all of them. It was only as the first stone fell that he gathered his wits enough to throw up a wall of power to shelter him and the girl.

He crouched, wincing, as the slabs thudded heavily down on the invisible wall, until a slab bounced off the wall sideways and hit something softer.

There was a sharp cry of pain and suddenly it was as if Nian was seeing everything from a different place. This murderous creature was not Rik, but the result of the bogging plague which had made Nian himself scrape a whole section of his precious garden down to the bare dead rock.

Yes. It was the plague he had to fight, not this poor thing.

The plague was all round them, in the air, in the dust. It had slept for hundreds of years, but now it had found a host it had awakened and . . .

. . . Nian, crouched under the low roof of his power wall, called together all his strength. He had to scour the whole of this great labyrinth, sterilize every fragment of everything.

He looked within himself for some way to do it. His powers were much better at healing things than killing them, at strengthening rather than destroying.

Nian had been studying with the Lords for a long time, and he had been taught a lot. He could squat there and use the wisdom and discipline of the Lords; do everything carefully, thoroughly, rationally, or . . .

. . . it was done before he knew it. Power and anger came out of him in a great rush, and for a moment every stone in the walls around him was outlined in brilliant blue fire.

And now the dust under Nian's feet was beginning to squirm, like mud in a pond. The dust dissolved under Nian's feet and they sank down until they touched the rock-hardness of the bare stone floor.

Then all was still in the dark tower again, and the air hung empty around him. And there was a clearness, an after-the-storm feeling about the place which told Nian that the plague which had haunted this place for so long had been destroyed.

Nian pushed up one end of the wall of power so all the slabs of stone slid off, and then he let the wall dissolve.

And then, weary and apprehensive, he went over to look at what had become of Rik.

38

Rik's body was resting on the black rock of the floor. Even to Nian's pale power-vision he looked little more than a mound of rubble, except that he was glowing with heat and that Nian could sense a large heart galloping along in a triple-beat: *thud-thud-THUD, thud-thud-THUD, thud-thud-THUD.*

'Who are you?' asked the girl, wonderingly.

'The Truth Sayer,' said Nian.

Nian squatted down beside Rik. Rik had been so much affected by the plague that he was hardly more than a barrow-load of iron and flesh.

Nian placed a hand on the jagged ridge of Rik's crooked back. Every cell in Rik's body had been altered by the plague, and now they were collapsing, buckling, bursting.

Rik began shuddering. Nian put out his power in a fierce burst of concentration: each cell had to find its way back to its rightful shape—but it was more complicated than that, because the great bones must not contract while the tender organs inside Rik's chest were still swollen.

Thud-thud-THUD . . . thud-thud-THUD . . .

Nian was concentrating so hard that he didn't notice the noises from outside, though he must have heard them.

Thud-thud-THUD . . . thud-THUD . . .

The first thing he noticed was a bright light shining in his face, and then a voice from the middle of a jostling of bodies, high with amazement, saying, *'There's people in here!'*

Nian turned his face away from the light. Another voice was saying, *'What's that?'* But Nian was still concentrating on the *that*. The particles of what had been Rik were relaxing, coming back together, but Nian could feel sudden landslides and waves in the process that meant that Rik would never be quite as he'd been before.

'Is it a heap of clothes?'

'It looks more like . . . good grief!'

But Rik was changing so fast these people couldn't believe their eyes from one moment to the next.

There was a click and a sudden bright flash that left Nian with a red after-image floating sluggishly across his vision. And here was a man with a small writing block and some sort of stylus.

'Name?' the man said, eagerly.

'Rik,' said Nian.

Rik's body heaved a little under Nian's hand. Rik's tongue was still too big for his mouth, but soon he would be able to speak again.

It was Rik's mind that was changed the most. Nian wondered about putting it back as it had been; but that would not be right, because too much had

272

happened to Rik for that to be the Truth of what he was any more.

The man with the writing block was speaking again.

'How did you get in here ahead of the others?'

Nian looked at him. The man was a simple soul who was dreaming of telling his story to millions of people and becoming famous.

'Rik will be able to talk to you soon,' said Nian.

The man hurried away: there were many stories in this place and he had no time to waste.

The ridges on Rik's back were going down. Now his head was moving a little. He was making a noise.

'Not yet,' whispered Nian. 'You're not ready to speak, yet. Wait for a while.'

Rik's body was recovering, and his thoughts were joining together again. Nian could hear them.

I could see so much, Rik was thinking, bewildered. *So much, so far. And now it is all gone and I am only here. I am only me and only here and the rest is gone.*

Nian got up and went over to the girl.

'Go to Rik,' he told her. 'He needs you.'

She looked at him searchingly.

'Is he all right now?'

Nian was so tired.

'No,' he said. 'That's why he needs you. Go to him.'

Nian found Jacob by the mouth of the cave, looking out at the other-world sun and the other-world desert which was spread out under it.

Jacob looked round when he heard Nian's footsteps. 'Time to go?' he asked.

Nian nodded.

Jacob sighed. The whole plain was dyed red by the light of the sun.

'It's a bit of a pity, really,' he said. 'I mean, I've seen hardly anything of this place.'

Nian didn't reply.

'Ah well,' said Jacob. 'I suppose I've seen more of the worlds than anyone else from Earth.'

'You nearly saw too much,' said Nian.

Jacob's front room seemed grey after the desert. Even the clashing oranges and turquoises looked somehow muted and weak.

Jacob, looking round, didn't seem to be all that impressed, either.

'It's small, this place,' he said. 'It's funny, but I've never really noticed, before.'

'I must get back to my world,' said Nian. 'I've got to make sure Tarq is all right, and then I must put as much of the garden back together as I can while the plants are still alive.'

'Leaving me stuck here,' said Jacob. He didn't speak reproachfully, exactly, but what Nian might have called thoughtfully if it hadn't been Jacob speaking. 'Hey, Nian,' he went on. 'Dad wants me to do a course in lapidatherapy so we can offer it at the Health Shop. It's quite cool. You put stones on people's heads and it sort of channels their psychic forces.'

'Really?' said Nian, intrigued despite everything. 'What psychic forces do they have?'

Jacob grinned, slightly sheepishly.

'None, really,' he said. 'It's just a load of garbage, I expect, unless you believe in it. I think, really,' he went on, 'it's really that Dad wants one of us to stay around to look after him. He knows Robyn would feed him to the nearest shark before she'd let him cramp her style. Anyway, she'll be off to college soon.'

'I must get back,' said Nian, again.

Jacob looked out at the grey sky.

'I suppose I was lucky the sun was shining in Rik's world,' he said. 'I mean, you'd have to pay thousands of pounds to go to a place like that on holiday. Nian!'

There was a faint ruffle of entirely uncharacteristic agitation running through him.

'I did help save the world, didn't I?' he said.

'The worlds,' Nian corrected him. 'Yes, you did. That makes it twice, now.'

Jacob nodded.

'Look . . . the thing is,' he said, 'I'm not much good at anything. I'm pretty thick, and I always fall over at football, and I even think Robyn might be right about my Tex-Japanese pizza topping. It *is* a bit of a shock unless you're used to it. But I seem to be quite good at saving the worlds, don't I?'

Yes, Nian nearly said. *I'll tell you what, you take on being Truth Sayer and I'll go back to the House of Truth and play pockle.*

'You haven't got powers,' Nian pointed out, sadly, and Jacob deflated.

'No, of course I haven't. Yeah. Forget it. Stupid of me. Ah well. Hey, but it was just so brilliant to see all those places. Yeah, I just loved seeing all those different worlds. I mean, those incredible belly-slapper buskers! I don't think there's anything like them anywhere on . . . '

But then his mouth suddenly dropped open.

'That's it!' he exclaimed. 'That's *it*! Hey, Nian, *I don't know*. About the belly-slappers, I mean, and there being none on this world. And . . . I don't *have* to work in the Health Shop, do I? I can be a busker! Me and the band! As soon as we're old enough we'll travel . . . ooh, everywhere . . . and earn our money as we go. Hey, think of the places we could go. Hawaii, New Orleans, Timbuktu, Dagenham . . . everywhere. Hey, Nian, it'll be brilliant! And we'll get people to teach us all their music and stuff, because, right, everyone has their own music and there must be, like, a billion different drumming styles just here on Earth. And then we'll do recordings and sell downloads on eBay!'

'It is brilliant,' said Nian, because it plainly was, whatever Jacob was talking about. 'Live well, Jacob.'

Jacob nodded happily, but he was too busy making plans to take much notice.

'Yeah,' he said. 'Oh, and you too, natch. Hey, I wonder if you can get a drum kit in hand luggage?'

Nian stood on the edge of the world and felt sad for several seconds. But then he found himself grinning. He was soon going to be several worlds away from Jacob and his drum kit; and he suddenly realized that in lots of ways that was an extremely good thing.

'I must go,' he said.

'Yeah,' said Jacob, absently. 'Hey, Nian, if we go to Hawaii we'll be able to go surfing!'

Jacob's face turned towards him, alight with eagerness.

It was the last thing that Nian saw as the abyss took him.

39

There was a lot of tidying up to do in the House of Truth. Literal tidying up, like putting back the several tons of earth and half a hundred young trees that Nian had sort of accidentally thrown across the garden; and, even more importantly, the not-so-literal stuff like making sure the Lord Tarq was being looked after properly, and that Nian hadn't done such terrible things to Snerk's beloved kitchen that Nian was in danger of an expertly-wielded meat-cleaver dividing him into chops.

If he wanted to live to see another day, that needed sorting out at once. Nian took a deep breath to give himself courage and headed for the Outer House.

The state of Snerk's kitchen was even worse than Nian had feared. Apart from the Snerk-shaped hole in the wall, the explosion Nian had caused had brought down a whole shelf of glass jars and blown several grain sacks to bits.

The floor was all shattered glass, dark sticky pools, flakes of oatmeal, and quivering heaps of . . . no, where Snerk's ingredients were concerned, it was probably best not to know.

278

Snerk was in the act of prodding a grimy questioning thumb into one of the quivering heaps when Nian arrived, but when Snerk looked up Nian saw that his bloodshot little eyes were glowing with cleaver-wielding rage.

Nian swallowed.

'I'm really sorry about your kitchen, Snerk,' he said, inadequately. 'But . . . well . . . I wasn't really myself.'

'Hurrrrrrr!' said Snerk, the sound rumbling round his great belly like the war-call of a marsh ox. 'Nurrrrr!'

'Yes,' said Nian. 'Of course. I couldn't agree more. I'm afraid I sort of went a bit mad.'

'Hurrrrrrrr?'

'Well, perhaps more than a bit,' Nian admitted. 'Quite a lot. Totally, really. So I thought I'd come to see if there's anything I can do to help.'

'Grrrrrrr! Murrrrrrr! Nurrrrr-nurrrsoboggoff!'

Nian tried not to look too relieved.

'Well, if you're sure—'

Snerk stuck up his thumb at Nian in a very rude gesture, realized it was covered in glerp from the quivering heap on the floor, licked it off in one vicious movement . . .

. . . and then he froze.

The sudden change from violence to stillness was even more terrifying than Snerk's rage—and until then Nian would have said there was *nothing* more terrifying than Snerk's rage. Snerk stood with his eyes bulging and his tongue hanging out and he went so white that you could even see the paleness glowing through all the dirt.

'What's up?' whispered Nian, in alarm. 'You haven't . . . that stuff . . . it wasn't *poisonous*, was it?'

Snerk blinked slowly. Then he blinked again.

'Blurrrrrrrrrrr,' he said, softly. And then he lunged forward so swiftly that Nian was caught before he knew it.

'Murrrrrrr!' said Snerk, clutching the front of Nian's tunic with one hand and bunching the other into a grimy fist. 'Burrrrrrrrr-burrr-burrrr-burrrr! *Nurrrrr!*'

'Oh,' said Nian, disentangling his hammering heart from his tonsils. 'Well, if you really want me—'

'Nurr NURR-nurr!'

Nian sent his thoughts obediently into the glerpy stuff on the kitchen floor.

'Well, apart from the usual mud and stuff, there's quite a lot of oatmeal, some swift-spit, some bread-mould, a couple of squashed roaches and some spinach,' reported Nian. 'Oh, and a few bat droppings.'

Snerk let go of Nian's tunic and clasped his huge hands together. Nian would have fallen over if he hadn't stumbled back into the wall behind him.

Nian got his powers ready to protect himself—but then he noticed that Snerk was suddenly looking quite different. Not sullen or violently unhinged any more, but pink about the chops. Even his eyes were glittering a particularly brilliant shade of red.

'Nur-nur-mur-blurrr-GURR gurr gur?' he asked, hopefully.

Nian obediently sent out his powers to search the Outer House.

'There seem to be quite a few breeding in the boot-lockers,' he said.

'Grurrrrr!'

And Tarhun Snerk, the greatest cook in the mountains, if not the world, seized a saucepan, elbowed Nian aside, and set off at a brisk lumber in the direction of the Tarhun's boot-lockers. Yes, there were hundreds of roaches scuttling about round there: they liked to feed off all the old skin.

Nian decided not to think about it.

A voice called after Nian as he made his way back to the Inner House.

'Truth Sayer! Truth Sayer!'

Snorer's great fat chops were hanging in solemn folds as he shuffled up.

'I'm afraid . . . I'm afraid you've got a visitor, Truth Sayer,' he mumbled, apologetically. 'Someone . . . someone from home.'

Someone from home? But of course.

'Ah,' said Nian. 'My brother Tan's arrived, has he? Thanks, Snorer, I'll just nip along to the Strangers' Room and say hello. Hey, do you think you could organize a bit of supper for us at some point?'

'Hang on!' protested Snorer. 'Hang *on*! I was trying to break the news gently. How the *grot* did you know it was him?'

'Long story,' said Nian. 'I'll tell you tomorrow, all right?'

Nian and Tan had a good evening. Nian showed Tan all round the bits of the House where guests were allowed, and several of the places where they weren't,

281

and then they had supper (no, *definitely* don't ask, Nian told Tan, trying not to think about roaches and bread-mould), listened to the Tarhun having a colossal celebratory fight, and then finally fell asleep side by side.

They awoke side by side, too.

And it was Tuesday.

40

A DISCOVERY TO ROCK THE WORLD!

In the cinema, the clipped, excited voice of the news-reader began as the sound of the tinny trumpet fanfare faded away. Everyone wriggled their backsides into more comfortable positions and prepared to be enthralled.

'The opening of the Monument of Hasiris was always going to be exciting, but no one knew just what a shock was in store when . . . '

Rik watched himself on the screen. He wished he didn't look so shaky and idiotic, but even so it was quite something to be one of the most famous people in the country. In the world, very probably.

There was Aranna. He was really glad she'd been with him (though he was still a bit hazy about where she'd come from) because he'd hardly been able to think straight enough to speak.

Rik had got most of what had happened sorted out now. At least . . . none of it sounded very likely, but Aranna had been around for the last bit, so it really did seem to be true.

Rik had tried to tell the journalists all about it, but they'd been in too much of a hurry to listen properly.

They'd grabbed one tiny part of the whole incredible thing and rushed off to print BIG HEADLINES.

ANCIENT CIVILIZATION OF THE MONUMENT PALE! they all screamed.

Well, perhaps that was astonishing enough. Rik had tried to talk about Time, and Links to Other Worlds, but it had gradually become obvious that the papers weren't going to print any of it. Rik was the Hero of a Big Story, and the papers had no intention of publishing anything that would make him look like a nutter. No, Rik was a curious boy-genius who'd managed to open the door to the Monument where all the scholars had failed.

Rik found himself 'quoted' using clever-sounding words he didn't even *know*.

The newsreels, having a 'pale' story, suddenly needed quotes from pale people. Rolan had worked on the excavations for years and looked good on film: by the time he'd done half a dozen interviews it had become clear that women fancied him, and he soon became if anything even more famous than Rik.

The biggest film studio, seizing on the new craze, announced a series of feature films starring a pale comic duo. A smaller, but thrusting, studio offered Rolan a starring role in a romantic drama. He refused it, but they got someone else with golden floppy hair and even sharper cheek-bones to do it.

The young people flocked to the cinemas in droves—and no one cared very much about what the old people thought.

Suddenly PALE IS PRECIOUS was on every lip. Rik's mother even bought herself a dress that was based on a native apron, and thought herself very daring and modern in it.

Rolan used his fame to start a campaign for equality for natives. He appeared on so many newsreels, shaking hands with so many politicians, that in the end he had to be given a Very Important Position Indeed, and was quite often to be seen being driven around in a car which was much too big to get down the alleys of the Native Quarter.

The photographers who lay in wait for Rik wherever he went were always keen for him to be snapped with a native. Aranna was useful in this way, as well as being the best possible company, and Rik thought he would have gone mad without her. Mind you, he suspected himself of being mad, anyway: there were things he couldn't quite remember—marvellous, huge things full of beauty and terror. He kept trying to remember what they were, but it was never any use.

'Enjoy what you've got,' said Aranna, sensibly; and he found that usually worked, at least as long as Aranna was around. And Aranna usually *was* around: Rik's parents liked to show her off at dinner parties to shock their friends.

Professor Hallam was the only person who showed any interest at all in what had actually happened.

'Another world!' he said, with huge satisfaction. 'You see? I always *knew* it had something to do with another world!'

41

Tan had never been the brightest sun in the sky; he was fine with things he could understand, like ox-grot or hay, but he could never really grasp anything that wasn't actually there in front of him.

'But you *haven't* gone to another world,' he kept saying, doggedly, when Nian tried to explain the plague of Mondays. 'You've been here ever since I arrived, you have. What am I going to tell Grandy? She was that set on it that the paths of the worlds was all a load of cobbles. And that's why I came.'

Nian ruffled up his already exasperated hair.

'But I *did* go into other worlds,' he said. 'I told you!'

'Yes,' agreed Tan. 'But that was before I came. That won't be any good to Grandy, will it?'

'But it wasn't before you came,' said Nian, yet again. 'Not really. Or, well, I suppose it was, but only in a sort of way.'

Tan pulled down the sides of his mouth.

'Grandy won't half be mad,' he observed, glumly. 'She was that agitated about it.'

Nian hauled up some more patience.

'The thing is,' he explained, 'that . . . well, I saw you in a sort of dream, you see.'

Tan looked guarded.

'Did you? Well, what was I doing, then?'

'You told me all about Grandy,' explained Nian. 'And I was so worried that I went off as fast as I could to the place that was causing the problem so I could sort it out. And Grandy was quite right, tell her. She discovered the problem before anyone else. Someone had been digging round a tower-thing, and that had tumbled some stones through into the wrong world. That was what was making the worlds feel bumpy. But it's all right, now. You'll see. When you get home you'll find Grandy's not fussing any more.'

Tan sniffed.

'It was a waste of time me traipsing all the way up this bogging mountain, then, if you already knew all about it,' he observed. 'Grot, Nian, I feel as if I've been walking uphill for a month.'

Just for a moment Nian wondered how long poor Tan *had* been walking up the Holy Mountain. It might have been a month, for all Nian knew.

Tan hoisted his pack.

'Well, I suppose I'd better be off,' he said. 'I've been away from home too long as it is, especially at this time of year. The rutnips will be needing hoeing, or else they'll be getting the fly, they will.'

Nian walked with him as far as the bronzewood and iron door that led to the outside world.

'Well,' said Tan, pulling on his knitted cap.

'Well, then,' said Nian.

'We'll be seeing you mid-winter, I expect, as long as the snows don't block the passes.' But then Tan gave his brother a suspicious look. 'Though I expect you could melt your way through any amount of snow-drifts if you had to, couldn't you?'

'If I had to,' admitted Nian.

Tan shook his head partly in wonder and partly in disapproval.

'Well, it takes all sorts,' he said. 'It wouldn't suit me, mind you, but then I'm just a farm boy.'

He took two steps out through the doorway and onto the worn path that led across the hoppit-cropped grass.

Nian almost followed him. He could have done: no one could have stopped him. He could have walked over to where the track turned to head down the mountain.

But he didn't. He had a feeling that once he was on that homeward path then one footstep would follow another after another until the dawn rose on his father's farm. And he didn't want to be there. No. The farm held beauty and contentment, but Nian wanted . . .

. . . Nian shivered. He couldn't remember very much of all the things he had seen when the plague had had him in its grip, but he knew he had seen a long way.

Out there. Beyond the stars: a million million worlds filled with . . . he couldn't remember what they were filled with, but he knew that it had cast a darkness, a coldness, over his heart.

'The thing is, my powers are still growing,' Nian had told the Lord Tarq, earlier. The old man was eating,

288

but slowly, as if the spoon was almost too heavy for him. His frailness terrified Nian, but he still asked:

'What if my powers grow so much I end up like I was when I had the plague?'

The Lord Tarq had been very still and peaceful.

'That will not happen,' he explained gently. 'You are the Truth Sayer—and the plague showed you distance, yes, but not Truth.'

Yes, thought Nian. You could never judge anything just from one standpoint. However great his powers became, he'd never really have much of a clue. He'd always need the others.

He must be sure to remember that always. All the time.

Tan had reached the top of the mountain path.

Nian raised a hand in farewell.

'Live well!' he called.

Tan waved a sturdy hand in reply, and turned and walked along the path and then down, down, down, out of sight.

The giant beaver yawned, and opened a yellow eye. Its hibernation seemed to have lasted a particularly long time, this year. But ah, bless them, its cubs had been born while it slept. There they were, all golden and snuffling.

The giant beaver yawned again, hugely. It seemed to remember something about a visit from a pale pink gibbon-like thing. Ooh, that had been horrible: it'd been after her cubs.

She sighed with relief.

Now, that *must* have been a dream.

42

The others were on the pockle ground, practising.

'Great!' exclaimed Hani, when he saw Nian. 'We can have a proper game, now. *'UuuuuNITEd UuuuuuNITEd!'*

'I'm supposed to be working on putting the garden back together,' said Nian, weakly; but he caught the flipper that Emmec threw to him.

Nian was getting settled into the game when he saw a great mound of red Tarhun hastening across the garden. For some reason that really worried Nian, though he was concentrating too hard to think about it properly.

Alin ran forward into space and swiped his flipper hard. The pock went up, up, spinning past the trees, the wall, the grey and cloudy autumn sky . . .

. . . and slowed to a momentary stop and came down again.

The pock was going to go out of play: Alin had muffed the shot a bit.

A piercing, dreadful doubt shot through Nian.

Oh no! he thought. *No, not again!*

Tack!

The pock hit the smooth trunk of a stoneberry tree . . .

. . . and then it bounced up, dived down into the hollow insides of the wingnut tree, bounded out, sailed through the air avoiding seventy-three branches and one of Hani's old boots that had been stuck up the tree for weeks—and then plunged down, missing the drey by at least three reaches.

There was a complete and utter silence for about five seconds while everybody's eyes took in what had happened—and then Hani let out a howl of joy.

'*Rubbishhhhh!*' he howled.

Alin tried to look outraged, but he couldn't do it. A great grin of relief spread itself right across his face. Everyone was suddenly laughing—even Snorer.

Nian let out a whoop and hurled his flipper straight up into the air. It went up and up, turning round and round, spinning like a wingnut seed.

It was Tuesday. The Lord Tarq was getting stronger, the garden would soon be back as it should be again, and the worlds were safe. It had been a dark adventure, but he had got through in the end.

Nian ran forward, carefully avoiding being dazzled by the lesser sun, and caught his flipper.

The game was even, and there was everything to play for.

291

A GUIDE TO THE PRONUNCIATION OF FOREIGN WORDS

Alin   A-lin (a as in *hat*)

Aranna   A-r'na (first a as in *hat*, second a as in *about*)

Bulls-Eye   BULLZ-ei (ei as in *eider*)

Caul   KORL

Derig   DE-rig (e as in *leg*)

Emmec   EM-ek (e as in *leg*)

Fallan   FALL-n (first a as in *hat*)

Firn   FERN

florikale   FLO-ree-KAYL (o as in *bog*, ay as in *say*)

Gant   GANT (G as in *go*)

Gow   GOW (G as in *go*, ow as in *now*)

Grandy   GRAND-ee

Grodan   GRO-dan (o as in *go*)

grohl   GROL (o as in *go*)

Halad   HAL-ad (a as in *hat*)

Hallam   HAL'm (a as in *hat*)

Hani   HAN-ee (a as in *hat*)

Hasir   HASS-eer (a as in *hat*)

Hasiris   h-SI-riss (i as in *sit*)

hombat   HOMbat

Jof   JOFF

Marle   MARL

Miri   MI-ree (i as in *sit*)

Moram   MO-r'm (o as in *bog*)

mouselets   MOWSS-litz (ow as in *now*)

Nian   NEE-n

ornyx   OR-nix

pockle   PO-k'l (o as in *got*)

Rago   RARG-o (o as in *go*)

Reeklet   REEK-lit

rezkler   REZ-kla (a as in *about*)

Rik   RIK

Robyn   ROB-in

Rolan   RO-lan (o as in *go*)

rutnip   RUTT-nip

Snerk   SNERK (er as in *jerk*)

Snorer   SNOR-a (a as in *about*)

Tan   TAN

Tarhun   TAR-h'n

Tarq   TARK

worzel   WER-z'l (er as in *jerk*)

Yolek   YO-lek (o as in *go*)

Sally Prue first started making up stories as a teenager, when she realized that designing someone else's adventures was almost as satisfying as having her own. After leaving school Sally joined practically all the rest of her family working at the nearby paper mill. She now teaches recorder and piano and enjoys walking, painting, daydreaming, reading, and gardening. *Cold Tom*, Sally's first book, won the Bramford Boase Award and the Smarties Prize Silver Award. Sally has two daughters and lives with her husband in Hertfordshire. *Plague of Mondays* is Sally's seventh novel for Oxford University Press.

HOW IT ALL BEGAN...

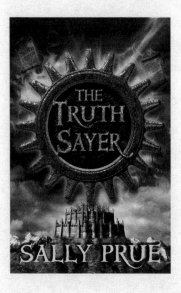

Nian is a boy with a destiny. Taken from his home and family
to live in the House of Truth, he must practise his skills
of mind-reading, weather lore and manipulation of
matter. Once he has achieved mastery, he will become
one of the elect, a Lord of Truth.

There's only one problem. Nian doesn't want to become
a Lord of Truth. He just wants to get away.
But his only means of escape is to step into another world.
To be precise, into Jacob's front room.
In Essex. Just before tea time.

Nian doesn't speak English, he doesn't know what to do
with a toaster, and he's got no idea what those roaring
lumps of metal speeding down the road are.

The truth is, this is going to be interesting...

It's all change in the House of Truth. The ancient
power of the House has been swept away, and now
there's a new energy about the place. For the first
time in years there are lots of new boys arriving
to study with the Lords.

It's all very exciting – but Nian, the Truth Sayer,
feels stifled. He's by far the most powerful person
in the House, but what good is that? Having
great powers isn't easy – especially when they can
be so very very dangerous. . .

Then the owlman arrives. It's terrifying,
and even Nian can't make it go away.

Who sent it? What does it want? And can it be
stopped before it destroys everyone in the House?

Other books by Sally Prue

'The Truth Sayer' sequence
The Truth Sayer
March of the Owlmen

Cold Tom
The Devil's Toenail
Ryland's Footsteps
Goldkeeper

The Truth Sayer

Plague
of
Mondays